GOD TELLING A JOKE

and Other Stories

GOD TELLING A JOKE

and Other Stories

BY

DAVE MARGOSHES

OOLICHAN BOOKS
FERNIE, BRITISH COLUMBIA, CANADA
2014

Library and Archives Canada Cataloguing in Publication

Margoshes, Dave, 1941-, author

    God telling a joke and other stories / by Dave Margoshes.

ISBN 978-0-88982-299-3 (pbk.)

    I. Title.

PS8576.A647G63 2014   C813'.54   C2014-902281-6

We gratefully acknowledge the financial support of the Canada Council for the Arts, the British Columbia Arts Council through the BC Ministry of Tourism, Culture, and the Arts, and the Government of Canada through the Canada Book Fund, for our publishing activities.

Published by
Oolichan Books
P.O. Box 2278
Fernie, British Columbia
Canada V0B 1M0

www.oolichan.com

Printed in Canada

This one is for dee

CONTENTS

DESERT ISLE
OR
THE COMPUNCTION OF NARRATIVE

Sarah Bingham, the distinguished Canadian author of the Giller and Pulitzer Prize-winning novel *The Centaur Speaks* and other celebrated works, is writing a story about an imagined character, but one of her favourites, a fellow she has called Margoshes. It's a name with rich angles that appeal to her. He, too, is a writer, and the story she's working on involves him writing a story about a woman writer much like her. Round and round the story goes, until she loses track of where she fits into the continuum—is she the narrative arc, tightroping along it, or in its shadow?

In Sarah's story—it's too soon to tell whether it will evolve into a novel, but seems headed in that direction—Margoshes is a washed-up relic of a writer (she doesn't use these terms but they will spring to the minds of alert readers), cast adrift in an inflatable raft after a terrible storm sank the sailboat he and his fourth wife had hoped to navigate around the world, and left stranded on a desert island, Crusoe like. Washed up for real. Sarah hasn't yet determined what becomes of the wife, but she's not on the island with

Margoshes—perhaps she'll reappear later. Sarah has cast herself—or, rather, a character much like herself—as a nubile Friday. The prints of her petite feet in the damp sand along the shoreline are driving the thirst-maddened writer to distraction, his imagination wilder than ever before. There is much to-ing and fro-ing, with skillfully built suspense, in and out of the dense jungle, up and down coconut trees, across streams, in and out of caves. Finally, when Sarah writes the scene in which Margoshes and the Friday character meet—she calls her Aras—she's pleased that it falls into neither of the two traps she feared: it is not love at first sight, which would tilt the story into romance territory, unacceptable for a writer of her standing; but neither is it instant antipathy, with all its hallmarks of irony, a literary device purportedly no longer in style. Rather, the two characters forming themselves into physical shape on the page out of wisps of imaginings in her mind circle each other like wary prizefighters, taking the measure of the other with the same acuity for detail with which one might examine a reflection in a newly acquired mirror.

"You certainly aren't what I expected," Sarah has Margoshes say, but immediately she backspaces the sentence out. She's noted for the sharpness of her dialogue, and that limp line is certainly not up to her standard.

She worries, too, if the metaphor isn't too obvious. Yes, of course it is, but if she can make the story believable, it won't matter, not too much. Regular readers will be charmed by it; academics, taking opposing views, will write essays about it.

𝄆

Sarah, whose star is on the ascendancy, especially in the U.S., since her Pulitzer win, is spending the year as writer in residence at Radcliffe, the prestigious former girls' college associated with Harvard University. On this wet, chilly day in October, she's been working behind a locked door in her office on the third floor of the Schlesinger Library, her nerves on edge. The previous week, a young woman was sexually assaulted as she hurried toward her dormitory on a shrubbery-choked path soon after dark, and the whole campus has been anxious, men as well as women, faculty as well as students. The shrubbery has been removed, security beefed up and lighting improved, but the assailant remains at large, and there's gossip on campus that the young victim, not so much physically harmed as traumatized, has been transferred to the hospital's mental wing for observation.

Sarah pauses in her writing, startled by a noise in the hallway, and thinks of this poor girl; perhaps inevitably then, her thoughts sweep her back to her own time, as a young woman, in a mental institution. This recollection is enough to stop her creative impulses in their tracks and, animated by a surge of restlessness, she pulls on her raincoat and heads out across Radcliffe Yard toward the river. Women have been cautioned not to walk alone on campus, day as well as night, but the rain is coming down so hard she can't imagine there'd be any danger. And she's in need of air—the story she's been working on is frustrating her with an unexpected development.

*

Years ago, when she was just starting out, Sarah went on a week-long writing retreat in the Canadian Rockies where she took a workshop with a writer much like the Margoshes character, and he'd made a strong impression. She was, to use his expression, "green as grass," an evaluation which smarted. She'd been wrestling with a particular story for years already and felt anything but green—if anything, the image that sprang to mind when he uttered that phrase was of withered grass. As a teenager, she'd experienced a breakdown after her beloved father's sudden death, and had spent some months in the secure wing of a hospital. She'd kept a journal of her dreams and the therapist she was seeing then encouraged her to expand the journal, so, after her readmission to the world, as he put it, she carried on, writing and writing. A tangled story of that painful time had slowly emerged—outlasting a failed marriage and several desultory low-level careers—but all her attempts to untangle it only seemed to pull the drawstrings tighter. Now this workshop fellow, a writer not much older than she was but with considerable experience and of some repute, with many books to his credit and a practiced way of explaining things, told her, "this isn't a story, not really, it's a cry for help. Now, ask yourself, is that what you're satisfied with, or do you really want to write a story? A real story?"

They were in the lounge, a lovely, comfortable room with a broad expanse of glass overlooking a snow-capped Rundle Mountain, having a private consultation. She had cried and the writer, after a moment, reached across the table to hand her a box of tissues. "Go on, cry," her told her, "don't be embarrassed. Tears are good lubrication for what we do. Cry, then write a scene in which a character cries."

Then he'd challenged her, explained things in a way she'd never thought of them before—"do you realize," he asked her, "there's not a sentence of dialogue in this? These people don't talk, they just *think* at each other"—and sent her off with an assignment. She'd spent the whole afternoon writing dialogue, skipped dinner, then wrote more dialogue, spent the whole evening till she fell asleep from exhaustion listening to the shadowy characters in her mind trade banter, quips, ripostes, their lines becoming sharper, shapelier. The next day, she brought the writer a couple of crumpled typewritten pages, held her breath as he read. "Okay, now you're onto something." He looked up, smiled. "Keep going."

She had. That "Keep going" was validation, the elixir all artists crave. A few months after that workshop, she'd mailed a letter to the writer thanking him. *I came home and re-wrote the beginning of another story, in a very different way than is normal for me,* she wrote, *so I am excited and unsettled and overwhelmed. Pretty good value for three or four days and a couple of hundred dollars, don't you think?*

I am trying to make my way out of the wilderness and just write and write. Easier typed than done, but you said one sentence that I'll carry with me for a long time. 'Don't squander it.' A directive to work, to just work at it. So thanks. Again.

He'd replied in a handwritten note she still had scotch-taped above her computer: *A pleasure to hear from you, Sarah. I'm glad you got your $'s worth. Writing fiction is hard work—hard to learn, hard to do. It's not just telling a story. Doing it well, I think, requires some qualities that we tend to think of as desirable in the people we know: intelligence, clear-headedness, clear vision, honesty, passion, compassion—oh, and the willingness to turn ourselves inside out, and to bleed. Then there's patience and persistence, because it takes quite a while before you start seeing real results. The main thing to remember, though, is this: make it believable. If you do, you can get away with anything.*

Turning yourself inside out—she'd done that over and over again in the years that followed. *And* bleeding. A few stories in literary magazines—oh, how she'd crowed with pride to him, her mentor, after the first one, and how pleased his reply had been—then a novel and another, good reviews, a small prize in her adopted home of Saskatchewan, another novel and the two big prizes (due to the peculiar circumstances of her birth, she was a dual citizen, so eligible for the Pulitzer, as Carol Shields had been), even, eventually, a better-than-modest income. These days, she leads workshops herself, channeling the advice he'd given her and she hadn't forgotten. Of all the advice she offers her students, the piece she doles out most often and with the most conviction, is that hoary "Make it believable." That's her mantra.

Starting a year or so ago, her old mentor began to appear—well, reappear—in the stories she was writing, complex, layered stories, the dialogue crackling. She called the character Margoshes, which wasn't his name but the name of a minor character in one his own early stories, a story that had appeared only in a book now long out of print but which appealed to her because of its freshness and naivety, so similar to her own when she was starting out. She'd asked him once about that character and his odd name, and he'd told her it belonged to a friend of his and appealed to him because it was, as far as he knew, unique in Canada. Now it held the same appeal for her.

You will make some grad student's day some day, her mentor emailed her, when the first of these stories appeared, in *The New Yorker,* a magazine he'd never managed to get into.

In Sarah's early, unpublished stories, the Margoshes character would often appear unbidden, in small parts, a waiter who brings the main character a coffee, a locksmith who arrives to save the day after she's locked herself out of her apartment, a mechanic who changes the oil of her car. In one or two of these stories, a romantic entanglement, or a sexual encounter, follows but is quickly extinguished. The Margoshes character is never allowed to dominate the story, and, in those early stories, he's never called Margoshes. Nor does he look like or in any way resemble the writer upon whom the character of Margoshes is based—rather, Sarah believes, these minor characters are informed in some small way by the spirit of the man who helped her at a crucial time of her life, as both writer and woman, and she so admired.

Later, as her assurance and success as a writer of short fiction grew, he would occasionally take on a larger role, perhaps that of the love interest or the adversary— "antagonist" is the technical term. As depicted in these stories, he was very much like the writer who had inspired Sarah, quite ordinary physically except for a slightly larger than normal head which implied superior brain power, long-haired and bearded, dark sombre eyes, an intriguing mixture of shyness and brashness. In some stories, he chain-smoked French cigarettes, Galloise; in others, foul-smelling Turkish cheroots. Sometimes he drank expensive Cognac; other times Irish whiskey, single malt. As with the earlier stories, he was never called Margoshes; nor was he ever depicted as a writer.

But in her more recent efforts—he played a small but key role in her latest novel as well—he has finally come into his own, occupying the stage of her stories as a writer in all his humble glory, and named Margoshes. At the same time, the character has morphed into almost a caricature of his former self: scrawny, except for a noticeable thickening around the middle, grey all over, much like a broken tree branch rimed with frost in the early morning grass, his once charming conversation now rancid with bitterness. She's already written two such stories since her late-summer arrival at Radcliffe. To this sour portrait, she is adding more details in the current story, this fanciful desert island tale.

For one thing, he walks with a limp, just as her old mentor does (or did—it's been years since she's seen him), a condition which he used to flippantly attribute to "an old war wound," without specifying which war or offering details.

Sarah steps gratefully out of the rain into a small, almost deserted campus coffee shop to pick up a latté in a cardboard cup. The bell above the door jangles, startling the barista, a slender young woman with dangling earrings, out of a reverie. "You surprised me," the girl says. "I didn't think anyone was out and about today." She appraises Sarah cautiously through large chocolate eyes while taking her order.

"Are you alone, dear? That doesn't seem safe, what with…"

"No, my manager's in' the back," the girl says, laughing stiffly, but it strikes Sarah as false bravado. She cocks her head toward the rear but hears nothing.

The drink this latest Margoshes character prefers, it comes to Sarah as she watches the barista's skilled hands juggle espresso and hot foam, is Guinness, served at room temperature. Not that there'll be Guinness or anything like it on the desert island.

After Margoshes and the Sarah-like girl Friday meet on the island, the ship-wrecked writer is inspired for the first time in many months to put pen to paper. Of course, he has neither, but he is able to improvise, using the quill end of a feather from a large seabird as pen, juice from crushed berries as ink, dried fronds of the large-leafed trees that cover much of the island as parchment.

The language barrier between the two of them is

formidable, but Margoshes and the Sarah-like young woman have learned to communicate, and he sets her to work preparing these writing instruments. Soon she's supplying him with enough ink and pages of parchment to write a thousand words a day, which once—in happier days—was his normal quota.

Thus equipped, he finds himself freed from the debilitating effects of writer's block which has so crushed him, for so long. The primitive woman on the island, her womanly attributes barely covered by animal skins, her language little more than gibberish, has nevertheless reminded him of someone, a fledgling writer he met years ago while she was struggling with learning the craft and still battling the aftereffects of a crippling childhood bout of depression brought on by her father's death. He remembers that his frank assessment of the story she was struggling with brought on a torrent of tears, which hadn't moved him. "Tears are good lubrication," he'd told the woman, and they had been. She had become a protégé of sorts, and eventually a successful writer. There had been no romantic or sexual entanglements between them, but a genuine friendship, though it had been some time since they'd been in touch. Now, he finds himself writing a fable-like story about a woman much like Aras, this primitive, his Friday, but attributing to her qualities and the personality of his former writer friend.

Naturally, he calls this character Sarah—though after first writing the name down, he crosses out the "h."

The work, once he gets accustomed to writing by hand, something he hasn't done in years, goes extremely well, and the words fly.

In his story, written in a flat, minimalist style reminiscent of Camus, Sara grows up on a desert island, not a native actually but a feral child, the product of a shipwrecked couple who succumbed to their injuries soon after her birth. She falls into the care of an old native man, the last of his race on the island, and, soon after his death, when she's a teenager, is discovered by sailors on a scientific expedition. She's brought to England, where she becomes the subject of intense public fascination, is lavishly educated by the state and becomes a world-famous writer of detective thrillers noted for her crystalline prose. All of this, of course, is the back story, revealed in bits and pieces as the main story progresses—this narrative involves the unexpected murder of a visiting female professor at a prestigious college, a murder of inexplicable, shocking violence.

The Sara of Margoshes's story—it's too soon to tell whether it will develop into a novel—has written more than a dozen novels featuring a female amateur sleuth, a wise-cracking refugee from the typing pool who, having worked herself up to private secretary to the head of a large multinational corporation, stumbles onto criminal activity—usually murders, once or twice disappearances—and brilliantly solves the related mystery. The first of these novels was called *An Aspect of Apricot*. It was followed by *The Beast Beyond, Crisis!, Duel at Dawn* and similar titles pegged to the alphabet. Although she's only up to *Murder at Montparnasse*, she's already grown bored with her character and the predictable situations she finds herself in. She decides to take a break from her series and write a serious literary novel, thus setting herself up to be a laughing stock should the novel fail.

Adopting an assumed name, and having cut her trademark long blond tresses and dyed the boyish remainder black, Sara enrolls at the famous McDowell writers colony in New Hampshire, where she hopes brushing elbows with serious writers will have a positive effect on her own work. She's soon caught up in a torrid affair with a poet from

Canada named Sehsogram (Margoshes spelled backwards, though Sarah, the real Sarah, is unsure whether in his story, Margoshes would spell that out. She leaves it in her first draft—she can deal with this problem later.)

Sehsogram is such a sensitive lover and has such a skilled tongue that he easily brings Sara, who has been unlucky in love ever since her first encounter with one of her rescuing sailors and has never before experienced orgasm, to unimagined sexual heights. She returns the favour by performing fellatio on him—something she had never before even dreamed of but which she appears to have an amazing talent for, perhaps inspired by his oral efforts. Unfortunately, Sehsogram is a devout follower of the Greek Orthodox church, while Sara comes from a long line of Lutherans, a clash that will likely doom any significant effort at relationship-building.

At this point, Margoshes stops writing. Several days have passed and he's already used up dozens of pages of frond parchment. What stops him at first is the puzzle of how Sara, having been raised in primitive conditions by a primitive, could possibly consider herself a Lutheran. No, if anything, she would be an animist of some sort, wouldn't she? Several times, he's noticed Aras, his own primitive, bowing before a figure fashioned of twigs and chanting in her own strange tongue. Yes, that's the sort of thing he should probably have Sara do, that would be just as incompatible with Sehsogram's Greek Orthodoxy, and serve the plot as well.

But as he ponders these strands and possibilities of his story, he's suddenly struck by its overwhelming banality— writer's block would be preferable to this, he thinks.

Sarah too—the real Sarah—has been troubled by the banality of what she's writing—or is it actually irony? She's not sure. Worse still than the banality, if that's what it is, is the lack of credibility. *Make it believable*—those words of her mentor come back to haunt Sarah now, ringing down through the years.

All of this is on her mind as she walks across the deserted, rain-drenched campus, sipping at her cinnamon-dusted foamy coffee. The rain is falling harder now but she doesn't mind. As always, going all the way back to those days in the mental hospital, it's walking, more than anything else, that frees her thoughts, as if the mere motion of limbs and joints somehow sets mental processes into motion as well, like a lubricant. *"Tears are good lubrication for what we do."* Another mantra from her mentor. Would she never outgrow him, be her own woman? But no, that was hardly the way to think of it. He was mentor, not taskmaster. Unlike Margoshes in her story (writer's block, banality) or Aras (primitivism, exaggerated sexuality), Sarah has nothing to free herself from. Well, that isn't right either—she's never completely freed herself from her own personal demons. Her mentor has helped her, as the psychotherapist before him had, and writing has empowered her, but always the shadowy figure of her father lurked at the back of her mind—and it was he, she suddenly realized, who the character of Margoshes had evolved to most resemble, not her mentor at all.

This bit of Freudian clarity—or was it Jungian?— stops her in her tracks and she stands for a moment on the sodden path, a drenched woman in an expensive but inadequate raincoat, improper shoes and no hat, rain water streaming from her hair, tears down her cheeks. The Charles River is not far away—she hears the mournful cry of a foghorn— and she presses on, hurrying across Mount Auburn Street.

She finds a bench on the Memorial Drive walkway and sits down—she can't get any wetter, so what difference does it make? She'll have a cold tomorrow for sure, but so what? She finishes her coffee and concentrates on the lazy spirals of a seagull, allowing her mind to empty itself. But Sarah is a disciplined writer, and after a while the story she's writing creeps back in and demands her attention.

The epiphany of a few minutes ago has cast the story in a whole new light. She gazes at the lazily moving river, imagining its course into Boston Harbour and the wide Atlantic. On his desert island (no matter that it's in the Pacific), Margoshes is gazing out to sea as well, she imagines, as perplexed by the story he's become entangled in as she is by hers. Perhaps his gaze is picked up by a peripatetic gull, and hers is as well—or no, albatrosses! Regardless, some-where in mid-ocean, the two birds come upon each other, and there, in that vast expanse of nothingness, they settle gently down beside each other on softly lapping waves. Margoshes's gaze and Sarah's gaze fall from the birds' beaks onto the glassy water and connect—a trans-oceanic meeting of minds to rival or even best those first triumphs of Marconi and Edison. A magical moment. It's also a ridiculous conceit, fantastic, outrageous!

She's distracted by the sound of footsteps approaching on the walkway and looks up.

Make it believable, Sarah remembers. If you do, you can get away with anything.

AFTER THE WAR

When the war ended, they sent me home, but I didn't stay around New York longer than it took to kiss Pop and the girls goodbye. I wanted to get as far from my step-mom as I could without going back to Europe. With my mustering out pay, I bought a '37 Plymouth, hardly any miles on it and in great shape, from a neighbour—it had been their son's, a kid from my school but a couple years older. He'd put it in the garage when he went overseas, with a tarp over it so it wasn't even dusty.

I pointed the Plymouth's sweet nose west, that GI Bill burning my ass through my back pocket, and in my memory I just drove and drove and drove till I saw the Pacific, but I know that couldn't be right. I must have stopped on the side of the road and grabbed a few hours now and then, and a bite, but I don't remember that. What I do remember is that I felt better than I ever had. I remember one night, middle of the night, somewhere in Nevada or Utah, cold flat desert and not a light for hours, thinking, "I'm not tired, I'll never be tired again." I was still the same age I'd been when I went in, eighteen, but in the ten months in between I'd killed seven men that I knew of, maybe more. Still a virgin, though. Oh, I'd been to a cathouse in Paris the guys dragged me to, but I figured that didn't count. Still eighteen, all that behind me, and the whole sunset over the Pacific ahead of me.

When I got to the coast, San Francisco, I didn't even stop to look around, figured there'd be plenty of time for that. I went right to the Bay Bridge and would have been in Oakland in a minute, where my Uncle Jack was expecting me, except the Plymouth stalled, right in the middle of the bridge, the bay deep and dark below. There was a streetcar on the bridge and I remember thinking I should just abandon that bucket of bolts and take my chances, but a highway cop came by and before I knew it a tow-truck was there and got her going. Good thing, because that car served me well the next four years. I never did figure out why it stalled then.

Before I knew it, I was taking classes at Berkeley and looking for a job.

Uncle Jack had a boyhood friend who was a scientist working on something he said he couldn't talk about, but he got me a job as a gofer at a lab in Oakland. I was there for just two weeks before I was promoted to be an assistant to this Italian fellow named Fermi. Maybe you've heard of him? He'd been in on the Manhattan Project and now he was working on a hydrogen bomb, although I didn't know any of that. This sounds like more than it was. I had nothing to do with what was going on, didn't have any idea. All these years later, I still don't know what exactly they were doing there, and that suited me fine. I was always on the go with one errand or another. I would get Fermi his lunch, coffee, post a letter, clean his instruments—he was fussy about them, and after he showed me how to clean his microscope and scales and other stuff with an alcohol solution, he wouldn't let anyone but me touch them.

When there was nothing else, I would stack boxes, perfectly square boxes, exactly eighteen inches long and wide, heavy, wrapped in brown paper and tape, no markings, thousands of them. God only knows what was in them. The first day I worked with them, my mind went through some of the possibilities—chunks of uranium, body parts, dirty pictures. There was no profit in speculating, so eventually I just put it out of my mind. The boxes arrived by truck during the night and when I'd show up in mid-morning, they'd be waiting on the loading dock, some days a few dozen, other days a hundred or more. I'd stack them on a dolly and wheel them inside, down a long corridor and into a back room that had become a warehouse. One day in the second week, a stack of them fell off the dolly and one got sort of banged up, the brown paper torn in one corner. I shoved it into a utility closet and didn't give it another thought.

Fermi was a funny duck. Tall and skinny, like one of those concentration camp Jews we saw in newsreels, he had eyes that put me in mind of Bela Lugosi in *Dracula* or something. Even when he smiled he looked unhappy, like he'd seen too much of something wrong. He took to calling me Finger. That's what the guys in my rifle company had called me, I don't know why for sure, Trigger Finger, I guess. When I got home, Pop and the girls called me Isiah, which is my Hebrew name, and Uncle Jack called me George, the name I'd used in school and went into the army with, so I'd almost forgotten that nickname. But when Fermi took me on, he asked what to call me, and, I don't know why, I just blurted out: "Some people call me Finger." I got to see his unhappy smile for the first time.

"Finger it is," he said. It seemed to tickle him—like I said, a funny duck.

I spent a lot of time at the lab, but, really, it wasn't ever more than a part-time job. Mostly I was in school taking all sorts of courses, trying to figure out what I really cared about, and hanging around at a coffee shop on Lantern Avenue with a bunch of guys I got friendly with, all veterans like me. And, of course, screwing every skirt I could get my hands on. I was no longer a virgin, a dozen times over. I'd made up my mind I wasn't going to fall in love—there'd be plenty of time for that later. Uncle Jack had put that idea in my head.

"Don't get yourself tied down, Georgie," he told me. "Be wise, play the field. Otherwise, it's diapers and mortgages and the supper dishes." We were sitting at the supper table, and he waved his hand to indicate the dishes in front of us, empty and dirty now, but I knew the gesture was meant to encompass the whole of his life there in that little bungalow in Oakland. Not that Uncle Jack was complaining, I knew that too.

He was Pop's youngest brother, the one Pop had talked about the most when I was a kid, but his life had been completely different from Pop's, without the politics and the melodrama. He'd gone out to California young, and had a good life. A good job in the post office, suit-and-tie job, nice house and car. His first wife died on him, and Pop always said Jack never got over that, but if it left any scars I couldn't see them. His kids, my cousins Cookie and Seymour, who I never really got to know, were grown and gone, and his new wife Joan—over ten years already, so not so new—was nice enough, and very nice to me while I was living there in their basement suite. Nothing like Pop's new wife, who was driving my sisters crazy back in New York.

But what Uncle Jack meant was, I knew, when you're eighteen and nineteen—which I'd finally turned, a wise old man I was now—that isn't the life you should be thinking about. Sow your wild oats and all that. I took him at his word and I sowed as much as I could.

The war in the Pacific had ended by this time and veterans were pouring back; Berkeley was filling up with restless guys. It was too late for most of them to get registered, so they just hung around, waiting for the Christmas break and the next term. Some of the guys I drank coffee with were taking classes, others weren't. Some of them were looking for jobs. One of the guys claimed to have helped load the bomb they dropped on Nagasaki. There was another guy, a Navy guy who liked to talk about destroyers in the North Atlantic, that sort of thing. But most of them didn't talk too much about the war, except maybe to tell funny stories about furloughs in Paris or poker games. Or killer doses of clap! Me, I never said a word.

What I did like to talk about was the stuff going on in my classes. I was taking a lit course, psychology, poli-sci, the usual first year liberal arts stuff. My brain was banging around inside my skull in all directions with ideas. I loved hearing this stuff, talking about it, but I wasn't too keen on the studying part, I admit. I didn't have the time.

Sure enough, try as I did to sow those oats, some girl got her hooks in me. I don't mean that in a bad way. Just that I was wanting to be thinking about the next skirt but I couldn't keep Brenda out of my mind. There wasn't even anything extraordinary about her, no girl-of-my-dreams. She was good looking, but not beautiful. Had a good body but not exactly a pin-up. Smart but not too smart. So why did I go so head-over-heels for her? I don't know.

Worse yet, she lived in San Francisco and now here I was wasting a lot of gas and oil driving back and forth across the Bay Bridge to see her almost every night. She had a place with a roommate, but the other girl was deep into something with some rich guy and she wasn't around much and we had the place to ourselves. Here I was in a routine, sort of what Uncle Jack was warning me against, but not quite: up early, classes, coffee with the fellows, then to the lab and a few hours' work. Back to Uncle Jack's for a shave, shower and shit, then into the city and an evening of supper out somewhere, dancing maybe or a movie, or drinks at a jazz club in North Beach, then to Brenda's place and screwing our brains out. Then drag my weary ass back over the bridge to get a little sleep before starting over again. In a rut, yeah, but I was loving it.

One night, coming back to Oakland around three in the morning, I noticed this car, an old Chevy, I think, pulled over in the emergency lane, lights off. The bridge was deserted, so I stopped, thought maybe somebody was having motor trouble, although the hood wasn't up. Right in the middle of the bridge. I didn't see anybody around.

"Hello? Anybody here?" I called out. No answer. I went around the car and there was this guy sitting on the edge of the bridge. He'd climbed over the railing and was sitting on the narrow lip, his legs dangling over.

When I was a kid, before Mom died, sometimes we would drive out to Long Island in the summer to see a friend of Pop's who lived on a farm. There was a river nearby, with a little steel bridge on it, and the water was deepest right under it so kids used to jump off, waving their arms and kicking and screaming. The girls and I would always bring our suits and go for a swim while Pop and his friend were talking politics. I remember sitting on the edge of that bridge in the sun working up my courage to push myself off. That's what this reminded me of except there wasn't any Sunday swim under this bridge.

"Hey," I said. "Whatcha' doing?"

This guy looked up. "What's it look like?"

"Nothing good," I said.

"Well, that's your opinion."

I came a little closer, but I didn't want to spook him, so I moved slow, a step or two at a time. Between steps, I'd stop and gawk around, like I was a tourist stopped to take in the view. I could see he was just a young fella, not all that much older than me, but with a beat-down expression, unshaven and sort of hollow-cheeked, scrawny, like he'd missed too many meals. When he glanced up, I could see a sort of dull cast in his eyes, like he was dead already. Not a crazed look, like you might expect. He reminded me a little of Fermi with that gaunt, haunted expression, even the same sort of miserable half-smile when he said, "What's it look like?" I don't know what I was expecting, but it surprised me that a young guy would be thinking of taking a dive. What could be so wrong?

"Mind if I sit down?" I said.

"It's a free country. Ain't that what the war was supposed to be about?"

I wasn't about to climb the rail, but I squatted down close by. The way the railings were, there was nothing between our faces. I was close enough to grab hold of him through the railing, but all he'd have to do is wriggle around a bit and lean over and he'd be out of my grip and gone—I knew that.

"You overseas?" I asked.

"Sure. Wasn't everybody?"

"I was in France and Germany myself, infantry."

"Italy, same thing. And Africa. That was sumpthin'."

"Yeah?"

"Hell, yeah. Those Ay-rab wimmin." He flashed me a black-toothed grin. "Drink?"

He had a pint of bourbon and he twisted around a little to hand it to me. I'm a boy who never tasted alcohol at all before going overseas, except for sweet wine and a cup of foamy beer one afternoon under the bleachers at Yankee Stadium. In France, I developed a liking for brandy, and it's still my drink. I'd never tasted bourbon before but I took a little sip. Must have made a face because this guy laughed.

"What's the matter boy, you never have a drink before?"

"Not this stuff."

"This is the only stuff there is." I'd handed the bottle back and he took a long swallow. "Go on, give it another try. It'll make a man outta ya."

"I think the army did that," I said, but I took another drink, a little more this time. It wasn't all that bad. I remember the brand was J.T.S. Brown, the same stuff Paul Newman drinks in *The Hustler*, but that was years later. I never saw a bottle of it or heard the name in between. I don't know why that name stuck in my head.

"Ain't that bad now, is it?" this fellow asked.

That was too good an opening to pass by. "I'll ask you the same."

"Whacha mean?"

"All this." I gestured with my hand the way Uncle Jack had at the supper table.

"Oh." He took another swallow of bourbon, and gazed out across the dark water of the bay to the lights of San Francisco. "Sometimes..."

"I mean, you got through that shit overseas," I butted in.

"Some of that was easier. Just bullets and shrapnel."

"Yeah, but why give Hitler the satisfaction?"

"Can't say anything to that."

Something about this fellow's look made me think suddenly of the last man I know for sure I killed. It was somewhere in western Germany—I've blanked out the name of the place, but just this side of the Rhine—on May seventh, the day the war in Europe ended. I was at a forward position, up a tree, waiting for our tanks to come through. The Germans were in position just across a little wooden bridge over this dinky stream, but there wasn't much to them, old men and boys mostly, and guys with bandages on their heads, the walking wounded. Still, they had guys in trees too, and you couldn't be too careful.

It was funny as hell, this skinny Jewish kid from the Bronx a sniper. I'd never even seen a rifle before I went in, let alone fired one, but I had a good eye and a steady hand—I used to say I owed it all to playing poker with my Pop—and that's the job they gave me. It always gave me the creeps, actually seeing the guy at the other end of my scope getting hit after I pulled the trigger, but I got to be good at it.

I was just scanning the scene over the creek through my scope and I caught sight of someone in one of the trees near the edge of the bridge. I couldn't see his face, so I didn't know if he was young or old or somewhere in between. I just caught a glint of sun off his helmet, saw the motion. I took a bead on him, but I wasn't planning on getting off a shot, just being ready.

Just then, one of our jeeps came up the road, a string of tanks behind it. They were heading for the bridge. There were two guys in the jeep, a GI driving, and an officer. I had one eye on them, the other eye on the tree. I didn't know what was going to happen.

Then I saw motion in the tree and I figured my man was

going to take a shot at the jeep. They were wide open and it would be one point for the other side for sure, maybe two. I squeezed one off and I knew it was good. When you're placing a shot, sometimes all you see is the jerk and you don't know if your man is dead or wounded or maybe not even hit at all. But this time I saw the flash of red, and a moment later he fell right out of the tree, wham onto the ground. Didn't move. I got that sick feeling in the gut you get. The only job in the world you get sick for doing too good.

The jeep jerks to a stop and the officer jumps out, looks around, then comes charging over my way, moving like Charlie Chaplin in one of those old silent movies. He can't see me, but he heard the shot, saw the Kraut fall, he knows what's up, knows I'm there. "Where the hell are you, you jackass," he yells. He's a captain.

"I'm here," I say, and I show myself.

"Well come on down. The war's over, you jackass. The Krauts signed the surrender this morning. I sent someone over, didn't you hear?"

For days afterwards, I thought about that German, how he'd fallen from the tree, just the way, I imagined, a grouse would fall from the sky if you got it with a shotgun. Not that I'd ever been hunting.

I thought about that German a lot, in ways I hadn't thought about any of the other men I'd killed. He wasn't one of the kids or old men, I was sure, not even a young guy with a good eye like me, but an old hand, a professional soldier. Someone who'd been around and knew the risks. I thought about his wife and kids back home, their photos in his wallet. But no, more likely he was a bachelor, a guy on his own.

I'd been quiet for a while and the guy on the bridge cleared his throat to get my attention. "You look like a nice young feller. Whyn't you get on about your bizness, leave me to mine."

"I'll stick around a bit longer, if it's all the same to you. Don't want you hogging all that good bourbon."

He laughed and took a swallow, handed it over. "Suit yerself."

I took a drink. The stuff was growing on me. "What do they call you?" I asked.

"Jim, just Jim. What about you?"

"Finger."

"Finger!" He laughed again. "Ain't that something. Here I sit broken-hearted and the world gives me the Finger!"

"Ouch."

"Ouch is right. You a college fellow?"

"I am tonight. Can't say for sure about tomorrow."

"Yer a philosopher," Jim said.

"I think about things, sure."

"That's what's wrong with this world."

"What'd'you mean?"

"Too many fucking philosophers. Too much fucking thinking."

"No," I said. "God, please, no…." But it was too late. He'd leaned forward already and then he was falling through darkness. I heard the splash, small and faraway sounding.

There wasn't anything to do but stand up and wait for the cops. A trooper came along after a while, someone who'd seen two cars parked there must have stopped and called. I think it was the same cop who'd stopped and got me a tow on my first day. "Why the hell couldn't you have come five minutes ago?" I said.

It's funny the way things come together. The very next

day, I got fired from the lab. When I came in to work, more bleary-eyed than usual, Fermi was raising the roof. He had a clipboard with sheets of paper, requisition forms for the brown-paper boxes I'd been stacking up. He had lists for what was ordered, what was delivered, what was in the warehouse. The numbers didn't add up, but just by one. One fucking box.

"I don't know where it is," I said. I'd forgotten about the bent-up one I shoved in the closet, didn't remember it until the next day, when it was too late.

"Then what good are you to me, Finger?" Fermi asked. He looked even sadder than usual.

A reasonable question, I guess, but you've gotta try, so I said, "Just one!"

"One is all it takes," Fermi said.

As it happened, it didn't matter. Next week was exams and I was a lost cause. I flunked two of them, didn't even bother with the third. Berkeley didn't have much patience for that sort of thing, not with other vets stacked up to take my place in classrooms.

Then Brenda and I broke up. It was no surprise but the last straw just the same.

There wasn't any point in hanging around. I said goodbye to Uncle Jack and Aunt Joan and hopped in the Plymouth and headed back to New York, got on with my life.

BUCKET OF BLOOD

The bar had no proper name but was known as the Bucket of Blood. The day that Archie Duggan died there, two Wednesdays ago, and the following day, when his death was mentioned in the news, it was the first time that the place, which had stood at the corner of 11th Avenue and Osler Street for over a hundred years, had registered in the minds of most of the people of the city in decades.

The bar was located in the basement of a rundown hotel that had once been called the Earle. The hotel had been built by a man named Louis P. Earle, a flamboyant former railway worker who had washed up in what was then still a town, not yet a city, after the construction of the CPR. In its heyday, the Earle Hotel was a good dignified address at which to spend a night or two, or even longer, though there was always confusion, among both guests and the residents of the town alike who had not had the occasion to ever meet Louis P. Earle, or hear his name said aloud, as to the pronunciation of the hotel's name: was it sounded *Earl*, or *Early*? Years later, all vestiges of Earle and his family having vanished, there were only a few who could say for sure. At any rate, the Earle Hotel had prospered, surviving the great cyclone of 1912 that destroyed most of the downtown and the ups and downs of the city's economy during its early decades, even the Great Depression of the '30s. Then Louis P. Earle had died and his son, Louis J. Earle, a reckless gambler, quickly lost the family business and most of its fortune. Over the years since, several owners maintained the Earle name, different owners pronouncing it differently, but now the hotel belonged to a numbered company, its investors largely immigrants or potential immigrants from Hong Kong and Taiwan, and the name Earle, once a proud name in the community, had lost all its significance. Even the word "hotel" had disappeared from the signage outside the building. In fact, what had once been the Earle Hotel, with a grand maroon canopy bearing its name in gold letters, was now a shabby, nondescript building of three stories, constructed of faded, chipped brick, that might have housed offices of marginal businesses, or tattoo parlours and pawnshops, or cheap apartments for people on welfare, and the only indication of its actual purpose was a small, hand-lettered sign on its doors that said "Rooms to Let."

Most of the occupants of this sad excuse of a hotel were retired railway workers living out their final years on pensions, the bulk of which they spent in the bar downstairs, a bar with no name above its heavy oak door, which opened with a creak. Archie Duggan knew that creak as well as he knew the click of his own dentures and the slight slur in his voice, which had appeared virtually overnight eleven years earlier when he was hit by lightning in the freakest of freak accidents.

The bartender and general manager of the establishment was a man called Danny O'Hara. That name, like those of the bar and the hotel, was somewhat suspect, since the bartender looked more Latin than Irish, and regulars at the bar speculated he was of Italian or perhaps Spanish origin. In fact, O'Hara was his proper name, and his father, who also had been called Danny O'Hara, was as Irish as any other true son of the Emerald Isle, but his mother was from Sicily and had been named Marianna D'Angelo, Maryann of the angels, and she was that, as Danny O'Hara the younger recalled her, though she had died while he was still in his early teens.

Danny had as black a temper as any Irishman or Sicilian might be expected to have, but he kept it tightly in check. He was a reformed alcoholic who, though he touched the stuff every day but Sunday, dispensing drinks by the thousands, had not brought alcohol to his own lips for fifteen years. He was a stalwart member of Alcoholics Anonymous and had been sponsor to several younger members over the years. He liked to say he had let Jesus into his heart, had given his life over to God, although he wasn't completely sure what either of those statements meant. He knew he believed in God and Jesus and that his life was better, saner, calmer, healthier than it had been when he was drinking and on a constant downward spiral. And if God and Jesus were responsible for that change, then he thanked them, though he had only the haziest idea of their form. He had been a tenant of the hotel for years and was one of the few who could remember when it was still called the Earle, even how to pronounce it, the final "e" silent so the name rhymed with pearl. He had been a railroad man, and had almost lost his life a number of times when drink had the better of him and the perilous rolling stock he worked with came close, almost too close. After he left his drinking days behind him, he became night manager of the hotel, and eventually had moved to take over operation of the bar as well.

O'Hara saw no contradiction in himself, a teetotaler,

tending bar for a clientele that was largely as dependent on drink as he had once been. In fact, he saw himself as a good shepherd, making sure that no one consumed beyond their capacity, keeping them from harm's way in the event a disturbance broke out, protecting them from pushers, grifters, conmen and hotheads who he barred from the premises. Danny even helped several of the regulars to their rooms at closing time, saw to them if they were sick, and was friend and confessor to all—he'd convinced any number of his customers to be his guest at AA meetings and at last a few had joined him, as he liked to put it, "on the right side of the bar."

The permit from the Saskatchewan Liquor Licensing Board, framed and hanging on a wall over the bar, read Earle Hotel Beverage Room, but, despite Danny O'Hara's watchful eye, the bar's nickname, the Bucket of Blood, persisted. It was well earned, if not very current. That was one of the things about the place that appealed to many of its patrons, the vicarious thrill of potential violence without the presence of much real danger. That was certainly some of the appeal to Archie Duggan, and even on the day he died he had not the slightest fear until the very last moment.

On that day—the 17th of August, a Wednesday—Archie came into the bar, smiling to himself over the reassuring creak of the heavy door, at his usual time, more or less fifteen minutes after three in the afternoon. Danny O'Hara, who had a railroad man's eye for detail, had often wondered about the significance of that time—never 3 p.m., never 3:30, but always 3:15, give or take a minute or two in either direction. Early on in their relationship—hardly friends, but bartender to customer, warmed by their mutual knowledge of the past they shared, the past they had, for different reasons, put well behind them—Danny had glanced at his watch as Archie took his preferred seat at one end of the bar, and Archie commented without elaboration "School's out." That was intriguing: was the man a teacher? A parent—or grandparent—of a school-age child? A student himself? From the looks of him, his neat but shabby suit, the Blue Jays ballcap on top a full head of snow white hair, his well-used face and rough hands, Archie was more likely to be a school janitor than any of the other possibilities. But when he died, the small write-up in the paper, the same story that invoked the name and reputation of the Earle Hotel for the first time in the public prints in many years, identified him merely as "a pensioner," so Danny would never know.

The first time Archie Duggan had walked into Danny O'Hara's establishment, six or seven years previous, he had stopped just inside the door to look around, get a whiff of the place. Then, apparently satisfied, he proceeded to the bar. He and O'Hara sized each other up.

"Nice place you got here," Archie said. O'Hara took note of the slight slur in his voice.

"It is," he replied. "What can I get you? Coke? Virgin Caesar?"

"That obvious?" Archie said, just a bit taken aback.

"Takes one to know one," O'Hara said.

After that, the two men were completely comfortable with each other.

On this day, the day he died, Archie arrived at 3:14 by the clock above the bar, an antique Budweiser clock circled by a brass team of heavy-footed draught horses. He took his seat, looked around at the almost-empty premises and nodded familiarly to Danny O'Hara, who had already poured the first of many ginger ales Archie would drink over the next few hours and placed it neatly, on a coaster, in front of him on the bar.

"She's a hot one," Archie remarked.

"She is. Not too bad."

This was more or less the standard exchange between the two men. Through the course of the year, it varied with the weather, Archie observing "she's a cold one," "she's a wet one," "she's a nice one," while Danny agreed but almost always added his cautious addendum, "not too bad." It took scorchers, streaks of minus thirty or blizzards to get the two men to completely agree.

Beyond that, along with the occasional observation about some patron's poor or exemplary behaviour, or remarkable attire, and O'Hara's good-natured joshing about the sagging fortunes of the Blue Jays, their conversation was limited to the bartender's "another?" and the customer's "I believe I will," delivered with his usual all-but-imperceptible slur that, O'Hara thought, gave Archie Duggan's voice a slightly exotic tone.

Archie took his first sip of ginger ale, let the satisfyingly sweet buzz play on his tongue and looked around the bar again. Including himself and the bartender, there were eight people inside the room, three at one table, two lone drinkers at tables and one solitary hooker at the other end of the bar. There was no air conditioning in the Bucket of Blood, so at this time of day, this time of year, when the days still puffed up with heat, there was unlikely to be a crowd. Archie knew all of his fellow patrons this afternoon—regulars, like himself—and he was able to register the satisfying conclusion that there were no threats.

The hooker at the bar was named Jeanne-Marie, after her grandmother, but called herself Crystal. She was mostly Cree—but with plenty of Irish, Scotch and German thrown in for good measure—and had a Rubensesque figure, with plenty of flesh top and bottom within a well-proportioned, well-toned body. She had a longish nose that gave her face a slightly mannish look when in repose, but she was very appealing when she smiled, which she did now, aiming it down the bar in Archie's direction like the beam of a flashlight.

Archie wasn't a fearful man—he had been a hell-raiser and a scrapper in his day—but a cautious one, a trait he had inherited from his father, who had been a soldier in the Great War. Wherever he was, he liked to quickly get the lay of the land, suss out the situation and potential dangers, and plot an escape route. At the Bucket of Blood, even on the day he would die, he had done all that and felt completely comfortable.

Years ago, obscured in the distant past, there had been a notorious murder at the bar, involving a well-known businessman of the day, his mistress, and a second man—a crime of deep passion. There was now not a single person alive who could tell Danny O'Hara more about this crime than those bare facts, that it involved a lot of blood, and that, at the time, it put the name "Earle Hotel" on the lips of the city. In more recent times, there at least two murders had occurred, not actually on the premises but close by, involving people who had just left the bar. Both of these killings were connected to drugs and O'Hara no longer allowed pushers and dealers or people known to have insatiable habits inside his doors. There had also been the usual run of arguments, brawls and assaults, including a nasty one involving a broken beer bottle just a year earlier, but these had become increasingly rare under O'Hara's watch. Trouble-makers were given the bum's rush and the place had a reputation among the residents of the downtown and the near east side who'd be likely to patronize such a bar as a safe haven. There was never a band and O'Hara had rigged the jukebox so it couldn't go over a certain decibel level. Even on a Saturday night, his bar was a quiet, orderly one. There was a lunch—soup and unfussy sandwiches, reasonably priced, made by a woman who came in for a few hours in the morning—that drew in a big noontime crowd, and leftover sandwiches, snug in plastic wrap in the bar fridge, and bags of chips and peanuts available through the evening. There were always a few hookers in the place at night, and some of the rooms upstairs were available by the hour. It was a self-contained establishment. Quiet. Safe. Despite its nickname, it was not a bucket of blood at all.

Like O'Hara, Archie Duggan was a recovered alcoholic but had beaten his demons in a unique way. God may well have taken a hand, but Archie was neither a devotee of the twelve-steps nor "born again," though he had certainly been reborn in an actual sense. And, like O'Hara—and like the hooker Jeanne-Marie—he was of mixed blood: his father, who also was a rolling stone, was a Scottish-Mohawk cross, his mother a high-yellow mulatto from Jamaica whose own father, she always said proudly, was a Jewish tailor from Minsk, in Poland.

Duggan's real given name was Reg, Reginald, actually, and that's what was on his health care card, but most of his life he'd been called Archie, a nickname derived from the comic strip of the same name—ironically so, because his shiny black hair made him more similar to his namesake in the comic, Reggie, than to the carrot-topped hero—and that's how he introduced himself. It's what Danny O'Hara knew him as.

In his traveling days, selling various lines of hardware and cutlery, he often went to Toronto. On this particular occasion, a sultry weekend in July, he was visiting friends there and, to beat the heat, they'd packed a picnic and taken the ferry to the island for the day. There was a concert of some sort, a cooler packed with beer and the flask of vodka Archie always carried in his hip pocket. Beyond that, his memory of the event was blank. He'd apparently fallen asleep in a copse of trees. When he awoke, it was dark. His friends were gone and he was the only person left in what had been a crowded picnic area. He made his way to the ferry slip but the boats were no longer running. Stumbling along the shore, though, he came upon a small aluminum rowboat, and he set out across the harbour—it couldn't have been more than a mile or two, he figured—toward the lights of the city, guided by the stern pulsing finger of the tower.

Thunder had been rumbling in the distance for some time but Archie had ignored it. As he rowed, he was entertained by occasional splashes of sheet lightning which turned the night to day for a heartbeat. Then the sky opened and a torrent of rain fell on him, soaking him to the skin in minutes. Finally, there was a jagged bolt of forked lightning.

With first light, the crew of the harbour fire-rescue boat found the rowboat drifting near the Yonge Street dock. The boat itself had been singed black, but the man inside it was, miraculously, alive and was rushed to hospital, where the jaded emergency room staff rose to the challenge and pulled him through. "It's a miracle you're alive," one of the doctors told Archie when he stopped by his room a couple of days later. He was a tall black man from Nigeria with scars on his face and an incongruous upper-class British accent. The only apparent effects on the patient were that his thick black hair had turned white—with a few stubborn patches of jet that gave him the appearance of a Dalmatian dog or a piebald horse—and a mild slur, barely noticeable, had turned up in his voice.

"Always been lucky," Archie said.

"Take my advice and hedge your bet," the doctor said, arching an eyebrow. "Lightning never strikes twice."

The lightning had left one other effect, although it wasn't apparent for several days. When he was released from hospital, Archie was reclaimed by his friends, sheepish over having abandoned him on the island. Celebratory drinks were poured but Archie declined. He'd lost his thirst, and it wouldn't return.

He remained, though, even in sedentary retirement, a man who liked to spend time in bars, who enjoyed the company of drinkers. He wasn't the sort of man who had ever frequented cocktail lounges, the bars of expensive hotels or the sort of pubs where well-dressed young men and women went to meet. He'd been a working man in his early life, and sometimes down on his luck. Even after he'd become a salesman and took to wearing a suit and tie, he continued to frequent working men's bars, dark, claustrophobic bars rank with the sour smell of stale beer, the fresh scent of sawdust and with just the whiff of possible danger, where men and even women down on their luck gathered. The Bucket of Blood was exactly the sort of place he liked, and he'd been coming to it for over six years now, since he'd moved to the city to be closer to a sister, his only remaining kin. The sister had died, unexpectedly leaving him a little money, but he'd stayed on, no other kin, nowhere else to go. His government pension and the inheritance were enough to keep him comfortable in his small apartment a few blocks down 11th Avenue. It allowed him to eat dinner at one of several Oriental restaurants further up the street or on the rabbits-warren side streets of downtown, just across Broad. There were several Vietnamese places he liked, and a Thai place, though he'd have been hard pressed to explain the difference.

Archie Duggan liked to sleep late, make his own break-fast, read the newspaper he had delivered to his door. He was the sort of man who prided himself on being up to date with the doings of the world. At exactly three p.m. by his kitchen clock, at the mid-point of the afternoon, the time of day when, back in his drinking days, he would begin his day's consumption, he would lock his door, carefully make his way down the one flight of stairs, sniff the outside air and leisurely stroll over to the former Earle Hotel, a walk of about ten minutes, arriving at just around 3:15. He would spend the afternoon there, chatting with the bartender and a few of the patrons, and drinking glass after glass—a litre or two—of ginger ale. This, he was convinced, kept his kidneys and bladder healthy.

Toward evening, he would walk to one of the restaurants he liked and have a modest meal, then return to the Bucket of Blood for several more glasses of ginger ale, the exact number depending on his mood. He liked to be home by eleven to catch Lloyd Robertson on the TV news. Then he would watch a movie if there was something decent on. Occasionally, Crystal, the hooker with the dazzling smile, or one of the other girls who hung out at the bar, would accompany him home for a while, but they'd always be gone by midnight. Late at night, he would sit by his window and watch the dark street below and think about his life. He'd made some mistakes, he reckoned, and was paying for them now, not with pain or discomfort but loneliness.

Bar—restaurant—bar—TV news—a movie…this is exactly the routine Archie followed on the day before he died, and for the days making up the week and two weeks prior to that. On the day before that, two weeks before he died, he had enjoyed, briefly, the company of Crystal. The days and evenings and nights previous to that stacked up like cards in a shuffling deck for years, each card slightly different but mostly the same, dating back to that momentous night on Lake Ontario, when his life had changed—for the better, he thought—and he'd begun to wait, to see if the doctor's prediction would be correct. "Lightning never strikes twice," he'd said. Archie never recalled that comment, day or night, without glancing up to the sky.

For supper on the night he died, Archie had his favourite, the rice noodle bowl with lemongrass, barbequed pork and spring roll, number 68, at Lang's Café on Broad Street. The slip of paper in his fortune cookie forecast, innocuously, "you will benefit from the company of friends," which provoked a rueful smile. He knew many people, but could call no person a friend, really. Once, yes, but that was all far behind him. On the back of the fortune was a series of numbers making up a possible lottery bet, but Archie didn't play the lottery. After the night of the lightning, he figured, he'd used up his life's allotment of good luck and was just coasting. The inheritance from his sister was so unexpected, though ultimately it could be rationalized as not involving luck at all, that he didn't let it alter his theory—or, conversely, it could be seen as using up the very last drop of good luck available to him. The two dollars or five dollars for a lottery ticket, he was sure, would just be thrown away.

In Archie's absence, the Bucket of Blood had begun to fill up. There was always a small crowd of men who came in for a beer or two before heading home to the family after the day shift at the steel mill. There were the usual array of linoleum and carpet layers, plumber's assistants and roofers, single men reluctant to give up the camaraderie of the shop before disappearing into the silence of their apartments and their solitary suppers. And, as darkness drew near, the regulars, the old-timers who lived upstairs, emerged from their cloisters, blinking their eyes, thirsty.

Nelson Bitternose came in to check up on his girls, an aura of slightly cooler air accompanying him. He wasn't particularly welcome but he knew Danny O'Hara would tolerate him as long as he kept his voice down. He no longer dealt drugs, the R&T packets that used to be his stock and trade, and he'd taken up body-building during his last stint at the correctional centre. He still drank, though not as much as before, but he liked to say his body was a temple. He watched what he ate, walked everywhere, and drank only a brand of beer that, he'd been assured, had no preservatives. He masturbated twice daily, morning and evening, as he'd learned in prison to keep the fluids of his body balanced, and avoided the girls, except for business. He no longer carried a weapon and rarely felt the need for one.

Bitternose went to the bar and slung one lean haunch on a stool. He and O'Hara eyed each other warily, as if they were adversaries on a square of canvas.

"Hey," Bitternose said.

"Hey," Danny O'Hara replied.

Bitternose ordered a bottle of the beer he liked, Labatt's Classic, and waved off the glass when O'Hara brought it. He drained the bottle in four or five long pulls. He sauntered over to the end of the bar, where Crystal had been joined by another girl, and had a brief word with them. The girls, like Archie Duggan, sipped ginger ale. The second girl finished her drink, picked up her bag and left. Bitternose went back to where his beer bottle still stood on the bar and ordered another.

After Danny O'Hara served him, from his vantage

point behind the bar, the bartender surveyed his domain. Except on Fridays and Saturdays, when he had a waitress helping out, delivering glasses of beer by the trayful to the tables, O'Hara was usually able to handle the load himself. Most people came to the bar to order—that was the custom when O'Hara was working alone, and the regulars were familiar with it. But some stayed at their tables, raising their heads occasionally to catch Danny's eye, or lifting an arm with two or three fingers extended, and he would, after a few minutes, bring them what he knew they wanted. On a Wednesday night, this routine was enough, he liked to say, to keep him on his toes but not run off his feet. Now, in a brief lull, at a little before 7:30 p.m., he was able to take stock. There were the steelworkers at their usual tables, there the construction guys, there the tradesmen, and, scattered about, the isolated men from upstairs. Archie Duggan had not yet returned from his supper and his usual spot at the end of the bar remained open. Should anyone attempt to take it, O'Hara would shake his head to warn him off.

One fellow whose absence O'Hara noted was Blossoms Dearie, one of the old-timers who lived upstairs. The man's real name was Lannie Miestre and he had come by his nickname because of his love of flowers. He'd first been exposed to them at the experimental farm near Indian Head, where he'd grown up and gone to residential school, learning something of horticulture. Later, in the city, he'd worked at greenhouses and for florists. Now, he lived on the third floor of the former Earle Hotel, in a small room filled with plants—various ivies, African violets, rubber plants and an abundance of other greenery which, on the rare occasions when Blossoms forgot to drop off the rent and Danny O'Hara stopped in to collect it, the stoop-shouldered man was at pains to identify for his visitor. On his windowsill, every summer, there was a large planter crowded with pansies and baby-faced petunias. Several crockery flower pots of various sizes, with begonias, more pansies and peonies, stood on the fire escape adjacent to his window. Blossoms spent his day fussing over these plants, watering, pruning and cultivating them, talking to them. As long as the sun shone on them, they filled him up, but usually by eight p.m., even in the height of summer, and long before that at other times of the year, he was downstairs, attending to his own thirst. O'Hara had lured Blossoms Dearie to AA a couple of times, and he seemed willing enough, but it never took, though he attended three meetings in a row once. That was several years ago.

Today, because it was so hot, he had lingered longer than usual over his plants, making sure they were well watered. Now he was having a supper of soup from a can and toast, all he usually needed to sustain him, regardless of the weather. In a few minutes, he would be going downstairs. He could taste the beer, bitter and sweet, already.

Archie Duggan had finished his own dinner but had lingered, in bantering conversation with the waitress, an old Vietnamese woman he liked. Her English was so poor, he could never be sure what she was saying, or if she understood what he said in reply, but they had developed a relaxed sense of understanding. When he ate at Lang's, he always sat in her section, or, if the place was crowded and she noticed him sitting elsewhere, she switched with someone else to wait on him. Her name was Violet, which she pronounced more like Vi-low. "Hello, Violet," Archie would say, on greeting her, and she would reply, "Yes, yes, Vi-low." Now, Archie dug in his pocket for a generous tip and rose from the table.

"Back to the grind," he said, his usual parting riposte. "No rest for the wicked."

The waitress replied jovially, but with words he failed to understand.

Archie nodded to some of the other patrons of the restaurant as he made his way to the door and stepped out onto Broad Street where hot air assailed him like a swarm of flies. The taste of ginger and garlic was still on his tongue but he was already looking forward to his first sip of ginger ale—ginger, ginger ale, so different. He had entertained this thought many times. It would take him no more than five minutes to walk back to the Bucket of Blood, even at his slow pace.

Nelson Bitternose finished the last swallow of his beer, gave Crystal a meaningful glance, nodded to Danny O'Hara and made for the door. It opened with a creak Danny could hear all the way from behind the bar.

At that moment, Blossoms Dearie, having finished his soup and washed the bowl, plate, spoon and pan, reached out his window with a watering pot to give one last drink to the simmering plants. His hand brushed against a small pot of multi-coloured pansies that was precariously perched on the fire escape, and, as he often feared might happen, it tipped over and went plummeting to the sidewalk three stories below. The flower pot narrowly missed Archie Duggan, just on his way in, and Nelson Bitternose, whose hand was still on the door, holding it open for the older man, but landed with a crash at their feet that startled them both.

Nelson spun around. He was being fired on and needed to take cover, back inside. Archie, who always had an escape route in mind, continued in the direction he was already headed, but at an accelerated pace, unsure of what had happened. He wasn't nearly as quick or agile as the big man behind him, though. Bitternose plowed into Archie, sending him flying. Adrenaline was already coursing through Archie's blood, producing a not-unpleasant sensation, so when he landed against a table filled with steelworkers, his snowy white head coming to a rest against a chair leg with a sharp crack, the last thing he felt wasn't pain but exhilaration. Then there was nothing. He never had time to reconsider the doctor's words, and there was no flash of lightning, not even stars. When the ambulance arrived, just minutes later, the paramedics unofficially pronounced him dead; it would take a doctor back at General Hospital—another swarthy man from Africa, as it happened—to make it official. His neck was broken, one of the medics said.

"Probably didn't feel a thing," he told Danny O'Hara.

"Jesus," O'Hara said aloud, and silently he said a prayer, for Archie Duggan, for himself, for all the patrons of the Earle Hotel Beverage Room, regardless of their various failings and sins.

The girl called Crystal went in the ambulance with the body to the hospital. She knew she was closer to Archie Duggan than anyone else alive, so it was no real lie to agree, when she was asked, that she was next of kin.

The police were at the bar even before the ambulance left, though. One of the men in uniform talked quietly to Nelson Bitternose, who sat at a table, stunned. Another went upstairs to have a chat with Blossoms Dearie. A sergeant took a statement from Danny O'Hara, who he knew well.

They agreed the whole thing was a tragic accident, to the extent, at least, that, in Danny O'Hara's cosmology, accidents were possible.

Afterwards, Danny bought a round for the house, a rare but not unheard-of occurrence, then closed the doors of the Bucket of Blood early. There was just a minimum of grumbling.

ECLIPSE

Papa sends me an email: *I've got a new drug of choice. Vodka. Ever try it? I mean* really *try it?*

I write back: *Sure. When I was in kneepants, I had the odd screwdriver or two. OJ killed the taste.*

Papa replies: *But that's the thing, there is* no *taste. It's the perfect drink for the new millennium.*

🎤

We've been calling him Papa so long, I have to think for a second what his real name is. It's Ernest, of course. But he hated that, even after he discovered Hemingway, never used Ernest. Surprised the shit out of me to hear Marliss call him that years later.

"Ernie Klein," he said, sticking out his hand, "German, not Jewish. But not *that* kind of German." Long drink of water, mop of brown curly hair, deep brown eyes, eyes that can fool you.

We're in the bar at the student union, Papa, me, Pam and Claire, maybe a couple of others. This is right after English class, first class of the term, our first term, University of Calgary. We've all just met. First-year English, "bonehead English," the prof had called it, grinning.

"Not *that* kind," I said. "What does that mean?"

"You know, the Hitlery kind, the kind that gave Germans a bad name."

"Sean McMullen," I said, playing along. "But not *that* kind of Irish."

"And what kind is *that* kind?" Papa, still known as Ernie, asked.

"You know, green beer, potatoes, 'When Irish eyes are smiling...'"

"'Oh, Danny boy...'" Papa began to sing.

"That's it exactly."

"Well, we're getting a pretty good idea of what everybody *isn't*," Pam said.

I worry about Papa. Living way off there in exotic New York City, no woman to keep him warm and safe from the temptations and dangers of the street, Rosemary long dead and Marliss gone, who knows what kind of shit he's getting himself into these days. Papa and shit have a magnetic appeal for each other. If they were co-stars in a movie, the critics would say they have great chemistry. That may be fine for shit, but it's not so great for Papa.

There are three Gods in Papa's life: Bob Dylan, Ken Kesey and I forget who the third is, Hunter S. Thompson maybe. Kesey died not long ago, which may have something to do with this vodka thing. I knew it would hit him hard, although exactly why is more complex than you might think.

The King is Dead, Long Live the King, he emailed me the day the news broke. Liver cancer, just sixty-six. So much promise unfulfilled. Then he added, *The King had clay feet.*

Papa is a man out of his time—either ahead of it or

behind, I'm not sure which. Living here in Saskatchewan, where we're on Mountain Daylight Time all year long, it's hard for me to tell.

~

It was in the bar that we started calling him Papa, not that first time but soon after. It was Pam who called him that first. Whatever it was we were talking about, Ernie took a slug of draught and pronounced, "It was good."

"Right, Papa," Pam said—she was usually the quick one with jokes, one-liners, rolled eyes. We all laughed and the name stuck. I never called him Ernie again.

It's not that he looked like Hemingway, or even had his macho sensibility. If anything, he looks more like Fitzgerald, or like one of those lost, star-crossed characters from *Gatsby*, maybe even Gatsby himself, forever gazing across the bay to the light on Daisy's dock. I'm his Nick.

If it were us having that famous Hemingway-Fitzgerald conversation, it would be him telling me that the rich are very different from you and me, and it would be me who'd be the practical one, saying, "Yeah, Jerk-off, they have more money."

But we'd just been reading Hemingway, and that week he was The Man. "Hills Like White Elephants," that's the one we'd been assigned, but "A Clean Well Lighted Place" was in the anthology too and we all read it. And Papa went right down to a used bookstore and got a copy of the *Collected Stories,* and he and I traded it back and forth for weeks, with annotations in the margins.

~

The day of the eclipse, Ken Kesey Day, as I think of it, Papa kind of lost it. Or did he find it? I've been refereeing hockey long enough to know that when you lose it once, it's usually just a matter of time till you lose it again.

But finding it? I don't know. I'm a high school English teacher, not a priest or a shrink. And a reader, not a writer.

~🎤

Scotch. For years, that's been Papa's drink of choice, so this turn to vodka is surprising, if not alarming.

I email him the next day: *The ghosts of all those bottles of Chevis Regal and Glenfiddich are going to haunt you for abandoning the spirit.*

He fires back: *What, the spirit of Scotch is a jealous spirit, put-no-other-spirit-above-me?*

Not jealous, I reply. *But it demands loyalty.*

Papa: *What about its loyalty to me? I've given Scotch the best years of my life. Why should it begrudge me a little fling with vodka?*

I start to write: *Well, how would you feel if your long-time lover turned her eye to someone younger?* but I delete that. It's been less than a year since Marliss left. Papa says he's fine now, but I know better. All this talk about vodka is leading to something, I know. I just don't know what.

~🎤

I wouldn't say Papa has a drinking problem; I would never call him a drunk. I've seen him drunk once or twice, and he does drink a lot, I don't deny that. But I say it's not a problem because I don't think he *needs* it. Sometimes he'll have one or two at lunch, if other people are drinking, but usually not till after work. One or two at the bar, then a few after dinner. Maybe a few more later to get to sleep. Where's the problem?

He has a real capacity. The first few times we went out

together, I tried to keep up with him, so did Pam and Claire. Of course, back then, university days, you think of drinking as part of the whole thing, rites of passage, that sort of stuff. It's never serious. In the bar at the student union, or wherever else we'd wind up, pitchers of beer, deadly stuff. Trying to keep up with Papa, we'd be under the table. We learned better pretty quick.

Still, me drinking half as much as him, it'd be Papa who'd drive us home, help me to bed more than once. Saved my life more than once too, most likely.

On our England trip, he was into sampling the local brews, every public house we came to. Single malt Scotches too. Then he scored that rock of hash, that was his undoing. From London, we drove south in a rented van to Brighton and along the channel coast to Portsmouth, and he was smoking all the way. By the time we came across Kesey and the Pranksters, he was good and gone. "Further" it said on the front of this bus, in the place where on a regular bus it would say Edmonton or Toronto. "Further." But Papa was already further along.

✎

Vodka? How do you even know it's there? I email him. *No taste, no colour, how do you know it isn't just water?*

That's just the thing, he writes back. *All that Scotch all those years, it muddled up my dreams, muddled me up. All that murky brown. Vodka's clear as god's eye. I can see right through it.*

What's to see? I email him.

Ah.... Papa writes back.

✎

Somewhere along the line in our planning, we had gotten wind that Kesey and the Pranksters would be in England too, on the same pilgrimage we were—amazing what you learn on the Net—and I'd brought along my copy of *Cuckoo's Nest*, a hardcover first edition. I've never had any serious hope of writing books myself, but I love them, and I can afford to be a collector. I have first editions of everything Kesey's done, but none of them signed. Papa and I were both excited at the prospect of actually running into The Man; I'm just an admirer, but with Papa it was something closer to idolatry. Hemingway had turned Papa into a writer, but after he read *Cuckoo's Nest* and *Sometimes a Great Notion*, Kesey was the writer he wanted to be. Well, that and all the tomfoolery, all that Acid Kool-Aid stuff.

✒

It's funny how friendship goes. It can be so intense, then fade away to nothing. Or last. Like love, I guess.

That first year in Calgary, Papa, me, Pam and Claire, we were it. The Four Musketeers of Bonehead English, that was us. For a while, the four of us were living together, in a big old house down in Hillhurst. Killed a lot of little brown soldiers, buried god and took care of the Meaning of Life. Played the odd hand of Hearts.

I think Papa had a thing for Claire for a while, short, dark and a rollercoaster of curves. And I know I was a little sweet on Pam, fair and all angles and sharp lines. But nothing came of it, no romance, no sex, though I continued to like Pam's disheveled blonde looks, her easy laugh. Just good pals. Lots of booze. Papa renamed us the Four Horse-people of the A-pack-o-lapse. Pam and Claire were both poets and Papa was a pretty fair hand with words on a page too. I was the hanger-on, not even a pretender, though they managed to talk me into joining them in a creative writing class winter term that turned out to be an even easier ace than it was knocked up to be. Papa's the only one of us who stuck with it, though. Still hasn't got a novel finished, but TV made his fortune.

Claire, always the romantic, married some British grad student and they both buggered off to England. The marriage didn't last long, but she's still there, says she likes the beer too much to ever come back. Likes it so much, in fact, she owns her own pub, which, after having a used book shop, strikes me as just about the perfect job. Pam's in Vancouver, divorced too, doing the single mom thing, a hotshot lawyer making a name for herself, human rights and feminist stuff. Me, I'm a small-town teacher and hockey referee, right back where I started, in Chopin, Saskatchewan, medium fish in a little pond, married, to the principal, no less, two kids, happy as can be as long as I've got a book and a glass of good scotch close at hand. Comfortable. Comfortable as all hell.

Papa's in New York, a big-deal writer-producer at CBS now, another hit show under his belt. The three of us, me, Pam and Papa, still get together once every year or two— well, we did up until the eclipse, two years ago now—and used to write and phone fairly regular. Now, with email, it's almost every day. Just as if we were living together again. Claire and Pam have stayed tight too, and Pam's been across the pond to visit a bunch of times. It was the two of them cooked up the idea for our get-together, the eclipse, turn of the millennium, twentieth reunion all rolled into one.

𝄞

Bill Kinsella was the instructor of that creative writing class we took, this was before he was famous. He's also the one who had used the "bonehead English" label the year before, and you could tell he didn't give a shit, for the class, the material, us. But in creative writing, he was a completely different guy. Even the stuff we wrote, he treated with respect, as long as we were serious about it and he could tell we weren't pissing around. "Forget about Art," he said, pronouncing the A as a capital. "*Don't* forget what Dr. Johnson said about a writer who doesn't write for money being a blockhead. You think the medical students and law students and engineers and commerce people are in it for Art?"

We had lots of debates about that, in the bar. "If it's not Art," Claire would say, "what's the point?" Pam was with her. I sided with Kinsella. I was reading mysteries, science fiction, thinking I could maybe write that sort of stuff, it didn't look so hard. I certainly wasn't adverse to making money. Still Art was Art. Papa didn't say too much in the bar on the point, but he listened close to Kinsella. And he's the only one of us who makes his living from the pen. Television isn't *lit-er-a-chure*, but it's writing just the same, and some of Papa's stuff has been damn good. All Pam writes is legal briefs. I'm a reader, someone who helps other people be readers too. Closest I get to writing is collecting books, first editions.

Still, Papa never turned his back on Art. He didn't say much on the subject, but I remember him saying this: "Why not make Art that makes money?" That's one of the things he admired so much about Kesey.

🎤

Some people say *Gatsby* is a perfect novel, *the* perfect novel. For Papa, it's *Notion*, all its sprawl and self-indulgence aside. Actually, that's part of what he loves about it. I guess Henry Stamper is a fourth God in Papa's heaven. If you don't know the story, it's all about freedom, about defiance, about fighting back. Stamper is this Oregon lumberman, crusty old bastard. In the movie version, he's played by Henry Fonda, at his crustiest, Paul Newman's one of his sons. There's a big fight with a union. Toward the end, Stamper loses his hand in an accident. He and his sons figure out a way of giving the finger to their enemies, to the world, literally.

                        🎤

The whole idea of the England trip was to see the eclipse, the last big one of the dying millennium, at Stonehenge. It was Pam and Claire's idea but Papa embraced it and made it his own, then he almost crapped out at the last minute. He wanted to marry Marliss there, at the moment that the lights went out. He'd gotten on the Net and found a funky Anglican priest willing to do the job. But by the time it came to start packing, Marliss was history. *What's the point of going?* Papa emailed me.

    You get your sorry ass on the plane or I'll break your arms, I wrote back. When I met up with Pam in Toronto for the flight over, I told her I still wasn't sure if we'd be seeing Papa or not, but when we got to Heathrow, there he was on the arrivals deck with Claire, waiting for us. He'd arrived less than an hour earlier from New York. "So what took you so fucking long?" he carped. "You think we got all millennium?"

                        🎤

Susan, the mother of my children, was my high school sweetheart. We broke up when I went off to university, but when I came home to Saskatchewan there she still was and the rest, as they say, is history. "You had your little fling with freedom at school," she likes to say. "Now you're mine." She's only half kidding, but I don't mind. With Papa, it was one damn thing after another, through school and the years after when he was trying to make it in TO, working on a novel and writing scripts for some dumb lawyer show. But then along came Rosemary, a make-up gal on the same show. I didn't believe it till I was best man at their wedding. He was as happy as I'd ever known him to be, and she kept him centred, focused, whatever. His show turned into a hit, he became a producer, said he owed it all to her. When she got breast cancer and died so quickly, it knocked him right off the rails.

Papa went a little unhinged for a while there, no surprise. He took an informal oath of celibacy in Rosemary's memory, but it didn't last long. They'd been together long enough, and he'd been faithful enough—in his fashion—he didn't think there'd be any point in even looking around. "Who'd be interested in a broken down old widowman like me anyway?" he said, only halfway ironic, and he sat around their Toronto townhouse for a while, staring at the walls and thinking The Big Questions all over again. This was followed by a new-girl-every-night-and-lots-of-coke period, a few months that burned out quick. Then he gave Rosemary's stuff to Goodwill, sold the place, told the Corp to shove it and made the big move to New York, where all the networks had been after him for a while. It was the move he'd promised himself years ago but put on the shelf when he and Rosie got together. Things just clicked for him there, a hit show, then another, and the next thing I knew he was on the phone, as out of breath as he'd ever been years ago, telling me about Marliss.

He snagged tickets for the Dylan-Van Morrison-Joni Mitchell show at the Gardens and talked Susan and me into flying down there. "He needs your approval," Susan said.

I raised my eyebrows.

"Well, wants anyway. You two are still in school together. You always will be."

Pretty smart, my wife. She didn't mean it as an insult.

Before the show, we all went out to dinner and I got my first look at this girl he'd been raving about. Marliss was a looker, no question, and young enough to be his daughter. She did something in the film biz I couldn't quite figure out but my jaw really dropped when she mentioned, just in passing, that Dylan left her cold. Van too. That's about all Papa listens to.

"Let me get this straight," I said. "You don't like Bob Dylan?"

"No."

"Don't like Van Morrison?"

"Not much."

"Now you're going to tell me you don't like Ken Kesey."

"Ernest gave me a copy of *Cuckoo's Nest* but I couldn't get into it."

"Ernest," I said. I gave her a long look. She didn't blink. Ice blue eyes, long lashes.

"So do you two have anything in common?"

"Well," she said, straight-faced, "...I love sex."

I looked over and Papa was grinning like Pooh Bear, his head bobbing up and down.

🎤

As it turned out, Marliss was an awesome girl, as my kids say, and she and Papa were as happy as could be, living in the Soho loft he'd bought—his monthly payments are about as much as all my worldly goods combined. Whatever it was he'd been looking for, she had it, said he was happy as he'd ever been with Rosemary in the best times. I had my doubts because, deep down, Papa is a one-woman man, like I am, and Rosie had come first.

And, young as she was, it didn't seem to me Marliss would stick around all that long. Still, he settled down, got back to work on the novel and was sending me chapters that kept me wide-eyed through the night. He'd always been good, but this was better than anything he'd done. Of course, it all went in the crapper after Marliss left. It was just like Rosemary dying all over again.

Papa was in a foul mood from the get-go. He didn't like the English weather, which was horrid, the English food, or the drafty English inns Claire had lined up for us. Even the English ale left him cold. It seemed like he just wanted to get to Stonehenge as soon as possible, see the eclipse and get it over with.

Claire led us on a merry tour of museums, pubs and a couple plays in London before we hit the road. It was great the four of us being together again—the first time all of us since Calgary twenty years before—without spouses or kids, just the Four Horsepeople of the A-pack-o-lapse together again, except this time we were the Horsepeople of the Eclipse. Well, "three horsepeople, one horse's ass," Claire said. She'd put on quite a bit of weight but otherwise seemed unchanged. Pam too was the same fun-loving girl I remembered so well, and I like to think I'm not all that different than I was. Papa, though... Everybody was having a great time, except Papa, who wasn't really trying. He was drinking a lot, smoking cigarettes again after having quit, and the hash—squirreled into a back seat with the window cracked open, gazing out at the grey, impacted sky—but none of it was making him any happier. He had nothing good to say about anything and plenty of snark. Pam kept tossing me these exasperated looks—*do something*—but I'm a past master at indulging Papa. Pam's got a teenaged son she's used to handling on her own and only so much patience, so it wasn't long before she was telling Papa to stop being such an asshole.

He started sulking for real after that. "I could be in Majorca, sipping rum through cigars," he growled. "Who needs this shit?"

"So what's keeping you?" Pam shot back. "Who needs this shit indeed?" But she was grinning, and she and Papa have too much between them to sour the whole deal. Still, it was a relief there were just two more days till the eclipse. We'd all planned on another few days in Paris afterwards, but Papa let us know he'd changed his reservation and would be splitting the day after The Big Dark. No one was really sorry.

The whole idea had been to see the eclipse at Stonehenge. Papa and I had never been there, Pam and Claire raved about the place. Somewhere along the way, though, we heard that Van Morrison would be doing a concert at Penzance, at the tip of the Cornish coast, while the dragon ate the sun over the Celtic Sea. Kesey and the Pranksters were heading there too, we heard, and would be doing some sort of a show, and that all sounded too good to miss. We got to Stonehenge two days before the eclipse, a day behind the Pranksters. It was stark and spooky, what we could see of it in the unrelenting grey light. The stones seemed aloof and lonely. We gave it a good shivery look and pushed on.

We spent the night at a hostel near a place called Bodmin Moor, a couple hours' drive from Penzance, and we got wind that the Pranksters were already there, had set up a big tent and were holding court. "Hot damn," Papa said. It was the first thing he'd said in hours, and there wasn't any question what we'd do. At first light, we piled back into the van and took off. We had no trouble finding the place, just followed the thickening flow of traffic, but it took longer getting there than we thought. There was the rainbow-coloured bus itself, big as life just as Tom Wolfe had given it to us, and freshly painted, lots of oranges and pinks. There were a couple of BBC vans parked alongside it and a crowd had gathered to watch Kesey being interviewed. What good timing! I grabbed my copy of *Cuckoo* and we all pressed in. I didn't know if I'd get a chance to get it signed, but I didn't want to miss any chance there was. Papa, I noticed, hung back a little, like a schoolboy suddenly struck shy. Not like him at all.

Kesey was waxing eloquent. He was still a good-looking man, but soft in the gut, white haired, and every trip he'd ever taken had left a wrinkle on his mug. He was wearing a shirt made out of a U.S. flag and a woolen white cap, and talking like a Yankee Doodle Dandy, which might not have gone down so smooth with the BBC crowd. It was hard to hear everything, there was such a press, but he was saying something about acid in the water supply doing more to end wars than all the missiles in Bill Clinton's quiver combined; something about too many fat women in the U.S. because people were too focused on the corporeal—I could see Pam and Claire gnashing their teeth; and I heard the word "Jesus" two or three times, which was two or three times more than I would have expected since he wasn't using it as an epithet. It was hard to tell if he was being straight, ironic, or putting them all on.

But then there was Papa at my elbow, whispering, "*Jesus* is right. What a crock of shit."

That got my attention because, as I said, Kesey is to

Papa what Gretsky is to my boy Eric, who's fourteen and a pretty fair left-wing in his peewee league.

Just about this time, even Kesey seemed to realize how weird he was sounding and he cut it off with a weak joke and a grin: "Have to go practice for the eclipse now, you know, holding my breath." He began heading back toward the bus, where some of the Pranksters were going at it with fresh day-glo spray cans. They were paunchy and grizzled too, so I knew they were probably originals, real Merry Pranksters from the first bus tour back in the Sixties, which made me all the more tongue-tied, but I barged ahead with the book. I don't know what had become of Papa at this point.

"Mr. Kesey" would have sounded pretentious, just "Kesey" too abrupt. "Ken Kesey," I said, "Sean McMullen," and I stuck out my right hand just as if we were bumping into each other in the hallway of my school. On an impulse, I added: "Irish, but not *that* kind of Irish."

The Great Man looked a little confused for a moment, but he shook my hand and gave me a frank expression. I grinned back. "I'm acting brave but my knees are trembling," I confessed. "I've got a first edition of *Cuckoo's Nest* I've brought all the way from Chopin, Saskatchewan, in Canada. Would you sign it for me?"

"I've been in Saskatchewan," Kesey said, and that's all he said, but he took the book from me, waving off the pen I offered. He looked around, found a small lettering brush on the table the bus painters were using and selected two small jars, one of orange, the other purple. He got down on the grass, sprawling out like a kid with the open book. I couldn't see what he was doing, but the motion of his shoulders made it clear he was writing. He took so long, the BBC guys noticed and came over. The next thing I knew, I was being interviewed.

"What exactly does Ken Kesey mean to you?" The guy with the microphone had eyeglasses falling down his thin nose, and I couldn't help focusing on it. I started bullshitting about the whole Magic Kool-Aid thing, how it changed my life, which wasn't exactly *not* true, and thinking they really should be talking to Papa, and where the hell had Papa got off to, anyway? My attention shifted from the guy with the mike to the girl in a tight green t-shirt holding the shoulder camera, a girl the Beatles were thinking of when they coined the term "fab," and just then, over her other shoulder, I saw Papa with one of the spray cans sneaking around the end of the bus, except he was sneaking the way Charlie Chaplin or Buster Keaton might, with slow giant steps and one finger up to his nose. Kesey was still on the ground happily defacing my copy of his book, but, hey, it was *his* book. All of a sudden there was this commotion from the other side of the bus, and a woman screamed.

Did I say Charlie Chaplin? I should have said Groucho Marx. What happened next was right out of *Horse Feathers* or *A Night at the Opera*. Everybody except Kesey dropped everything and made a beeline for the end of the bus, including the fab girl, who jogged along prettily with the camera bouncing on her shoulder, dragging the guy with the mike in her wake. Me too, because I had a pretty good idea that Papa was at the other end of the string that led to that scream. Sure enough, there was Papa on the ground with these two big lugs straddling him, Pranksters, it looked like, and there was this woman in what looked at first to be a multi-colour party dress standing with eyes bugging out staring at them. I say "what looks to be a party dress" because when we got closer I could see it was actually a pale blue cotton shift but someone had sprayed the front of it with pink day-glo paint, a broad swath that actually started at the woman's chin and went straight down her bosom to her waist before petering out. The same colour paint was splattered over the side of the bus in big broad strokes, where someone had painted a crude raised fist, middle finger extended, the famous symbol of defiance from *Sometimes a Great Notion.*

I worry about this vodka thing. If you're of a mind to drink yourself to death, that just might be the drink to do it with.

Papa sends me an email with a bunch of happy faces and a bunch of slogans from vodka ads over the years, stuff like Absolut Pefection, Absolut Truth, Fun things happen with Smirnoff. There's even an attachment of a famous ad, Zsa Zsa Gabor in a party dress under a red balloon, sipping a martini.

At the end of the list is this one:

*********It leaves you breathless*********

All those years as a hockey referee doesn't count for nothing. I know how to cut an argument short. I had us out of there, and at minimum cost, in no time. To get the woman to quit screaming, I pressed two twenty-pound notes on her, which worked like a charm. "Buy a new dress," I told her, "buy *two* new dresses." To get the BBC crew to back off, I explained that Papa was a mental patient, I was escorting him to a funeral. This is a gag that dates back to our early days in Calgary, and I'm convincing at it. You could see the light go out of the eyes of the reporter with the sliding glasses.

Even with that forty pounds, which is around a hundred bucks Canadian, I figure I'm way ahead. That *Cuckoo's Nest* was worth a couple hundred already—it would have been more but the dust jacket has a tear on the back—and god only knows what it would fetch now, with what Kesey wrote, his name in orange, the date in purple, and "eclipse!" in both colours, alternating letters. Priceless, as they say. It took him ten minutes, easy, and covers two facing pages. He was just finishing up when I remembered and got back to his side of the bus. He'd ignored the commotion, kept right on with his lettering.

"Thanks very much," I said—it sounded lame, but what else do you say?

"S'okay, Saskatchewan," he said. He turned away and climbed through the door into the bus. He looked tired, old, suddenly.

We did the same, into our van, Papa as subdued as I've seen him since Rosemary's funeral.

The next day was socked in and there was no eclipse to see, really, just a darkening of the smudge, the grey sky pulsing like a heart for a few minutes, then a gradual lightening, the worst anticlimax anyone could imagine. "Looks like God got tired of the play and drew the curtain," Papa said.

Morrison did his gig and the Pranksters their show, something about finding Merlin, but we'd been too late to get tickets. Even Papa couldn't harangue them out of anyone. The whole thing was a bust all around. And the worst thing was we heard later the sky was clear over Stonehenge, the eclipse there spectacular.

We dragged ourselves to a late breakfast somewhere, watery eggs and greasy sausage, and headed back to the hostel. Papa and I had been up late the night before, not talking much, just drinking scotch and, Papa at last, laying some ghosts to rest, or so I thought. He cried real tears, first for Rosemary, then for Marliss, a few, I guess, for himself.

I was wiped and hit the sleeping bag for an hour. When I got up, Papa had flown, hitched a ride with someone, apparently, without a word to anyone. He'd left me a note, though: *I can't do this anymore.*

I thought again of the last sight I'd had of Kesey, climbing on the bus. A man in a ridiculous shirt, soft in the middle. There was something to the tilt of his shoulders that had seemed resigned, even forlorn.

For a while, I didn't know if Papa was alive or dead. It was as if he had disappeared off the face of the earth, just the way the sun had that day. There was no answer at his Soho pad, and at CBS he was still on vacation, even though weeks had passed. The next time I called, he was "in a meeting," but he didn't phone back. I stopped calling, and months passed. Finally, the emails began again, just as if nothing had happened.

There's more than one way to see an eclipse, he wrote obliquely.

It reminded me that looking at an eclipse is a good way to go blind, so maybe that overcast was a blessing in disguise. I remembered something Bill Kinsella had said back in Bonehead English: "In literature, not everything is as it seems. Just like in life."

We were supposed to get together last summer, take in a few Dylan shows, but somehow our wires got crossed and it didn't happen. Same thing this summer, but we promised each other Christmas in Mexico. Then Sept. 11, Ground Zero just a couple of miles from Papa's office at CBS. He wasn't hurt or anything but apparently shaken as a martini, and the vodka messages started to come. Two months later exactly, Kesey packed it in. Papa's emails became even bleaker. It occurred to me that he was either going to drink himself to death or finish his novel, one or the other, I didn't know which.

Like I said, I'm neither priest nor shrink, just a reader.

I've been thinking about vodka, how it's both more and less than it seems to be. A dandy metaphor. I'd try it out on my students but it's maybe not the most appropriate things for Grade tens and twelves.

Papa was always a big one for metaphors, ever since. Kinsella explained them to us. That and irony.

It appealed to Papa, saying one thing and meaning the opposite, talking about one thing but meaning another.

Not everyone saw it. "It's dumb," Claire said. "Why not just say what you mean?" This was before she really understood poetry and metaphor became her meat and potatoes. For me, it was no revelation. Lapsed Roman Catholic that I am, I see icons everywhere. I'd understood what Kinsella was saying right away, realized I already knew it.

"Saying what you mean is for squares," Papa said. "Suits. People without imagination."

"Imagination's a defence," Claire said, huffy.

"What's a meta for?" Papa shot back, grinning. "I mean, among friends."

Now he sends me this email: *I'm filling a tub with vodka. Gonna take me a long, slow bath.*

Bathtub gin, I write back. *Gin.*

You fill your tub your way, Papa writes. *I'll fill mine my way.*

LIGHTFOOT AND GOODBODY, IMPROBABLE AS IT SOUNDS

Lightfoot set out.

What he'd hoped to take with him was a change of socks and underwear, an apple, a wedge of cheese and a crust or two of bread, folded up in a red bandana and slung at the end of a stout walking stick into a thirties-style bindlestiff. Romantic though the image was, it proved impractical, as he had neither bandana nor stick. Instead, he stuffed essentially the same goods—the underwear and socks times two, augmented by two clean short-sleeved knit shirts, his usual summer attire, and a good-sized chunk of cheddar and half a loaf of Winnipeg-style Safeway rye bread in plastic wrap—into a small red knapsack, along with a plastic bottle of water, his reading glasses in a stout case, and a dog-eared paperback copy of *The Grapes of Wrath*, which he'd found the day before at Barney's Used Books for ninety-five cents. And it was with this, slung on his right shoulder, the one less prone to arthritic pain, that he set off on a bright June morning to find not his fortune so much as a direction, not *his* direction necessarily, but one that would do.

The romantic image, too, called for him to shuffle off

into the sunset. Instead, leaving early in the morning, the sun was still at his back as he headed west along the Trans-Canada Highway (a brief bus ride brought him to the edge of town), his thumb stuck out in the most desultory of fashion. The mountains, where he imagined himself laying his head beside a free-flowing stream, beneath rain-fresh resin-smelling pine trees, were many hundreds of miles away—he still steadfastly refused to use the word "kilometre" or any of the other metric vocabulary. They were surely too far to reach in a day's tramping, maybe two, even with good luck and many rides. Between them lay miles and miles of undulating fields of amber wheat, sky-blue flax, bright-yellow canola—his mouth pursed in sour annoyance at the made-up name for the perfectly legitimate rape his grandfather had once planted, some people's sensitivities be damned; miles of grain, then equal miles of undulating rangeland where, if he was lucky, he might see an antelope in the distance and a hawk observing his progress disdainfully from high above. Many, many miles, far too many for any man to walk, let alone a seventy-seven-year-old man with bad knees, a bad stomach, and a stroke, mild though it was, only two years behind him. Still, what lay ahead, he knew—*thought* he knew, at any rate—was do-able, weighted down merely by discomfort. And with all this in mind, and a hundred and seventy-seven dollars, in various denominations and combinations of change in his pockets, a VISA card in his wallet, a pair of poorly fitting sunglasses perched on his nose, and a jaunty porkpie hat set at an angle on his almost hairless head, Lightfoot set out.

God knew, there was little to keep him.

As he trudged along the gravelly shoulder of the highway, he once again recited the so-familiar litany of his misfortunes: wife dead, son estranged, daughter and son-in-law devoted enough but, damn it, they did have lives of their own; friends dead, moved away, confined to nursing homes or hospitals, or caught up in an indifference brought on by illness, medication, forgetfulness, weariness or some combination of same; job gone, profession barred to him by licensing rules and his own, reluctantly admitted, infirmity. What was left? An apartment for which he felt no attachment, a motley collection of furniture and furnishings, from which he derived little pleasure; a few acquaintances whose presence he would certainly not miss while, for them, his absence, he was, he was certain, would barely go noticed; a pathetic schedule of activities: the *Globe* and Peter Gzowski in the morning over two cups of coffee—no more—plus doctors' appointments, counselor's appointments, poker games, chess games, visits to the library, coffee or tea with this crony or that, classes at the university senior centre, swims at the Y, his notebook crammed with jottings almost immediately indecipherable to him, *Ideas* every evening at 9 on the CBC, then the late news, then cocoa, then bed. There, in a verbal nutshell, was the part and parcel of his life, compete with wrapping paper.

"Not an altogether bad life, Mr. Klebeck," the counselor at the senior centre had said to him not long ago. "There's a credit side to the ledger too. Your daughter *is* devoted, so's your son-in-law. Regardless of what you may feel about that, think about the many old people who have *no one*. Your health is relatively good. You have some appetites and sufficient income to indulge them. Believe me, there are many far worse off."

Lightfoot hung his head in mock shame. "You're right, I should thank my lucky stars, kiss the hem of the Goddess, light candles, tithe at the church, call the noon phone-in show and sing the praises of the government."

"All I mean," Trevor said, "is that self-pity, never a particularly attractive feature, is premature in your case."

Trevor! What kind of a name was that for a grown man. And that was just the start—the rest of his name was a double-barreled concoction Lightfoot could never get right, it was either Bright-Jones or Jones-Bright. Fancying a name like Jones up with something like Bright made sense to him; dragging a name like Bright into the mud with a dead weight like Jones made no sense at all.

"What I mean," Trevor persisted, "is that you have a life. You should try to make the best of it."

To which Lightfoot caustically replied: "This is a life?"

Trevor had made an exasperated sound and gesture. Still, there was something to what the obnoxious but well-meaning fellow said. True, he had a bit of an income, not enough for holidays in the Caribbean, but enough that he didn't have to worry about the rent or the grocery bill, that he could have as many coffees at the Empress Café, or ice cream cones at the Milky Way as he wanted without breaking the bank. His health was manageable—aches, pains, occasional shortness of breath, those ridiculous mini-strokes which would disorient and occasionally incapacitate him for a day or two but leave no lasting effect he was aware of, no chest pains as long as he wore his nitro patch, even his vision, which had seemed to be going on him a couple of years ago, had settled into a serviceable dimness and stayed there. The after-effects of the real stroke—numbness, weakness, forgetfulness—were almost all gone. And he had his appetite—he still loved to eat, would have loved to drink if he hadn't given that up years ago, would have loved to smoke except for the same, would have loved to get into the sack with some woman if there was some woman willing. He was pretty sure the equipment was still in working order.

Yes, he still had appetites, it was just his opportunities to fill them that had dwindled down. Sometimes he thought about taking up smoking and drinking again—what could they do to him? Kill him?

So what did he have to lose? Nothing but a life which was rapidly losing value.

But about which his son-in-law, Richard, a good fellow he'd grown fond of, would occasionally, trenchantly, observe: "Better than the alternative, right, Pop?"

"Thank you, Richard, for so clearly stating the obvious."

With all that in mind, he set out, humming a tune by a country singer he was fond of, Mary-Chapin Carpenter: "I take my chances, I take my chances every chance I get."

🎤

His first ride, with a Mercedes-Benz salesman delivering a brand new SL500 to a customer in Swift Current, got him as far as the Pilgrim truck stop just west of Moose Jaw. The salesman made amiable company and would have been glad to take him as far as he was going, and the car's leather upholstery was a pungent-smelling dream, but Lightfoot was hungry and he'd always liked this place, especially the pies. He had no schedule to meet and his one rule for this adventure—that's how he thought of it—was to go where his whims led him. "Sure I can't buy you a coffee, eh?" he asked the salesman but the fellow was in a hurry.

He passed a pay phone on the way in and thought about giving a call to his daughter, who, this evening, when he didn't answer her regular phone call, would be worried and by tomorrow morning frantic, but he hadn't figured out yet what he wanted to say.

It was the middle of the morning and the place was filled with truck drivers, farmers and families headed east or west on highway holidays. The waiters and waitresses were all students at the nearby Bible college, fresh-faced and perky. Lightfoot let one of the waitresses, blonde ponytail bobbing, lead him to a small table set for two even though he would have preferred a booth. He figured she could read him as a small tipper, which was true enough. He'd once been a money manager who ran large sums through his hands on a daily basis; now, he watched his pennies, though he was far from destitute. He'd made some poor investments, though, on his own behalf and that of others—errors in judgment that had finally convinced him to retire five years earlier— and wasn't as comfortably off as he should have been.

"Pie and coffee," he said. "What've you got today."

The waitress rattled them off with practiced ease: "Apple, cherry, blueberry, saskatoon, lemon meringue, chocolate cream, flapper, sour cream raisin."

"Maybe I should I have them all."

The girl smiled at him indulgently.

"Flapper. I had a girlfriend once who was one."

The girl nodded and moved away without giving any indication she'd understood the remark. Well, why should she? The pie, at least, was good, and Lightfoot allowed himself a second cup of coffee to wash it down. He read a few pages of Steinbeck as he ate. He hadn't read the novel in years, but it had been a favourite when he was young. The evening before, dipping into the first few chapters, the story and its characters had come vividly back to him, Ma and Pa Joad, Tom, his malnourished sister, Rose of Sharon, the preacher, their desperate journey from drought-ridden Oklahoma to California and its so-called pastures of plenty.

That's what had made up his mind to actually do this. He'd been thinking about taking the plunge for a while, since the weather had started getting nice in late April.

Taking the plunge—that was it exactly. Who knows where he might land, and if he broke his neck in the process, well, so be it. There were worse things to be afraid of, he figured, his son-in-law's mantra notwithstanding.

He finished his coffee and, to spite the waitress, left double what he usually would. He didn't think he'd need money much longer.

A farmer in a pickup took him half an hour down the road, hardly worth the trouble, and then there he was on the side of the Trans-Canada in the middle of nowhere, where the chances of being picked up were slimmer than they would have been at the truck stop. Blue smudges of hills—the Dirt Hills, the farmer had called them—lay shimmering in reflected sunlight to the southwest. Beyond them, he knew, were the Cypress Hills, highest point between Labrador and the Rockies, his son-in-law, who collected such trivia, had told him. So high, Richard said, it had escaped the most recent ice age and was home to fossils found nowhere else. He didn't know if he'd really make it to the Rockies, but the Cypress Hills seemed like a reasonable goal, so he readjusted.

He counted more than a hundred cars and trucks whizzing past him in the next ten minutes. Then a blue truck camper slowed down, went by, slowed more, steered into the shoulder, stopped, backed up. He was no runner any more but he walked briskly up to meet it. He opened the passenger door and found himself staring into the tongue-lolling snout of a collie dog. Behind the dog was a white-haired woman wearing blue jeans with patches on the knees and a khaki down vest over a red plaid shirt. "Where ya headed, old timer?" There was a rough-hewn quality to both her appearance and her voice, suggesting she'd just stepped out of a country and western song.

"Old timer? Thataway." He gestured down the highway with his thumb.

"I figure I've earned the right to call someone my own age 'old-timer,' or anything else, for that matter." The woman was plump and red-cheeked with a pleasing, jolly air to her. "Hop in. Come on, Lady, in the back."

The collie jumped over the seat into a narrow half seat between the front and the back of the cab. Lightfoot put his pack at his feet and strapped himself in. The dog nuzzled the back of his neck. "Hey, boy," he said, scrunching his shoulders.

"Girl. Settle down, Lady. Don't you mind her." The woman edged the truck back into motion. "Thataway, eh? You're in luck, sir. Thataway just happens to be where I'm headed too. No offence, but aren't you a little old to be hitchhiking all the way to thataway on your own?"

"Maybe I'll just get as far as thisaway. I'll be satisfied with that."

The woman laughed out loud, a good healthy laugh. Now that he'd gotten a better look at her, he could see she really was practically his age, in her late sixties or early seventies for sure, with curly white hair, the sort of woman he ran into all the time at the senior centre where he took classes. But he liked her laugh.

"Thisaway or thataway, I like that. I'm Doris Goodbody, and no cracks, please. Goodbody was my husband's name. What's *your* name?"

"Lightfoot."

"No first name?"

"Well, it's Bob. Bob Klebeck, actually. But today I'm Lightfoot, just Lightfoot."

"Like the singer?"

"That's it. Always liked his name."

"I always liked his voice. And you're lightfooting it, that it?"

"Hotfooting it."

"Pardon?"

"Hotfooting it, that's the term. But, yes, I guess I am. Hotfooting it, lightfooting it. As you said, at our age, we've earned the right to do what we damn well please. And be *called* whatever we damn well please."

"Well, Mr. Lightfoot, I'm pleased to make your acquaintance."

"Likewise. What's with the Farmer Jones outfit? You're no farmer."

"Good eye. No, I'm just a retired schoolmarm widow, on my way to Banff. These clothes are just for comfort. Well, maybe to get me in the mood, too. Like you calling yourself Lightfoot or Hotfoot or whatever."

Lightfoot shook his head. This was getting to be too good to be true. "Banff is where I'm going too. I mean, really. It's the *that* in thataway."

She laughed again. "Well, aren't we just two peas in a pod."

They stopped an hour or so latter at a little park to stretch legs, use the spartan toilets and let the dog run around a bit. Doris Goodbody had plenty of sandwiches and Lightfoot was talked into having one, baloney with lettuce and tomato on good homemade bread, with enough Dijon mustard to make it interesting, and to accept a cup of still-hot coffee from a thermos.

"I just had a cup and pie at the Pilgrim, but this hits the spot," he admitted. "Of course, with all this coffee, we'll have to stop again in five minutes. And five minutes after that. Old man's complaint."

"Don't worry about that, Bob. Weak bladders is another thing we have in common. The Pilgrim, eh?"

"Best pie," Lightfoot said. "Of course, I haven't tried yours."

"I'll ignore the false flattery. I usually stop there myself, but today I wanted to get some miles on."

"You got a date waiting?"

"On me? Sure. It's Paul Newman. We slip away for a weekend every chance we get."

Now Lightfoot laughed. "Paul Newman, yeah, I can see driving all day for that. Those icy blue eyes."

"Who would *you* drive all day to see?"

"Now *there's* a question. I'll have to think about that one. But, you know—and this isn't a flip answer, school-marm lady, and God knows, at my age, it isn't a come-on—but right now there's no one I'd rather be sharing a baloney sandwich with."

"Well, that is sweet. Thank you, kind sir. But if you really mean it, that's kind of sad too."

That stabbed Lightfoot right where he lived. A sixteen-wheeler roared by, raising clouds of dust and giving him the time to compose himself.

"A well-meaning fellow of my acquaintance is fond of reminding me that self-pity doesn't become me."

"Hey, it doesn't fit any of us very well. Sorry if I made you uncomfortable."

"No apology necessary. There's not a lot going on in my life. Or maybe too much but no good reason for it. It doesn't bother me usually, but you just touched a nerve. Perceptive."

"I'm sorry. Really."

"No, really. No need to be sorry. It's good to look things in the face. That same well-meaning fellow keeps reminding me of that too."

She turned to him and he found himself looking her square on, a once-good-looking woman still handsome enough. Too much of her, but he was getting used to that already. Beautiful blue eyes, good teeth that she showed a lot when she smiled, strong chin. Another pang ran through him.

"So no wife?"

"Dead."

"Sorry. Recent?"

"Nope, quite a while ago. I'm used to it."

"Same here. But you never really get used to being alone, do you?"

"No, guess not. And not just to being alone, to missing them."

"That's why I've got Lady. Hardly the same thing, but she's a dear. Girlfriend?"

"Me?" He chortled. "My son-in-law says something funny sometimes: 'get real!'"

"So you've got a daughter. A loving one, I'll bet."

"She is that."

"Suffocating?"

"You say something about succotash? I love that stuff."

Doris Goodbody pursed her lips and shut up.

Lightfoot drained the last of his coffee. "A son too, but the less said about me, the better he likes it. He's in Toronto. Haven't seen him in quite a while."

"Hmmm. So maybe thataway should be *that*away."

"No, I'm running away, not toward."

They got up and brushed crumbs away. The collie came running, snuffed around expertly at their feet and bounded into the truck and over the seat without being told. Back on the highway, Doris asked: "Running away really what you're doing?"

"Thinking about it. And you? You never did say."

"Just going for a hike." She grinned. "Sounds silly, I know, but sometimes I just like to take Lady and go off somewhere. You wouldn't believe how many miles there are on this camper. You mentioned succotash—I've got four kids, all with kids of their own, they're all in Regina. Well, five, really, but one died." To Lightfoot, it looked like her smile got a touch fiercer. "It's OK, it was long ago. We're the original happy family Tolstoy was talking about. I *don't* feel suffocated, but I'm still who I am, not just mom, grandmom and that nice Mrs. Goodbody. I'm still Doris, always was and always will be. And sometimes I just feel like a hike in the mountains."

"A hike in the mountains. God, that sounds good." He looked out his window for a moment at the speeding landscape, then turned back to her. "I had this cockeyed notion of lying down next to a stream, letting all the bad vapours in me just rise out, evaporate. Then of hiking into the sunset and just, you know, disappearing. Poof."

"I don't think it's that easy."

"No, I know it isn't. But just going for a walk, smelling the pines, hearing the birds, that's not exactly what I had in mind but…."

"It's hearing the birds I especially like," Doris said. "I hear them in the backyard all the time, but in the mountains it's different."

They were both silent. A minute passed, then another. Doris turned on the radio, but there was just static on the FM. They passed a highway sign, "Swift Current 20 km." The blue smudge of hills was growing larger, sharper.

"How does dinner in Medicine Hat sound?" she asked. "I know a good place."

"That sounds great."

"Maybe stop for coffee in Maple Creek, first, though. There's a great old hotel there, cowboy place."

"That sounds good too. But I'll need a pit stop before that."

"Me too. You're awful agreeable all of a sudden, Lightfoot. Everything I say sounds good to you."

"Well, it does, Goodbody. Everything you say *does* sound good to me."

"Lightfoot and Goodbody. Sounds improbable, doesn't it."

"*Improbable*. Sounds impossible."

"Nothing's impossible this side of the grave, Bob. That's what my daddy used to say. He was a CCF MLA, so he ought to have known."

"No, nothing impossible," Lightfoot agreed. "My daddy was a died-in-the-wool Jimmy Gardiner Liberal. And here we are."

A quick stop in Swift Current, then off again, 130 km to Maple Creek, by the first sign they passed back on the highway, 226 km to Medicine Hat. *Kilometres.* He rolled the word around in his head, tried it out on his tongue: "A hundred and thirty kilometers, two hundred and twenty-six *kilometres*."

"What's that?"

"Just thinking out loud." He chuckled under his breath, then laughed out loud.

Doris smiled at him. "Going to share the joke?"

"Oh, it's on me."

Lightfoot stretched out his legs, felt the warm, moist breath of the collie on the back of his neck. He swiveled his head around so he was nose to nose with her. "That true what they say, Lady? About old dogs?"

He thought about Tom Joad, Ma Joad, the anemic Rose of Sharon, the thin milk from her breast that kept a starving man alive, if he was remembering that right. Maybe he'd call his daughter from Medicine Hat.

ROMANCE

The year I was nineteen, I was in love with a girl for the first time, but it turned out badly. This was years ago, when things were different between boys and girls, men and women. Were they simpler then, or more complex? I don't know.

There had been other girls I'd dated or liked or mooned over, but this was something else, adult love or something close to it, that transforming love they show us in the movies.

Her name was April. She was a desk clerk in a pink sweater, pleated grey skirt and black flats at the summer hotel in Pennsylvania's Pocono Mountains where I was a waiter. My mother had sewn a black satin stripe along the outer seam of my black chinos to make it official. April was blonde, brilliantly blue-eyed, always smiling. Her face poured out light. She was as different from me as day is from night, but she made me shine like a new penny. We didn't get together until late in the season, just a week before she was to go home to Long Island early. Her parents had promised her a quick tour of Europe so she could decide if she wanted to spend her third college year there. It should have been a summer romance except that already it was something more.

At night, the basketball and shuffleboard court below the patio outside the bar became a dance floor, propelled by the music of bands on the weekends, crackling, hissing records the other evenings. We danced, the Everley Brothers and Dion and the Belmonts and the Five Satins tinny through the loudspeakers, then wandered down the moonlit path to the dock, the strains of "The Great Pretender" still in our ears. We walked along the lake, where night birds called from the bordering trees, to a sandy beach. We kissed and I put my hand on her thigh. She said "I don't" or "I won't" or perhaps "I can't." She was speaking so softly I couldn't be sure, but without her actually saying so I understood she was a virgin, and I hesitated, drew back. "It's okay," I said, kissing her again, and in my hesitation—in that moment between things—something happened I wasn't familiar with. The arc of my desire rose and rose and was transformed into something else. It surprised me, the feeling that welled up, not just then but later, as if my lungs had rapidly inflated with pressurized air and were bursting, a sensation I couldn't put a name to.

In the fall, back at school, me in Vermont, she at Penn State, we wrote to each other, almost every day, and phoned, once a week, our letters and calls filled with news, trivial and urgent, and sweet talk. Neither of us had said the word, but I understood I loved her, and that she felt the same. The fact that we were apart, that there was so much distance between us, and that hesitation stood between us like a wall, made it all the sweeter.

At Christmas, my vacation began a few days earlier than hers. That timing allowed me to go home, just outside New York City, talk my parents into loaning me the family car, an old Chrysler, and drive to Pennsylvania. It was a long trip, through New Jersey on one Interstate highway to the Delaware Water Gap, then straight west on another halfway across Pennsylvania to State College. She lived in a dormitory and she was waiting in the lobby when I drove up—I'd called from a rest stop an hour or so away and said I would be there at three.

"Hurry," she had said, and the briefness of our exchange struck me, yet it seemed in every way authentic.

The sun was still shining brightly in a blue sky that was clouding over as I began the last leg of the drive. The first flakes of snow started to fall only as I took the freeway exit. I followed her directions and found the building quickly and pulled the car up beside a sign that said "10-minute loading zone only" and got out, shaking my stiff legs. April came running out, an oatmeal wool cardigan over her shoulders, a yellow skirt swirling around her bare legs. It was certainly not an outfit for winter driving. She would have to change, slowing us down, but I understood that she had dressed for me, that it was a gift. We kissed and held each other in the gently falling snow, our cheeks growing wet, but we didn't feel cold. No, we burned.

She had already brought her suitcases down and I loaded the car while she went back up to change into jeans, a pullover and ski jacket. Then we took off into a gradually increasing storm.

It had not been our intention to make it all the way to Long Island that day, and it was just as well. The snow came down in ever-thickening sheets, all but overpowering the windshield wiper. We sat cozy in the Chrysler's front seat, the heater blasting on our feet and the windshield, April curled up beside me with her head in a red wool knit hat on my shoulder. She wouldn't let go of my right hand, which was entwined with hers, and she lay them both in my lap, at the top of my right thigh. Even with just my left hand on the wheel, and the poor visibility, I felt as if I could drive that way forever, but gradually it grew colder in the car, the light leeched from the sky and the combination of snow outside and fog on the inside of the windows made driving almost impossible. Traffic dwindled, but occasionally we overtook and passed a big snowplow spraying sheets of slush into our path, the windshield wipers clogging with it. In the rear-view mirror, they loomed for a moment like great yellow beasts, their snouts snuffling the highway, their eyes burning fiercely for just seconds before fading, then disappearing altogether. We had thought we would go as far as Stroudsburg, where I had made a reservation at what I'd been assured was a good hotel, then revised that to Bloomsburg, barely a hundred miles from State College. Now I wasn't sure we could go even that far.

The question was decided for us when we approached the exit near the Susquehanna River. The state police had closed the highway and we had no choice but to get off. There were signs, just barely visible through the fog rolling off the river, indicating services in the town, called New Columbia, a few miles away, and soon we were pulling up to a motel. It didn't look very good but the Vacancy neon was still lit. That was all that mattered, and April put on a brave face. "This looks good," she said.

I had never done this sort of thing before, checked into a motel with a woman, registering as Mr. and Mrs. As I stood in the lobby talking to the clerk, the condom in my pocket burning against my upper thigh, I was sure he could see through me. His bland features seemed to reconstitute themselves into a leer, and a *frisson* of danger arced through me, but when I blinked my eyes, the clerk was the same tired-looking middle-aged man who'd greeted me when I entered. He gave me the key and directions, and bade me goodnight.

The room was dimly lit, one bulb out, and shabby, but we hardly noticed. Through the window, thick with frost, we could see the light of the diner the clerk had told me about, pulsing weakly behind fog and snow. We were hungry, but we were starving for each other more and couldn't wait. For almost four months, we had phoned and written so often, the flow of words between us constant, words stripped of artifice and freighted with meaning, but now words were not what we needed. We fell upon each other, our kisses so deep my jaw ached. We stripped off each other's clothes, except our underpants, and embraced again, fell on the bed entwined. I kissed her mouth, the hollow of her throat, her breasts—so beautiful—her navel, covered with soft downy hair just barely visible. I was as hard as I'd ever been, and she touched me there. I felt that arc again, that surprise, that mixture of expectancy and restraint, that catch of breath, the long held breath. It would have been so easy to enter her, but when I touched her she gave her head the slightest of shakes. It didn't matter. We lay as close as any couple could lie. We pressed close, our hips moving, my knee between her legs, hers between mine, until I felt release, and continued on until April too gasped with surprise and pleasure. We were slick with sweat, and when I lifted my head to gaze at her there was a sucking sound as my chest parted from hers, as if skin were kissing skin.

"I love you," I said. The words seemed enormous, as if I were shouting them.

"I love you," she echoed.

And if there was any uncertainty there, in my voice or hers, any hesitation, it was indiscernible, drowned out by the pounding of our blood in our veins.

We parted, pulled reluctantly away from each other as if it were life itself we were relinquishing. We lay on our backs, panting, overwhelmed.

After a while, I went to the bathroom, stripped off my underpants and ran them under the hot water tap, left them there to soak. She came in and looked at me naked for the first time and, without a word, she pulled her panties down. They fell to the floor and she stepped out of them. I couldn't help myself. I fell to my knees on the cool tile floor and wrapped my arms around her hips, my face close to her heat. After a moment, she bent and kissed the top of my head. There was a tub with a shower head and plastic curtain. We got in and turned on the shower, letting the warm water splash over us, soak our hair. We soaped each other with slick washcloths until our skin glistened. Inasmuch as such a thing is possible, we baptized each other, emerging as new people, raw.

We dried each other and I remember thinking those stingy towels were a poor omen, so thin, almost threadbare, after the richness that preceded them. I almost said this but I stopped myself, and laughed out loud.

"Why are you laughing?"

"Just something I thought, something stupid."

"But funny stupid."

"Funny stupid."

"Tell me then."

"No." I kissed her instead, and she accepted that.

We went out into the storm, walking with our heads down, our hair turning white in a minute. The diner was almost deserted. A waitress with brown curly hair under a cap brought us hamburgers and French fries and cokes and cherry pie and coffee and tea. "You kids have a good night, now," she said when we paid. We walked back to the motel through the storm, a light moving through darkness. We lay in each other's arms, April in a pink nightgown, me in the bottoms of flannel pajamas, and exhaustion overcame us.

Just before we slipped off to sleep, she said: "This is what it must be like to be married."

"Yes," I said, although I wasn't completely sure what she meant.

"This close," she said after a moment. "This much comfort."

"Yes," I agreed. And then we were asleep.

In the morning, the storm had passed and the sun burned with fierce brilliance across the wind-glazed snow. We had breakfast at the diner—enormous platters of eggs and chopped potato and bacon and toast dripping with butter—then headed off. We followed the flashing red lights of a yellow snowplow for miles along a narrow track carved out of the ocean of snow covering the highway. It was warm and snug in the car, and we traveled slowly and safely through that ocean, like submariners. The sun was so bright it was hard to see.

Over the holidays, we saw each other several times. I was invited to her home in Seaford, out on the Island, had dinner with the family and stayed overnight in her older brother's room. I didn't like her parents much and it seemed plain they didn't care for me, but everyone was polite. Another time, we met in the city and had dinner at a French restaurant, Larré's, went to see Paul Newman in *Sweet Bird of Youth* on Broadway, had time for one drink afterwards before I put her on the last train home. Whenever we could, we embraced and kissed—the night I stayed at her home, we met in the finished basement after everyone else had gone to sleep and kissed for an hour—but went no further. That great urgency we'd felt the night in the snow had passed, and

I didn't know if we would feel it again. But it didn't seem to matter. The possibilities appeared to be endless, and that was more important.

Back at school, the letters and phone calls resumed, the measured diary of our days, classes and profs, exams and papers, friends. Deprived of the chance for kisses and my addled gaze into her cornflower eyes, we fell back on words, and for months they sustained us. But in spring something happened. Although I continued to write as often, her letters became less frequent. On the phone, her conversation was halting and there were silences like puddles on the street after a rain. I knew something had changed, was changing, but I didn't know what, and I didn't have the courage to ask. Easter came and went but our breaks didn't coincide. There was just six weeks left till the end of term, then five.

"I've got to talk to you," she said on the phone.

"We're talking now," I replied, willfully blind.

"I mean really talk. See you and talk."

"We'll have the whole summer," I said. We had plans to spend the summer at the resort hotel again. I'd been rehired as a waiter and she as a desk clerk. I'd be in the narrow dormitory they crowded the waiters and busboys and bellhops into, but she would share a small cabin with just one other girl, and the possibilities for us would be endless, there and on the beach by the lake under the moon in the perfumed nights.

"That's what we need to talk about. I...."

"Go ahead."

"I'm not going to the mountains. I'm going to Europe."

"But that's not till fall." She'd been accepted in the third-year exchange program and would be spending it in France, I'd known that, we'd talked about it endlessly. The letters would take longer, the phone calls would be more expensive, shorter, but nothing would change really. She'd be home for Christmas, and the year would go quickly. I'd even thought, though I hadn't mentioned it, of maybe quitting school for a semester or more, bumming to Europe on a tramp steamer, if such things even still existed, meeting up with her there, sleeping on the beach in Greece under the stars.

"No. I'm going now. I mean, this spring, as soon as school's over."

"But...."

We agreed to meet. It was Wednesday; on Friday I hitchhiked down to the city, leaving after breakfast and getting there just before dark. I stayed at my sister's. April had a ride in, but she hadn't said where she'd be.

The next day we met at noon as arranged on the steps of the library on 5th Avenue at 40th Street, by the stone lions. She was late and I stood in front of a lion watching a bewildering world rush by in the blaring spring sun, lilac already in bloom. *April in April*, I thought, not for the first time. I was rehearsing things she might say, feeling dead inside. I think I already knew everything she'd say, without actually knowing it, and that everything that followed would just be rote.

When she appeared she was as beautiful as she'd ever been, her hair loose and longer, her eyes masked by sunglasses. She didn't take them off, and offered me only her pink cheek to kiss, and I knew that whatever we'd had was over.

"I don't understand," I said.

"I don't either."

"But you know something I don't know."

"Yes."

She took my hand and we walked in the bright sunlight. We'd meant to go somewhere for lunch but now, she said, she had only a few minutes. She was sorry.

"I've met someone else," she said.

That was the one thing I'd thought sure she would say, yet it took me by surprise. I didn't say anything.

"He's older." She looked away. "We were awfully young, we still are. I...I need someone more mature."

"We're a year older, April."

"Oh, I know that. I don't mean it as an insult, that isn't what I mean at all. I just need someone older."

Someone who doesn't hesitate, I thought, but I didn't really know if that was it.

"And you've already found him."

"I didn't mean for it to happen."

"It just did."

"Yes."

"But you let it."

"Yes."

"You didn't turn away."

"No." After a moment, she added: "I know, it's my fault."

We were in the little park behind the library, Bryant Park, and we stopped under a tree that was hesitantly in leaf, delicate strips of pale green. "It's not anybody's fault," I said. "Fault doesn't figure into it."

"Thank you for saying that."

She went on, trying to explain, but I tried not to listen. We crossed 6th Avenue and walked to the 8th Avenue subway entrance along 41st Street, which wasn't as crowded as 42nd. We went down the stairs to the downtown platform. We waited for the train in silence, still holding hands. She'd taken off her sunglasses finally and the sky was there with us under the ground in her eyes. "I'd like it if we could still be friends," April said.

"No. I don't think so."

"Please don't be that way."

"What way?" I asked petulantly.

"The way you're being now."

"All right."

"I'll write from France."

"Okay."

We could hear the growing roar of the train approaching, feel the vibration. As it rushed into sight, its headlight flaring, it was preceded by wind. A grimy newspaper on the platform fluttered like an ungainly bird trying to take off.

"You were wonderful," April said, and she called me by name. "Really."

I held her in my arms—I couldn't help myself—but just for a moment. The doors opened with a vacuum hiss and passengers poured out. We were pushed to the side. People pressed in blindly. At the last moment, I released her and she went wordlessly in with the others. The doors swished closed. There was a hesitation, then the train began to move. I could see her face, that crystal of light. Then it was gone.

I stood on the deserted platform watching the last car of the subway disappear into the black tunnel. The newspaper fluttered its pages, a settling bird. A feeling sprang up in me again that I thought I recognized from the summer and from the days before Christmas, a feeling I could put no name to.

THE KING OF THE JEWS
OR
THE CURIOUS CASE OF
L'ACHIEM MORDECAI MACLEOD

It was the coldest winter anyone could remember. Robert Grey Eyes, a Woodland Cree from the Beardy's reserve who had been calling himself Palliser Macleod since leaving residential school two decades earlier, came out of the northern woods laden with so many pelts, and of such good quality, that he strolled out of the Hudson's Bay post in Fort Labiche with more money in his pocket than he'd ever seen before. He caught the first bushplane out to Edmonton and bought himself a good three-piece suit, light blue pinstripe, and good quality brushed leather cordovan shoes. He set up headquarters at the Chateau Lacombe, checking in as L'achiem Mordecai Macleod, and placed this ad in the personals section of *The Journal*:

> Seeking descendants of the Ten Original Tribes of Canada. The Hebrews were the First Nation, we are the Second. Our rights have been repressed too long. Join me in a new crusade.

Over a hundred people came to his first public gathering, in a meeting room at the Chateau, but by fall, after a busy summer of organizing and consultations, he was drawing thousands to his Second Nation Crusade rallies in Edmonton, Calgary, Saskatoon, Regina, and Winnipeg. Even Lethbridge, Kelowna, Prince Rupert and Prince George saw sizeable crowds, and there were plans for taking the crusade into Ontario, Quebec and the Maritimes over the winter. People responded at a gut level to Macleod's theory that Canada's native population were, with some exceptions, Jews. Only on the West Coast did there appear to be outright scepticism, even hostility.

As he outlined his views in an early Edmonton *Journal* interview which was reprinted widely, the famous lost tribes of Israel had indeed, after many decades of wandering through the deserts and steppes of Central Asia and Russia, traversed the frozen Bering Strait into North America, millennia after an earlier wave of Asiatics had blazed the same trail.

"Those earlier travelers were true 'Indians,'" he matter-of-factly explained to the reporter, a young woman newly graduated from the Carleton University journalism school, "and almost all of them continued south into what is now the lower forty-eight states of the U.S., and Central and South America, where Columbus and the Spaniards came upon them."

The reporter scribbled furiously in her notebook, then raised her charming green eyes to indicate she was ready for him to continue.

"The so-called Indians and Inuit of Canada, and the Eskimos of Alaska, are from the second wave of immigrants," Macleod instructed. "They're not 'Indians' at all, but Israelites."

At that point in the interview, the reporter, who had been incredulous, was barely able to repress a smirk of disbelief.

Macleod smiled indulgently. "I see you're having trouble believing what I'm telling you."

"Well, perhaps a bit," she agreed. She was barely twenty-two, blonde and slender, and, despite her studied cynicism, eager to please.

"That's not surprising. Generations of brainwashing. Lies in the history books and the schoolbooks. Canadian governments, from the days of Sir John A. Macdonald on, have always known the truth, and their attempts to smear Canadian natives with the same brush as those in the U.S. were based entirely on anti-Semitism. It goes on today."

"But surely..." the reporter began, then fell silent, perhaps recalling a journalism school admonition against arguing during an interview.

"I'll prove it to you," Macleod said, and began to lead the young woman through a detailed analysis of the history of the Indian Act, deliberate starvation, disenfranchisement, residential school debauchery and forced integration, some of which made it into her story, which was carried on the front page under the headline *'Wandering Jew' theory expounded.*

"In short," he pronounced as the note-taking grew all but indecipherable, "genocide. Although the Canadians weren't nearly as efficient as the Germans. They've been working at it for two hundred years and still haven't gotten rid of us."

Macleod repeated these views, often making use of overhead projections showing genealogical charts, geological diagrams and lists of artefacts unearthed at archaeological digs, at his rallies, and in scores of interviews with the press and speeches he gave to business, fraternal and academic groups.

Most people, except for the fervent disciples who thronged the front rows at the rallies (many of them "Indians," some of them Jews and born-again Christians), responded much the way the *Journal* reporter had: first with scepticism, then incredulity bordering on hostility, then grudging interest. From there, of course, many went beyond to full acceptance and even ecstatic adherence, but Macleod was content, especially in the interviews, to successfully reach the third stage. He was confident that once shown the facts, most intelligent people of good will would come to see the wisdom of his views.

As he often observed, "Time is on our side."

In full flight, either at the podium, in a television or radio studio (he was particularly popular on the radio talk shows, where he would often amaze the host by turning a heckling caller into a follower within minutes) or alone at a restaurant table with an interviewer, he intuitively gauged the temper of his audiences and skillfully led them from one emotional response to the next.

At the mention of the word "Israelites," listeners tended to lean forward slightly, while the term "anti-Semitism" had just the opposite effect. Depending on the measure by which he released these claims, he soon would have his audiences rocking back and forth in a steady rhythm.

🎤

It was a report of one of the Western Canadian rallies that caught the attention of Tempest O'Neill, who was then dancing in a touring company of *Cats*. She was in a hotel room in Omaha, Nebraska, when she saw an item on the curious crusade on CNN. A brief video clip of Macleod on a makeshift stage brought her abruptly out of the half-sleep she'd fallen into after returning to her room, exhausted from the show and a few post-show drinks. First the immediately familiar voice, one tenth Cree, nine tenths Princeton, then the more difficult but not-impossible-to-identify physical presence, tall and rangy, with a slightly enlarged head caught her attention. The beard made him look different, and he was older, of course, but it was definitely Palliser Macleod.

"Son of a bitch," Tempest said.

Macleod's response to what he termed the "certain state of affairs of so-called Indian-white relations" was still evolving. In his lectures, he posited two possible satisfactory conclusions. One would be a demand that Israel allow, finance and facilitate the Right of Return for all Canadian and Alaskan "natives," with full voting and other rights of citizenship. The second was that the province of Saskatchewan be set aside for the exclusive use of these "natives," and that jurisdiction for the province be transferred from Canada to Israel, which would declare it first a colony, then, after a suitable transition period, a full-fledged province; this, he argued, had been predicted by Tommy Douglas in his famous "New Jerusalem" speeches.

Macleod himself was torn between these two options. "It is not for me to say," he declared, "but for the people to decide." He and his assistants, including two burly former members of the Indian Posse gang, began laying plans for a referendum.

Similar claims for sovereignty by Palestinian-Canadians, who identified Prince Edward Island as a possible location for a homeland, were dismissed and ridiculed by Macleod himself as mere "bandwagonism."

Indian Affairs Minister Robert Nault expressed interest in Macleod's views, and established a committee of bureaucrats, under the leadership of the distinguished retired judge, Mr. Justice Thomas Berger, to study them. He was particularly interested in Macleod's assertion that the treaties were illegal, since the Indian Nations had not truly been nations at all, but rather representatives of the Jews, who, at the time, had no nation of their own, and that treaty rights, therefore, were null and void. Instead, he argued, the "Israelite natives" should be considered full citizens of Canada, with full equality. As such, they were owed a rather sizable credit, including compound interest, as the result of having been deprived of their citizenship rights for over one hundred and fifty years. The Berger committee was charged with doing a costing of such a scheme, as well as the financial implications of losing Saskatchewan.

Prime Minister Chretien, for whom solving the Indian Question had long been a preoccupation, also expressed interest in Macleod's views and hailed Macleod as a "an innovative new voice, a source of new leadership," for aboriginal people. A private audience between the two men was arranged.

The existing Indian leadership, of course, was horrified. Grand Chief Matthew Coon Come called together chiefs from around the nation to discuss this threat. Macleod was invited to speak to them, but he declined, refusing to acknowledge the powers of the chiefs. "In Judaism, God is supreme and only the rabbis speak for Him. Political organizations and jurisdictions have their place, of course, but not in this particular debate, which is more scientific and theological than political."

Former national chiefs Fontaine, Erasmus and Cardinal were brought out of retirement to help meet this challenge to self government, and Coon Come threatened a massive campaign of civil disobedience if the government gave serious consideration to Macleod's "reactionary, racist" theories.

The Indian leadership was not the only camp that set out to battle Macleod and his beliefs.

In his cosmology, the Jews, as a people, were *the* First Nation, Israel being merely the modern geopolitical manifestation of that Biblical reality. The "native" Israelites, as he termed them, of North America, were the Second Nation. Christianity as a whole, and Islam as a whole, were the Third and Fourth Nations, in that order, based on the chronological appearance of Jesus and Mohammed. These four nations, he preached, constituted the "United Nations of God" and represented the benchmark for civilization. Although he took pains to emphasize that he bore no one any ill, Macleod made it clear that there was no real place in his theories for Buddhists and Hindus, whom he put on a par with animists and pagans in general. Understandably, feelings were enflamed among various Oriental and East Indian communities in Canada, and, subsequently, around the world. This seemed to bother Macleod not a bit.

In fact, he seemed to thrive on controversy.

Early editorials in the *Globe and Mail*, the *National Post* and other papers had painted Macleod as a buffoon and clown, his theories as nothing more than hot air. But as the numbers of people giving credence to these theories—both native and mainstream—increased, editors began to reassess their views. The tone of interviews with anthropologists and theologians, similarly, shifted. For example, early on, Michael deRaddison, Professor Emeritus of Anthropology at McGill University and an aboriginal studies specialist who was among a group of scholars who had exploded earlier Bering Strait migration thinking, dismissed Macleod in a *Globe* interview as "a poseur and charlatan." There was "absolutely no basis in fact for such a hare-brained theory," deRaddison declared. That was in June, soon after the Edmonton and Calgary rallies. However, by August, when Macleod was interviewed live on CBC's *The National* by Peter Mansbridge, he was followed by a panel including Princeton anthropologist and biblical scholar Louis Maysefield, who pronounced Macleod's hypothesis "the most important breakthrough in immigration pattern studies in decades."

What was most striking about the Mansbridge interview with Macleod, notwithstanding the absolute self-assurance the interviewee projected, was the way in which the television anchor, usually so demonstrably objective in his demeanour, was so visibly moved by Macleod's arguments.

This brief excerpt from the transcript of the interview will illustrate:

> Mansbridge: The name *L'achiem*, I believe, is Hebrew. It means "to life" and is often used as a toast.
>
> Macleod: You're absolutely right, Peter. But it is also a Cree word, meaning "water of life" or "spirit of life."
>
> Mansbridge: Is that right?
>
> Macleod: Absolutely. But so much of Cree derives from Hebrew. There are significant cultural differences, of course. No one is saying the North American Israelites are like the Ashkenazi, say. Any more than the Jews of Ethiopia are like those of Latvia. These differences have had a profound effect on the evolution of our indigenous languages.
>
> Mansbridge: That's fascinating.
>
> (NOTE: Macleod's assertions of the Cree-Hebrew

link were confirmed later in the program by Prof. Eugene Orbachs, a Harvard linguist.)

The Mansbridge interview and panel, which were carried internationally via the Internet, proved to be a watershed. They were seen by hundreds of thousands of people, including Tempest O'Neill, who caught the streaming video at an Internet cafe in Billings, Mont., where *Cats* played both a matinee and evening show.

"That son of a bitch," Tempest exclaimed out loud.

"What's that?" asked a man in the turtleneck sitting at the next terminal. He'd been ogling her openly since she'd brought her latte over and sat down.

"I said 'fuck you,'" Tempest said.

✒

Earlier in his life, Macleod had been a VIA rail porter and was present the day Pierre Trudeau famously gave the finger to farmers as his train passed through Winnipeg. Macleod witnessed the event and was impressed by this eloquent exercise of power. Afterwards, an exhilarated Prime Minister ordered a vodka tonic brought to his compartment and Macleod, remembering to squeeze the twist of lime just the way M. Trudeau liked it, earned a prime ministerial thanks and a dollar tip.

This was not Macleod's first brush with the power elite of Canada. As a boy at the St. Christopher of the Birds Residential School in Lac la Biche, he'd shaken the hand of John Diefenbaker, who'd come to visit the school in the wake of a student uprising put down by Mounties firing rubber bullets and wielding fire hoses. As one of the organizers of the rebellion, but now rehabilitated, at least in the eyes of the Jesuit fathers who ran the school, he'd been as keen to meet the tall, stern-looking Prime Minister as Diefenbaker had been to meet him. They posed for photographs, their hands clasped, and their eyes locked together, as if equals.

Macleod had come a long way since St. Christopher's.

He'd been born of mixed blood heritage on the Beardy's reserve but was fortunate to have been classified as a Treaty 7 Indian, thus qualifying for dental care. As a result, he had excellent teeth.

He was a tall, ascetic but handsome man, with a definite Old Testament quality, to which his slightly larger than normal head and a scraggly beard contributed. His dark flashing eyes, high cheekbones and firm chin gave him a regal look that the camera loved. In fact, he bore a striking resemblance to Archie Belany, the famous "Grey Owl," and, like Belany, he possessed a charisma that effortlessly drew people to him. His speeches were galvanizing.

At St. Christopher's, he had become very familiar with both the Old and New testaments and this knowledge, along with a photographic memory and analytical skills inculcated by the Jesuit fathers, gave him an awesome command of Biblical scholarship. He'd gone on to do his undergraduate studies at McGill, where he'd had a serious run-in with deRaddison, who failed him in Anthropology 101 when he mocked some of the distinguished professor's theories. Later, after a year on the railroad, he moved on to Princeton, where, studying with Maysefield and others, he did field work in Fiji and wrote his dissertation on the dwindling survival of threatened cultures. His McGill and Princeton studies were all courtesy of the Canadian taxpayer, of course, as had been his earlier education at the hands of the Jesuits.

In Fiji, where he'd first begun to question his own identity as an "aboriginal"—a questioning which would ultimately lead to development of his ground-breaking theories—he'd worked side by side with Prof. Lionel McTaggert of Harvard, who was sufficiently impressed to insure that Macleod would be offered a teaching position after his postdoc work at Princeton was completed.

This would likely have happened, and it's possible that his revolutionary theories would have come to fruition earlier, but for a chance encounter that altered Macleod's life.

While doing his laundry at the Suds & Duds, a combination Laundromat/bar on Princeton's Einstein Street, not far from his bachelor digs, he met a young theatre student named Tempest O'Neill, the illegitimate daughter of Eugene O'Neill's own illegitimate son Franklin and the Shakespearean actress Vanessa Mills.

"I don't suppose you have change for a dollar?" Tempest asked.

The exchange, which would prove to have historical ramifications, was entirely innocent.

Macleod's nose had been buried in the most recent copy of *The American Anthropology Journal*, and when he lifted his eyes they locked on Tempest's, which were lavender.

"I think I have some quarters," Macleod said. He stood up, shaking a cramp out of one long leg, and dug his hand in his pocket.

Before the end of the spin cycle, they were back at her place, tangled up in sheets that would soon need laundering.

Macleod stayed at Tempest O'Neill's apartment for seven days and nights, and it was in her company that, one evening, they walked through warm, soft April twilight to the Princeton Theatre on Fulford Street, where they saw Robert Redford in *Jeremiah Johnson*. This 1972 film by Sydney Pollack, about a white man who "goes native" as a trapper in the mountains of the American northwest, had a profound effect on Macleod.

The very next day, he kissed Tempest O'Neill goodbye, went back to his own apartment to pack and disappeared from the halls of academe.

The thought of a man like Palliser Macleod, a cultured, citified man a dozen years—and light years culturally—away from the reserve, going "back to the land" and even surviving, let alone thriving, was laughable. Indeed, Macleod might well have perished that first winter North of 60, all his new Hudson's Bay and Eddie Bauer catalogue equipment notwithstanding, had not Muskrat Andy Calling Home come upon him. Muskrat Andy, who some people swore was part Ukrainian, was legendary in those woods. It had been years since anyone had heard the man speak a single word, in any language. However, Macleod, who was being menaced by a pack of wolves when Muskrat Andy—much like the character played by Will Geer in *Jeremiah Johnson*—made a sudden and timely appearance, found the old trapper remarkably gregarious. They spent the rest of the winter together and Macleod, in effect, became apprentice to Muskrat Andy, learning at the older man's knee and, some said, occasionally bending a knee of his own.

It was during the seven years that Macleod spent in the north, far away from the white noise and mental taint of academe and the political arena, that he developed the theories that would so revolutionize the anthropological, theological and linguistic worlds.

Of course, not everyone was convinced. DNA testing was proposed, to see if there were similarities between Jewish and "Indian" gene patterns. Some testing was done but the results were declared inconclusive and further tests were scheduled. Geneticists, including no less an authority than

David Suzuki, hypothesized that, after two millennia, genetic differences were certain to have evolved. Macleod declared that he welcomed and encouraged any manner of scientific scrutiny.

In the meantime, Jewish comics had a field day, with both Woody Allen and Seinfeld working a little "wandering Jew" material into routines they displayed on the Letterman and Leno shows, respectively. Picket lines by Buddhists and Hindus at Macleod appearances became increasingly rowdy. And catcalls from hecklers, who loved calling him "king of the Jews," were more vociferous. Scrawled swastikas began appearing on tombstones in Indian graveyards throughout the West.

Would it be too much to expect that when a serious obstacle to the progress of Macleod's ideas arose, it would be in the shape of a woman?

Tempest O'Neill, Macleod's former lover, was a practicing Shintoist with a strong interest in Buddhism and was enraged by his theological expressions. She had no views on the Indian Question and his immigration theories, and she cared nothing for Macleod's views of Judaism, Christianity, Islam or Hinduism. But the slander against her own religious beliefs was blasphemy and could not be tolerated.

Although their affair had lasted just seven days, one precious week, and there had been no contact between them since his mysterious disappearance, Tempest had gotten to know the man intimately, better, in fact, than anyone in the world, except, perhaps, for Muskrat Andy Calling Home.

She knew a secret.

On a brilliant October afternoon, barely six months after his first Edmonton meeting, Macleod emerged from the lobby of the Chateau Laurier in Ottawa. A chauffeured limousine was awaiting to take him to the Prime Minister's residence on Sussex Drive. The two men had already had a number of meetings, both official and unofficial; tonight's was to be purely social, a relaxed "family-style" dinner with Chretien, his wife and several close friends. The Chretiens' adopted native son would also be in attendance, and Macleod looked forward to meeting this troubled young man.

As frequently occurred when Macleod was out in public, a small crowd had gathered. The man's charisma was such that, even among those who knew next to nothing about the Indian Question, and had little interest in politics, there was a desire to see, to touch, to speak to L'achiem Macleod. He was usually more than willing to oblige, to pause and share a word with an elderly admirer or provide autographs for a group of excited children. Today, among those in the throngs being held back by velvet ropes, including two Vietnamese monks carrying gasoline cans, there was one face Macleod instantly recognized.

"Tempest!" He went directly to her, nodding reassuringly to his heavily tattooed bodyguard.

"Hello, Pal."

"It's great to see you. You look...wonderful." Although it had been quite a while, she did look every bit as lovely as he remembered her, her fiery hair rolling around her shoulders.

"It's been thrilling seeing you on television," she told him, "but I just had to see you for myself. It's been seven years."

"Is it really that long?"

"You know it is."

"Are you....?"

"Married? No."

"And is there..."

"Anyone in my life? No."

"I'm sorry about leaving so suddenly back in Princeton."

"My heart was broken, but I got over you, Pal."

"Not entirely, I hope." He smiled flirtatiously.

"No, not entirely." She put her hand lightly on his.

The security man returned to Macleod's side and whispered in his ear. The car was waiting. A hurried exchange revealed that Tempest was staying at the Chateau as well. They arranged to meet later for a drink. Then Macleod was whisked away.

The lure of sex has been the downfall of so many great men, and so it was with L'Achiem Macleod. Well, yes and no.

At the appointed time, Tempest came discreetly to his suite. The bodyguards had been dismissed for the night. She was fetching in a short, tight black skirt that showed her dancer's body to good advantage and an equally flattering mauve sweater set. She carried a largish tooled leather bag on a shoulder strap. Macleod was in a dressing jacket and loose slacks, barefoot. A fire had been set in the living room grate. There was a moment of shyness at the door, but then they were in each other's arms. He was unfastening, she was pulling...and then they were naked. He embraced her and Tempest gave him a passionate kiss, her hands running up and down his thighs. Then she leaped back to get a better view, reaching for the camera in her bag. You can imagine her surprise.

"Wha.... Shit! How in hell did you manage that?" She pointed the camera at his mid-section.

"What are you taking about?" Macleod said, dumbfounded.

"You weren't circumcised," she spat at him.

"Oh, that." He looked dejected. Then he glanced with surprise at the camera, as if really seeing it for the first time. "Say, what's going on here, anyway?"

Tempest was starting to put her clothes back on. She paused, her arms twisted behind her back. "I was going to reveal your dirty little secret. Some Jew! But you anticipated that, you bastard. I just hope it hurt like hell."

Macleod flopped back on an amazingly comfortable sofa and stared at her. She was bent over, her back to him, adjusting her stockings, and, even in the black panties she'd already slipped back into, her backside was remarkable. Rarely, if ever, was he at loss for words, but this was one of those times.

"But, I don't understand, Tempest," he finally managed to get out. "Why?"

"Why?!" Tempest O'Neill spun around and glared over Macleod's shoulder, as if addressing some third person. "He dismisses Shintoism as if it were a piece of lint on his Pierre Cardin shirt, and he asks why! Is he brain dead?"

"Shintoism?"

"What, you're claiming to forget what you said?"

"No, it's paganism, but..."

"And all your redskin Great Spirit hocus pocus isn't? *Turtle Island!*"

"Tempest! Tempest!" he cried in exasperation. "Were all those expensive years at Princeton wasted on you? Do you know nothing? Haven't you even read the Bible? Don't you know, we are the chosen people. Do you think that was *my* idea? Do you think enduring all that shit over the millennia was easy? Do you think it was a cakewalk in the park for Jesus lugging that cross up the hill? Do you think Mohammed...."

"What about Buddha?" Tempest spat.

"What about him?"

"You're hopeless." She slipped the sweater over her head, stuffed the camera in her bag, shouldered it and headed for the door. "Just rot in Hell," she cried over her shoulder. The door slammed shut.

Macleod continued to lie on the sofa, various sounds ringing in his head. "Rot in hell, hell, hell hell hell hell." The slamming of the door. "What about Buddha?" The door, the door the door the door. "What about him? What about him?"

The first grey emanations of dawn found Macleod still slumped on the sofa. He may have slept a few minutes from time to time but he couldn't tell, the vibrations of the diaphanous membrane between sleep and waking adding to the pealing in his ears.

What *about* Buddha?

Was it possible that, somehow, Macleod had gotten it wrong? He had contemplated his theories for seven years before springing them on the world, but was that enough? The lost tribes stuff, the second wave, that was a certainty. But the theology, the first and second nations, all the rest...

He rose and stood in an eastern window watching the arrival of the day. When at last he roused himself, his mind was made up. Better to go quietly. He dressed, took only his laptop computer and a few books and his notebook and slipped out the door, down the corridor to the service stairway.

He was spotted by a reporter at the Ottawa airport later that day, and there were unsubstantiated reports of him in Edmonton, then Whitehorse. Then he simply dropped off the media's radar.

And so, like Jeremiah Johnson before him, L'Achiem Macleod disappeared into the mountains of the Yukon

Territory, and has not been heard from again.
Not yet.

TRUE LIES

Gillian phoned this morning, early. I wasn't surprised. She had emailed to say she'd be coming, that she had the papers for me to sign. *There are things we need to go over,* she'd written. She's a bit hard of hearing and doesn't like to use the phone. Never has. So she's come to adore email. It had been almost three years since I'd heard her voice, but I knew it from the first word. Even before that, actually, from the hesitant intake of breath. Afterwards, as I sat waiting for her taxi to arrive, I kept hearing her voice playing over and over in my ear: "Hi, it's me. I'm at the airport. I haven't woken you, have I? Tell me your address again."

"*It's me,*" she'd said. What did she mean, *me*? "Me" could be anyone.

🎤

Wake me? No. I don't sleep as much as I used to. I go to bed late, get up early. I work from home, mostly at my desk and computer, so I keep my own hours. I was making breakfast when the phone rang.

I have a routine. I make my breakfast at the counter next to the sink. A box of plastic bags sits at the end of the shelf above the sink, along with wax paper, aluminum foil, a few folded sandwich bags, a few cookbooks. It's only today, with Gillian on my mind, I realized I've replicated the arrangement of these objects from the kitchen shelf in the house where she and I and our son lived, before I left.

As I work, putting cereal into the bowl, and slice in a banana, my head is at the level of the shelf and just to the left. As I take my vitamin pills and drink my juice, I find myself reading from the side of the small rectangular red box: "Here are some ways to use Baggies for freshness, protection and easy storage," or: "Lunchbox Foods, Leftovers... Fresh Fruits, Vegetables, Cheese... Household items." I read these sentences almost every morning, always with mild interest, as if there is some possibility the meaning has changed over-night. I read these messages always as if for the first time, with no real comprehension.

But this morning, after Gillian's call, and perhaps for the first time, I noticed, at the very bottom of the box, the Colgate-Palmolive trademark. I stared at it, the juice glass cold and wet in my hand, breaking the words down into their parts: Col-Gate, Pal-Mol-ive, no, Palm Olive. Do olives grow on palm trees? Of course not. Palms grow on olive trees? No—but what exactly is a palm anyway? Or do they mean the other kind of palms, the kind that might be olive-coloured if you didn't wash them with Colgate's....

I shook my head, drank my juice. Thought no more of it. Breakfast as usual, cold cereal with sliced banana, two cups of coffee. I'm reading a novel, *Clara Callan,* and it absorbs me through the second cup. I used to read the newspaper with breakfast, but I've let my subscription lapse. I don't trust the words in the paper anymore, and I take my news on the television in the evening instead. It's not that the words spoken by the anchor or the reporters are any more reliable, but hearing them, rather than reading, provides a layer of insulation from the shadow behind them.

Is it Gillian's call that makes me think of Boo today? Of course, but maybe it's also that novel, *Clara Callan*. It's in the form of letters, two sisters back and forth. They're very convincing, and it feels like the letters are written right to you, or that you're eavesdropping on a conversation. Boo and I exchanged letters for years, though not as detailed, as well written. Ours were filled instead with puns and oddball observations. After growing up and moving away, me in one direction, Boo in another, my marriage to Gillian, the birth of our son—all these things didn't come between us but they did keep us apart for years on end. So we wrote letters. They were a reliable way of staying connected. I've kept a lot of his letters, even the last one, the one that made me wish him harm. They are all I have left of Boo—several rubber-banded bundles of letters sent sporadically over the years, in a plastic bag in a closet. Including that last one, the one with Gillian's name, the letter torn in half, then Scotch-taped back together.

Why did he have to tell me? I've wondered that a thousand times. We never got to discuss it, but I've imagined the conversation we might have had.

"Why did you tell me?" I would ask.

"I had to, Shithead," Boo would say.

"But why? I didn't know—I didn't need to know. Gillian wasn't going to say anything."

"You did, though. You needed to know. I needed to tell you. We're friends, remember? I couldn't deceive you."

"But you had."

"Don't I know it. I couldn't do it any longer."

"All right, stop doing it, fine. But tell me? Why do that? Why pour vinegar into my wounds?"

"Elementary, my dear Watson. I just had to. I had to."

Since Boo's death, I think of him often. Anything can spark his memory. It's not sadness these thoughts bring, though there is that too, of course, rather a recollection of myself. Or maybe *reflection* is the word, from Boo's eyes.

When I was a boy of ten or eleven, my best friend was Robbie Dowell, a solid, generally humourless but loyal and steadfast boy as different from me as headlamps from stars. My *special* friend, though, the one in whom my interest most often lay, was Boo Toglin, a tall, gangly, perverse boy who was my natural soulmate, my distorted double. He was the only one of my boyhood friends I kept up with in later years, and if there was anything in his character when I knew him as a boy or a man that hinted at the hurt he would someday cause me, I certainly wasn't aware of it.

It would have made more sense for Boo to be my best friend but circumstances made that difficult, if not impossible. We went to different schools, and Boo had to endure parents who allowed him very little freedom. He was a moody boy with preferences as ephemeral as sunlight and, while I was much like that myself, I also had a need for constancy in others. I never had to doubt Robbie's friendship, any more than he, in his darkest moments, would have had to question the love of his parents, who were solid, fair-minded people, much like the man he would himself grow to be.

His father was a carpenter, a tall, angular man with powerful hands and a jaw that appeared to be welded shut. In the evening, he sat in the living room watching sports on television and puffing on his pipe, agreeing "Yes, Mother," to the occasional comment of his wife, a rail-thin woman who did cleaning for other people in the area and who was famous for her pies. If he spoke more than a dozen words to me in the seven or eight years I was a constant visitor in his house I don't recall them.

We all lived in the country, in and around a small community called Michaels Mill, named for the old abandoned mill by the river. People said the mill had been there for over a hundred years, but it had been abandoned so long no one could remember what had been made there, or who Michael or Michaels was. The mill itself was a crumbling wreck; the millrun upon which its fortunes had hung given over to muskrats and water moccasins. A dozen or so houses had sprung up on the other side of River Road from the mill, for a quarter of a mile in each direction. The road took a sharp turn to the south after the last of these houses, leading to a trio of small bridges, two of them metal, one wood, crossing three strands of the braided South Raritan River, which dominated Robbie's and my lives.

Robbie, tousle-haired and sunburned, had a passion for fishing that I acquiesced to, and we'd spend hours each day dangling the lines of our spinning reels into the swiftly moving water; or, in the shallow, rocky water downstream, scavenging for bait, tiny crawfish and hellgrammites; or, in poor weather, poring over old *Field and Stream* and *Outdoor Life* magazines, reading fishing articles and ogling the tackle ads, which were pretty much the extent of Robbie's interest in reading, one of many differences between us. In the heat of summer, we were part of a gang of kids who swam in the river, leaping from the bridge into the deep spot, and launching ourselves in inner tubes into the current that rushed us downstream into the rocky shallows, always keeping a watchful eye out for the water moccasins that plied the river for small fish, the distinctive moving V that indicated their presence as they swam. They kept their distance, as leery of us probably as we were of them.

Robbie and I also played a lot of baseball and watched a mind-numbing amount of the major league variety on TV, in the company of his dad in the evenings or on our own on rainy afternoons. We rode our bicycles, often with other boys, screaming our pleasure as the wind battered our faces and tore through our hair.

In the winter, we spent hours after school and on weekends fussing over Robbie's traps and inspecting his trapline, and sledding on the big hill on the other side of the river.

Most of these pursuits had been prohibited to Boo, though we would occasionally cross paths with him. Sometimes, he would flaunt that prohibition and join in the baseball playing—he was a decent fielder, with a borrowed glove, but he couldn't hit very well. He loved to hurl insults at the batter from the safety of right field, "Hey, Shithead, don't be afraid of the ball, go on, hit it, no, don't just wave at it as it goes by, *hit* it, you schmuck, *hit* it."

As for fishing, trapping and so on, Boo would never be more than a casual spectator. He was an only child and his parents, who had no genuine affection for him that I could see, were extremely protective, as if determined not to lose what little they had, no matter how unworthy it might be. He was not allowed to have a bicycle, because those ungainly vehicles, which the rest of us boys in the neighborhood doted on in the manner of movie cowboys with their horses, were dangerous. In the summer, when the rest of us spent most of our afternoons at the river, Boo was forbidden from swimming for fear of his catching polio from the muddy water. Nor could he fish, for fear of germs, or, in the winter, sled or skate, for fear of injury.

Boo was unhappily enrolled in a private school attached to the college where his father taught. He went and returned with his father every day by car while Robbie and I and the other kids of the area took the yellow school bus to the grade school in Middlesex, then later to the high school in Somerville. So there were often days on end that I didn't see Boo. On Saturday afternoons, though, when Robbie was busy with his traps or a bait business he'd started and I was no part of, or on Sunday mornings when he'd go to church with his family, I'd often stop by Boo's house. His mother, as tall and angular as Robbie's dad, regarded me at the door with a suspicious look but she would always allow me entry. She had been a teacher and knew something of the dynamics of boys; I think she realized her son's need for a friend and saw me as the least of numerous possible evils, until, that is, I did something unforgivable in her eyes.

Boo had a sharply developed sense of humour and imagination, qualities which I admired and aspired to myself. His real name was John, but he had appropriated Boo for himself from the character of the scary neighbor in *To Kill a Mockingbird*. I never called him anything else, though when I came to the door I would always take care to ask his mother if John were at home. He was eleven when his family moved into the old Baker house down the road from Robbie's. By then, he had already created a large cast of imaginary friends, all of them ghosts patterned after the carefree, cynical duo in Thorne Smith's *Topper* stories, which he had begun to consume a year or so before. Each friend had its own name, history and personality and only Boo could see and hear them. On my visits to his bedroom those first couple of years, he assured me they would make themselves known to me as well if I could only prove myself worthy. This was something I longed to do, though I never really believed in his friends, marveling rather at the intensity of Boo's own belief.

Robbie, on the other hand, had no use for Boo's ghosts, and not much more for Boo himself.

"He's weird," he said the first time we met the new boy, and that pronouncement seemed to colour his attitude toward his neighbour from that point on.

"Not weird, just, well, eccentric, maybe," I said in Boo's defence. My father was a bit eccentric—that was his own word for himself—and I had an appreciation for that state.

Robbie just shrugged.

By the time Boo was thirteen, his ghosts had been dispelled and he had turned his attention to collecting. His father, whose field was economics, had been an avid stamp collector as a boy. After a visit to his parents in California, he came home with his boyhood album, retrieved from the family attic. This he presented to Boo with solemn formality, as if initiating him into a family rite of passage, with the comment: "Maybe you can be good at this."

Boo had no real interest in the stamps, though he spent time with the collection, adding to it, going through the motions to please his dad. His real passion for collecting showed itself in quirkier ways. He had a huge, constantly growing ball of silver foil collected from the inside of cigarette packages, which Boo picked up wherever he came upon them. Of more interest was his passable collection of pornography—photos scissored from the girlie and nudist magazines of the day and a handful of grimy, dog-eared cards from a French deck that depicted a dark-skinned man and an overweight woman in several of the reputed fifty-two positions. I had no idea where Boo came upon this stuff. He left the foil ball out in the open, on the top of his dresser where his prying mother could inspect it anytime she wanted to. But he kept the taped-up cigar box the photos and cards secreted away in a constantly changing hiding place—sometimes under the mattress of his narrow bed, sometimes on the top shelf of his closet, sometimes in the easily reached attic, sometimes in his school bookbag, sometimes even in his locker at school. Boo liked to change the location daily and he'd become adept at finding hiding places.

"Do you ever lose track of where it is?" I asked when he explained this routine to me, and he admitted he did forget once.

"I was shitting bricks for days until I found it. It made me think, 'Christ, if I could find it, my mother can too.' Then I was *really* shitting bricks, thinking about the bricks *she'd* be shitting."

His pride, though—and kept well hidden in a hole he'd dug under a loose board in the garden shed—was an assortment of empty foil condom packets. These were gathered at two nearby lovers' lanes: one down the overgrown path beside the abandoned railroad tracks to the old, broken dam on the main channel of the river, across a cow pasture from the mill; the other the turnout beside the railroad bridge atop the hill on the road that passed the three bridges. I accompanied Boo on several of his treasure hunts. Sunday mornings were prime time, before the prizes discarded during the previous frantic evening had fallen prey to the elements. I knew that his real interest was likely in the rubbers themselves, and the vicarious thrill that seeing them, not their packets, brought. He'd stopped short of making a collection of the rubbers themselves and transferred his attentions to the foil, which did, in fact, hold a certain interest. They had evocative brand names, like Trojans and Sheiks, and had bold, suggestive designs of helmets and Arabs on the crinkly packages.

Regardless of brand, there was one message common to all these packages: "Use for the prevention of disease only."

"Oh, baby, let me prevent disease with you," we would mimic, in a variety of voices, low and high.

"Yes, doctor, prevent me, prevent me."

I enjoyed reading the foil packets as much as Boo did. Even then, I had a compulsion to read and was a real bookworm, a tendency that, later, when Gillian and I were first married, caused her some amusement and, sometimes, irritation. "Oh, he'd rather stay home and read," she'd always say if we were invited out somewhere. At home together in the evening, I'd be engrossed in the paper or a magazine or a book after supper and Gillian would playfully throw a pillow or something at me to get my attention. "Remember me?"

There was a used bookstore near where my father worked in the city and he would often bring me treasures. I had Kiplings, Jack Londons, all sorts of Dickens in hardback, and many others in paper. I devoured them all as fast as my father brought them. "Bookworm," my father called me, but he pronounced it with affection. My prize was a collected Sherlock Holmes stories in soft leather binding my father had brought home when I had the measles.

I tried to interest Robbie in Sherlock Holmes but he merely shrugged halfway through the first story. But I turned Boo onto the great detective. He delighted in the book too, as much for the woodcuts which decorated the beginning of each story as the stories themselves. Boo came to our house sometimes. My parents liked him. They took a dim view of his mother's and father's parenting skills, and always welcomed him warmly. Often when he came over, he'd read a Holmes story, and afterwards we'd re-enact key scenes. Sometimes I would take the part of Holmes and Boo Watson. Other times, we would reverse.

We both took glee in saying "Elementary, my dear Watson."

From somewhere, Boo obtained a deerstalker cap just like Holmes', which he wore in the privacy of his room. Walking to the bathroom one night in his pajamas, with the cap on his head, he told me, he ran into his father, still wearing his necktie, in the hallway. His father regarded the deerstalker first with curiosity, then distaste.

"I suppose that's supposed to be a joke," his father finally said. "Very good."

"It's a Sherlock Holmes hat," Boo said.

"Yes, I know," his father replied, and went past Boo and down the stairs.

But, while Boo and I shared a passion for the great detective, our focus was different. Boo loved Holmes' idiosyncrasies, the violin and the opium, while I loved his skepticism. Like me, Holmes was suspicious of what people said and preferred to put his trust in what he could read from them—not from printed words, but their clothes, their gestures, the way they walked. These were statements that never lied and sometimes betrayed them.

Boo lived in his mind, his imagination. I preferred to live in other people's minds, finding access through their writing.

I couldn't fall asleep without a magazine and a flashlight under my pillow. I couldn't eat breakfast without the box of Cheerios in front of my bowl. I couldn't go to the bathroom without a comic book. Try as I might to connect with my friends—not just Boo and Robbie but the whole assortment of boys and girls in my life, from school, the neighbour-hood, children of my parents' friends—and try as I might to connect with my family, it was always the printed word that had the most meaning for me. People were fickle, their personalities mercurial, their opinions and positions unstable as sand, their affections unreliable. The word—the *printed* word—was, in contrast, the rock of Gibraltar. It endured, it spoke plainly and honestly, unwaveringly.

Only with Gillian was I ever able to get past my instinctive distrust. I loved her completely, so I trusted her completely. Isn't that what love is?

With others, I kept my guard up. Even lies, once committed to writing, lost their ability to deceive. If you read the words over and over, often enough, you could see through any duplicity they might contain.

Sitting here now, waiting for Gillian, the image of her dark-eyed beauty still sharp in my mind, I can't help but think of the papers she'll be carrying for me to read and sign. I think about the lies they'll contain, the truths.

*

The July Boo turned thirteen, just four days after my own twelfth birthday, his mother had a so-called party for him. It was held in mid-afternoon, on a weekday, when Boo's father wasn't at home. Even in summer, when there were no classes, he made the hour-long drive to the college every day. Boo said his father felt restless at home.

I was the only invited guest. There were no games. There was a cake, though, a plain white cake his mother had baked herself, with "John" spelled out in icing, along with Happy Birthday. We were seated at a table on the screened-in summer porch and served modest slices, each one topped with a rounded scoop of vanilla ice cream. Afterwards, we moved into the living room and Boo's mother, who could play reasonably well, sat at the piano and we sang "Happy

Birthday." She and I sang, that is. Boo stood silently, studying a water spot high on the wall behind her. I remember Mrs. Toglin had a surprisingly rich contralto voice and small circles of red appeared on her cheeks as she sang.

Then the gifts were presented: from me, a Louisville Slugger as good as my own, which my father had purchased and my mother had gift-wrapped in different coloured tissue paper and scissor-curled ribbon; from his parents, in store boxes decorated with a single taped-on bow each, a pair of summer-weight pajamas, a short-sleeved blue and red checked shirt, and a flannel shirt of more or less the same colour scheme for the winter. There were a few other boxes with similar gifts from aunts and grandparents who lived in California and Boo rarely saw.

Boo accepted all this—the cake, the song, the gifts— with the quiet equanimity he customarily adopted to receive his parents' fussings, scoldings and left-handed compliments. He showed neither pleasure at my gift, nor annoyance or disappointment at his parents'. His mother, though, couldn't mask the annoyance she felt over the bat, though she stumbled over herself with embarrassed false praise for it.

"What a thoughtful gift," she said.

"It was my folks' idea," I said, somewhat lamely.

"Be sure to tell them how much John appreciated it."

I had told my father the bat was a waste of money, that he'd never be allowed to play with it, but he wouldn't listen.

"If he has a bat, how can his mother not let him play ball?" my father asked.

Afterwards, while his mother cleaned up, Boo and I sat on the steps outside the porch, the boxes of presents around him. He rolled the Slugger in his hands and quietly whistled "Take Me Out to the Ballgame" while I smiled ruefully. As usual, Boo was dressed as he would be for school, with an ironed white shirt and charcoal pants with a knife-sharp crease, his hair carefully combed.

"Thanks for the bat, Shithead," he said after a while. "I can use it for beating off. *Toglin gives it a good whack, it's a base hit—a very base hit—no, no, it's lifting, it's rising, folks, there it goes, omigawd, it's a grand slam.*"

"I've got something else for you too," I told him. For some reason, I hadn't wanted to bring it in. This was the present I had meant to give him until my father came up with the idea of the bat, and the thought of giving two gifts was mildly embarrassing. It was in the basket on my bike, which was parked in the driveway. "Hold on, I'll get it."

Boo put a finger to his lips and cocked his ear toward the porch. "Mom, we're going for a walk," he called. Walking was one activity his parents approved of.

"Not too far," she called back.

"Come on, let's go down to the river," he said to me.

Across River Road from Boo's house was a branch of the Raritan no wider than a creek where the old mill stood, a few hundred yards east. I thought that's where he was leading me—Robbie and I often went there to fish in the deep water of the millpond, although we had to be wary of the moccasins that lived in the broken concrete rubble. But after we crossed the road, he plunged into the bushes and disappeared with a crash.

"Boo, where the hell are you?" I called, the gift-wrapped book in my hand.

"Down here," he called back. When I peered closer, pushing my arms and head through the tangled branches of a willow, I could see a narrow trail leading at an angle down the steep embankment to the river. By the time I got to the bank, Boo was sitting cross-legged on a rock beside the water, removing a pack of Camels from a plastic bag he'd pulled from a crevice beneath the rock. Looking up, I could see that the angle of the embankment and the dense shrubbery made it almost impossible for anyone to see us from the road. I sat beside him and lit the Camel he offered. In exchange, I handed him the present.

Even with the gift-wrap on it, it was clear the gift was a book. It was the Sherlock Holmes I valued so much.

"This is great, thanks, really," Boo said, admiring the illustration of Holmes and Watson on the cover, though he had seen it many times before.

"Elementary, my dear Toglin."

"You are a loyal and true member of the River Road Irregulars," he said grandly. He laughed sourly and turned the book over carefully, examining its frayed binding. He was just about to say something else when we heard a sound that made us both freeze.

It was the snapping of a branch, followed immediately by his mother's icy voice: "John!"

She was at the top of the embankment but had pushed through the branches and shrubbery and was peering down at us. "Is this how you repay me for your party? Smoking? Sneaking behind my back?"

Boo didn't say anything but his face had gone as white as mine must have been. We both scrambled to our feet, tossing our cigarettes into the water.

"You get up here immediately! Bring me those cigarettes! We'll see what your father has to say about this when he gets home."

"Oh, shit," Boo said under his breath. He slipped the Sherlock Holmes under his shirt, into the waist of his chinos. I crunched the gift-wrap paper and ribbon into a tight, crinkly ball and crammed it into my pocket. Together we clambered up the steep path and through the willows onto the road where his mother stood waiting, her crossed arms pressed tightly against her midriff. Her lips were almost white.

"Get home right this minute and go to your room, John. And you," she hissed, turning to me, "I suppose you're responsible for this?"

"Honest, Mrs. Toglin, I...." I began, but I realized that denying blame would only make things worse for Boo and I didn't finish the sentence. "I am," I said. "It was just a sort of birthday gift. I'm sorry."

"And so you should be. You'd better get home, too. I'll be calling your mother, you can be sure of that."

I *was* sure of it, so I told my mother first, and my father too. He just laughed. Surprisingly, Mrs. Toglin didn't call, and, inexplicably, didn't tell her husband, either. Boo was banished to his room for the rest of the afternoon but freed just as his father was coming home. A few days later, Boo told me, he checked the stash where he kept the plastic bag with his collection of condom packets and found it empty. His mother said nothing about it either and Boo turned his attention to other pursuits. The cigar box with the pornography collection, he assured me, was in a place beyond detection and wouldn't be found. I never saw or heard him refer to it again.

The Sherlock Holmes was a casualty, though. Boo's mother had noticed it in his shirt and confiscated it along with the pack of Camels. Who knows what she did with the book. I told my father and he found another copy, not as good, which we gave to Boo for Christmas, from all of us, making it less vulnerable. Even now, thinking of the wood-cuts in the first copy, I get angry.

Years later, when we all lived out in California—Boo in Berkeley, Gillian and I in San Francisco, and we used to get together a lot—I mentioned the birthday incident to Boo and was surprised that he only barely remembered it, while getting caught that way had left a permanent mark on me, even though I'd been relatively innocent. I can still remember the *snap* of the branch, the sting of his mother's words, the whiteness of Boo's face, the book in his hands, the wisp of smoke from the cigarette in his lips, the hiss as the cigarettes completed their arc into the flashing river. I can remember my own confusion. I can see every detail, as clearly as if it were a photograph preserved under plastic.

But why am I thinking of these things today?

I sit in the window seat and gaze out at the street, waiting for Gillian's taxi. All sorts of memories could be in my mind, so why these? There are birds in the spruce, a quarreling cacophony of birds, small, indistinguishable sparrows. I think of Robbie, who I haven't seen or heard from in years. Like me, he married, and seemed to flourish. Then, I heard, something went wrong. His passions, whatever they had become, even his steadfastness, were insufficient. I think of Boo, who is dead. All his parents' carefulness shattered by a moment of his own carelessness behind the wheel of his car.

His death came within weeks of his revelatory letter to me and my cursing him, a freak coincidence. I could not believe my words, or even my anger, were in any way responsible, so I felt no guilt, certainly no vindication, only sadness. Despite everything, it seemed to me, he was a good friend. Although now, as I await Gillian's knock on the door, I wonder if that's true.

I think of my son—Gillian's and my son—thirteen now, the same age I was when I stopped implicitly believing what I read, though I didn't stop reading.

I think of Gillian herself, the way light used to nest in

her hair when it was long. In a minute or two, her taxi will arrive, slowing to a halt outside the building. She will back out of the door, her shoulders bent under the collar of what I imagine will be a dark blue raincoat, not a trench coat exactly but with epaulets on the shoulders, London Fog printed on the label. I'll press the buzzer to let her in. I'll hear the click of her heels on the steps as she mounts them, wearing attractive blue pumps. There'll be a hesitation at the door, an awkwardness. We won't embrace, though our arms may ache. Inside, she'll put her briefcase on the coffee table—grey, leather, Armani, the leather of the handle slightly worn. She'll tell me about our son, the house we used to live in, nervously chattering on. Boo won't be mentioned—none of it was his fault, really. We were all friends, thrown together. One thing had led to another. Was there deception? Of course. Betrayal? Of that, I'm not so sure. Holmes deceived Watson many times, but there was never betrayal, not in his heart.

Gillian will perch on the edge of the sofa. As I pour her coffee, she'll reach for the briefcase. She'll speak, but in her hand there will be papers for me to read.

BREASTS: A MEDITATION

My mother had beautiful breasts, was famous for them.

Now that they've been stripped off her, like rusty bumpers from an old Chevrolet, it hardly seems to matter. Not just flat, but actually concave, a barren moonscape of flesh and jagged scar tissue. That's what her chest looked like in the brief glimpse I got as the doctor was changing the dressings. "He saw them when they were there, so why not now that they're gone," my mother told him, Dr. Schwartzman, a very decent man, in an amiable but not-to-be-argued-with tone when he gestured in my direction. To me she snapped: "Don't you dare look away," a dare I'm sure was directed not just at me but at the world. I did, though, I had to.

I saw that ruined chest again at the fitting, weeks later, the scar tissue smoothed over now, almost glossy.

She was wrong when she said I'd seen her breasts. I never did see them first hand. She was an independent-minded woman—she had me on her own—but she was still too caught up with her figure to risk breast-feeding me, so I was a bottle baby. And what mother—even mine, even the notorious Lana Lamark—allows her son to see her breasts as he's growing up? I guess she forgot that.

But I did see them plenty in magazines and in the movies, though even then I usually had to look away.

My mother was one of the early *Playboy* bunnies and a Playmate of the Month two times. She slept with Hugh Hefner lots of times, she used to tell me, but, she said, she knew for certain he wasn't my father. "Anyway," she said with a wink, "everyone knew he was shooting blanks." So, even though I share a certain leanness of jaw with the great philosopher himself, I always believed her. Oh, the thought crossed my mind of getting a lawyer to write Hef a letter— thought of writing it myself, after I got my law degree— advising him of my existence, the timing of my birth and its circumstance, asking for a blood test, but, as I said, it just crossed my mind. For about ten seconds. Then I shrugged it off, just like I had to teach myself to do with other things. When I was a teenager jerking off over girlie magazines, the thought of other boys doing the same over pictures of my mother would sometimes intrude and deflate me, but just for a minute. I'd swallow, shake my head to let some happier thought click into place and get on with it.

After *Playboy*, she was in movies, a star at a certain level, not exactly the Graumann's Chinese Theatre sidewalk of stars variety. I don't mean porn. She was in westerns and mysteries, a few comedies, legitimate shows that came to the theatre near you but never got more than two stars, never won any awards. She played a waitress, a secretary, a wife, a mistress, a showgirl, the woman who got killed, the woman who was the killer. She could act—she got better over the years—and she was good-looking in a blowsy, soft-blonde way with clear blue eyes and a throaty voice that could be thrilling when the part called for it, in the Monroe mode, though she was no Marilyn. Mostly her job was taking off her blouse at some point. That's what sold the tickets. Of course, in the Fifties, even the early Sixties, the bra never came off, but even with it on, you could tell how beautiful her breasts were. By the late Sixties and into the Seventies, she was taking the bra off too. I don't know how how she did it, but her breasts were just as beautiful when she was in her forties as before I was born.

Over the years, until she retired at forty-seven, she was in over four dozen movies. She made good money but never got rich. Never did a TV show, not a single one, not even a guest spot on Jack Paar or Carson. No breasts allowed on TV, not in those days.

She never married either. So my last name is Lamark, the same made-up name as hers, though after Hef and the nameless man who was my father there were plenty of other guys in her bed. Until I was eighteen and went off to college, she always said I was the only man for her, all the man she needed, as though she thought I was blind and deaf, since that was clearly not the case. She still says something like that. When I visit her at the Rehab Centre, where they're helping her regain strength in her arms, she calls out to the nurses and other patients, "ah, my man is here." Again, it's a dare to the world: *don't you dare think that just because I no longer have breasts I am no longer desirable.*

🎤

My wife had beautiful breasts too, and, just as my mother had, she knew it. The first time I saw them, the third or fourth time we'd been out together, I made an appreciative sound and she made one back, a sound that struck me as a satisfied acknowledgement of what she expected as her due. That thought made me smile, which she may have misunderstood. "What are you smiling about?" she asked, a faint hint of belligerence in her tone.

I don't know why I blurted this out, but I replied, honestly, "I was thinking of my mother."

This made her laugh, but a look passed over her face that seemed to indicate she was thinking, *why am I wasting my time with this man?* Up to this point, I think perhaps I had said, only in passing, that my mother had been in show business, but I hadn't elaborated or mentioned her name. Now, in response to Sandie's laugh, I laughed myself and said, "It's not what you're thinking. My mother is famous for her breasts. She's Lana Lamark, the actress." At that point, it had been a few years since she'd been in a picture, and more years than that since she'd been even a semi-star, but her name still had purchase.

"Oh," my wife said—well, she wasn't my wife yet. "Oh," Sandie said, an appreciative "oh," a sound that indicated she understood everything now. Maybe I was wrong, maybe *this* was the point where she was wondering why she was wasting her time. Certainly she must have thought, *uh oh, wouldn't she just be the perfect mother-in-law storm,* but before she could develop that thought any further, I was kissing her breasts, kissing her, and we were swept up. It was at that point, I believe, that we started being serious about each other. So, in a sideways way, I owe my married life to my mother.

🎤

They have convinced my mother to give the prostheses a try.

After the surgery, she proclaimed that she had no need for them. "No falsies for me, thank you very much," she said loudly, when one of the nurses suggested it. "I've *had* breasts, dear. No need to try to duplicate them." Her meaning was clearly "like you'll never have, eat your heart out."

She's seventy-six now, and luring a man is the farthest thing from her mind. Well, I think that's the case, though prior to her surgery she was certainly aware of the admiring looks she still got from men, and it pleased her.

But she still is highly conscious of the opinions of other women. If Sandie were here, they would have had a discussion long before the surgery even, had it settled, an appointment for a fitting long made. In Sandie's absence, it is the glances of other women my mother is contemplating— admiring or pitying. At first, she'd thought they would admire her for her courage and stubbornness. But she's been persuaded by the nurses that appearances will trump those virtues. It's something that, it seems to me, goes far beyond mere vanity.

"There's also balance to consider," the technician is telling her. "After walking around all your life with those melons strapped to your chest, you take them off and you'll find a tendency to tip over backwards."

"Surely you jest," my mother retorts.

My mother is sitting up on the side of her bed in the blue cotton nightgown with muted yellow daisies I brought from her closet in Connecticut. It's very demure, a far cry from some of the lace and satin see-through jobs she'd worn on the screen. I'm sitting across from her, on one of those uncomfortable hard-backed chairs hospitals favour, presumably to keep visits sort. She gives me a glance that suggests she could eat this well-meaning woman for lunch if she was of a mind to.

"I'm jesting in my language, sure, but not my meaning," the woman says. "You're going to have to relearn how to walk, posture, how to lift, everything really. This is not like a hernia operation, a quick fix-up, then stitch-up and away you go. You have a completely different body now.

These babies"—she holds up one of the silicone moulds she's brought to the fitting—"make all the difference in the world. You sure you don't want me to kick him out?" She tilts her head in my direction.

"No, he's fine," my mother says. She gives me a bleak smile. "He's harmless."

I never called or referred to my mother as Mom, just Mother. Well, I guess I did when I was little. As soon as I was old enough to have heard and understood the word "mammaries," I stopped. Mom, Mam, just too close.

I was apprehensive about taking Sandie to meet my mother. She had disapproved, for a variety of reasons, of other girls and women I'd brought along on that archaic rite of passage, the parental inspection. I was in my thirties already, so there'd been a few of them. And I thought sure she would not like Sandie, that they would not like each other, some sort of a girl thing. Breast envy, maybe.

We had always lived in New York, where my mother grew up. She commuted back and forth to Hollywood, with me often in tow. After she retired, she bought the place in Connecticut, an old farmhouse lovingly restored, lots of trees, a pond. I had a life in New York, but I often got out there to see her. I put off taking Sandie up there as long as I could—I was crazy about her and I didn't want my mother's disapproval putting the voodoo hex on things. But Sandie kept asking, and it was becoming obvious that I was making up excuses. I called my mother to let her know we were coming. She had already sussed out that I was seeing someone, that it was serious. We drove up on a

Friday afternoon in May, with the idea of making a weekend of it. I'd arranged for a friend to phone me there Saturday around lunch time so, if things were going badly, I could announce they needed me at the office for an emergency.

Sandie was nervous as a cat. I had a key, but I rang the doorbell, to give my mother warning. "It's open," she sang out—obviously a careful strategy, forcing the meeting to occur in the setting she'd chosen rather than at the doorway.

We found her in the living room, seated on a divan in front of the French windows overlooking the garden. It faces the west, and the room was flooded with light. My mother had positioned herself on the edge of the seat, angled so that our first sight of her was in profile. At fifty-seven, she looked as stunning as ever.

My mother got up and I went over to hug her, then stepped aside. "This is Sandra," I said, aware of the stiffness of my movements, the formality in my voice.

"Sandie."

"Of course," my mother said. "How nice to meet you at last. This naughty son of mine has been keeping you all to himself." That word, "naughty," hung in the air above our heads for a moment, like an echo from one of my mother's early movies.

They approached each other coolly, apprehensively, like prize fighters taking each other's measure or like cats in an alley, their ruffs stiffening. Then my mother dropped all defenses and embraced Sandie, anointing her as the one for me. It was a generous gesture for which I have not stopped being grateful.

To my utter surprise, they took to each other and became close almost immediately. It was a brilliant weekend, no need for that escape clause phone call at all.

After Sandie and I married, I would sometimes have the

feeling that it was I who had married into the family, that Sandie was my mother's daughter. Throughout our marriage, Sandie and I, and, after they came, the kids, were frequent visitors in Connecticut, at least one weekend a month. They were always a little different when they were together, like girls home from school reuniting with old chums, childhood best friends. Together, they seemed to regard me as an acceptable specimen of a somewhat inferior species.

In company, they liked to announce, accompanied by uproarious laughter, that they were "bosom buddies."

Sandie and I had two children, fine sons, identical twins, but no daughters, so we never got to see what sort of breasts my genes and hers might have produced.

~✒

I am taking my mother home today. She is dressed and waiting for me, in the lobby, not her room. She's wearing a black skirt, a tailored white blouse, stockings, heels, not too high, standing up straight. Classy, and stunning as ever, even now. The physical therapists have done a great job, having her lift weights, strike poses. She's strong, balanced, composed.

"You look great, Mom," I say.

"Well, well put together," she replies dryly. She gives me a wink.

On the drive to her place, she broaches the subject she's obviously been thinking about for some time.

"You should move in. Living alone's no good for either of us. Besides, the city's no place for those boys of yours."

"It was fine for me, Mom, remember?"

"That was different. For one thing, I had a career, remember?"

"Not on Broadway. You were always flying off to

California. You actually live closer to an airport now than we did in Manhattan."

"Well, I had a public. It was important that I be seen. If we'd lived in the country then, I'd have been branded a recluse."

She's probably right about that, so I don't reply, though my mother was hardly a Garbo.

"For another thing, the city's different now. So much violence, hostility. I worry about the boys."

I laugh. "Hello. Does the name Rudy Giuliani ring a bell? The city's actually safer now than ever. Definitely safer than when I was a kid."

"But so much pollution," she retorts. "The boys shouldn't be breathing that foul air."

Chemicals in the atmosphere is a sore subject with both of us, so again I don't reply. Besides, the idea is not completely outrageous. Brett and Bart are fourteen now, and still miss their mother something awful. They'd grumble about losing their friends, but a change might be good for them. My mother will be seventy-seven soon and we can't expect her good health—if that's what you call what she's experiencing now—to last forever. The downward slide is just ahead. She'll need me then. I might even enjoy the commute.

"We can think about it," I say, but I can tell my mother's already made up her mind.

/

My mother used to say, "Life doesn't give a shit," a little piece of show biz wisdom she picked up from Clark Gable or some other dime store philosopher on one picture set or another. Yes, my mother was in a film with the great Gable, they had a steamy clinch scene together, him toward the end of his career, her at the start of hers. And she probably bedded him. She was always discreet, didn't boast, other than about Hefner, who I came to realize was really more mentor than lover, and I never asked.

Even as a kid I understood that aphorism to mean there's no justice in this world, that you've got to play the cards you're dealt—another little piece of show biz wisdom.

The cancer that took Sandie was brutal, merciless. And so unfair. But when is cancer fair? Yes, I suppose it strikes "bad people" too—not that I know any really bad people, just good people doing bad things or being stupid—but it always seems like it's the good who die young, the all-suffering people who suffer the most.

Not that Sandie was an all-suffering type. We had a good life. My law practice thrived and still does. The boys were and are happy, healthy, smart, well adjusted. We all enjoyed frequent visits to my mother, and occasional ones to Sandie's parents, in Kansas. A very good life.

And Sandie definitely was good. Good wife, good lover, good mother, good person. She was still at NYU when we met, in commerce, not because she had a head for or interest in business, but because she'd always been good at organizing things—"bossy," I used to kid her—and a guidance counselor had suggested business administration. Her first job after graduation was as admin assistant to the ED of the Lung Association New York chapter, and she went through two or three similar jobs before the boys came. Committed to non-profits, to charities. She stayed at home till our sons started kindergarten. Then she got right back into the fray, was ED herself at two agencies before the opening came up at the place she really wanted to be—at the Cancer Society, the end of an arc that began when she was a girl and her best friend died of leukemia.

Cancer Society head succumbs to cancer, that was the headline in the *Post*, too good an angle to pass by.

The end came fast. She hadn't had an ill day, not even an off day. She felt something the size of a pea in one breast in the shower one day, knew her own drill well enough to make an immediate appointment with the best man available to her. They thought they'd caught it in time, but "this was a tricky one," that's what the oncologist said. Schwartzman, the top guy at Columbia Presbyterian. The cancer had been there undetected too long and had already spread, but for some reason that didn't show up. "This is as much art as science," Schwartzman said. "Black art."

This was after the useless lumpectomy and the just-as-useless mastectomy. After chemo, during radiation. The doctors threw everything at it. And finally came the marrow transplant, the last chance. It was long, painful, all-consuming. For a while, it seemed to be working. Sandie rallied and felt better. Her blood cell count was promising. Colour came back in her cheeks. That was the set-up, I figure. Cancer is a cat playing with a mouse. Life doesn't give a shit.

🎤

I had my own brush with the cat a dozen years ago. My mother called one day to say my father had just died, of prostate cancer, that I should get a checkup right away.

"My father!" It took me a few seconds for that to register. "You mean you've been in touch with him all along?" I protested. "And never told me?"

"It doesn't mean that at all. And I'm not going to tell you who he was now. Are you listening to me? The only reason I told you anything was to warn you to get tested."

I got the test but my mother was worried for nothing. My annual tests since then have always been clean, and the shiver that went through me that first day, after what my mother had told me finally sank in, hasn't returned. She never mentioned the subject again, either the disease or the man who died of it.

∮

My mother took my wife's illness and death hard, very hard. But there is something called the survivor syndrome, that little surge of joy—or maybe it's merely relief—you feel when you realize it's not you. Soldiers apparently experience that on the battlefield when the man next to them falls. It's inevitably followed by guilt.

So when something bad happens to you later, it might be easy to think God or something is punishing you.

That's what happened with my mother. It was barely six months after Sandie's death that she found her own small lump. I try not to think of this but I cannot *not* think of it. These were beautiful breasts still, even if over sixty years old. Breasts that were once famous, the world over or close to it. Breasts fondled and kissed by Hugh Hefner, Clark Gable and who knows how many others. Breasts jerked off over by legions of teenaged boys, dreamed of by thousands of men in stale or loveless marriages. My mother had been washing her breasts in the shower or bath, patting them dry with a fluffy towel, powdering them with talcum, rubbing moisturizer cream into them for six decades—that's what, eighty-five percent of her life?—examining them against just such a dreaded possibility, a lump no bigger than a pea. But forty mattresses can't alleviate the discomfort a pea can cause a princess.

We were well connected. It only would have taken one phone call to get into a doctor's office right way, a good one. My mother hesitated. She didn't phone immediately, the way Sandie had, allowed herself another day. Another shower. Another examination. Maybe she hesitated because she felt she was being punished. Maybe she thought she deserved whatever it was. Live by the breast, die by the breast, something like that. One more day, another examination, just to be sure. Then she phoned me.

"You won't believe this," she said.

My wife was only six months dead, I still didn't have a lot of patience.

"Mom," I said, maybe too harshly.

"I have a lump. In my breast."

That shook me out of whatever funk I was in. "Don't do anything," I said. "Hang up the phone. I'll take care of it."

The very next day the two of us were in Schwartzman's office.

"I think we got this one in time," he said. "I think you're going to be lucky."

Well, yes and no. Both breasts gone. Sick as a dog from the chemo. Bald from the radiation. But alive. A good chance. At seventy-six going on seventy-seven, that maybe doesn't mean so much—not as much as it would have to Sandie, that's for sure—she was only thirty-seven. But it's something.

Life doesn't give a shit. But sometimes it relents.

My mother is standing in the open door when we arrive, the moving truck right behind us. She is a striking older woman, still statuesque, her blonde-streaked grey hair falling over her shoulders. The cut is suitable for a much younger woman but it looks good just the same. We have made extensive renovations to the house that will make the boys and I feel more at home. In fact, it will really be *our* house, with my mother in the new wing that's been added on, a nice bedroom with *en suite* bath and a sunny sitting room.

Something about her pose in the doorway, the sun pouring into the house from the westward windows behind her shining over her shoulders, reminds me of the way she chose not to come to the door when I first brought Sandie here, almost twenty years ago. There was no malice in her that day, but guile. Today, I'm conscious that there is no guile in my mother, just pleasure that her "men" are with her. I used to be her man, the only man for her, all the man she needed. Now I have to share her with my sons. I see all this, think all this, as I get out of the car. I pause for a moment to take the time to say a little prayer that they'll have the deliciously agonizing pleasure of bringing a girl home to meet her some day. She probably won't like the first few, but you can't tell. She'll know when the right one comes, I believe that. Women know other women.

The boys clamber out of their own doors and run up the walkway. They're fifteen now, an age that could make them shy away, but they are still crazy about their grandmother. And no wonder. It's not just the cookies and cakes, extravagant gifts and other indulgences she gives them. They're still boys, but she makes them feel like men.

"I'm so glad my men are here," she says now, as she engulfs them both in a hug. She buries her face in their hair, first Brent, then Bart. She kisses them, then raises her head, looking over their shoulder to me. I'm next. I don't hurry, taking pleasure in the moment.

Still a beautiful woman. Still beautiful.

GEEKS

The best things and the worst thing that ever happened to Brownie came together on the same day.

It was mid-August, 1942—Aug. 14, in fact, which happened to be his nineteenth birthday—just outside a town called What Cheer in Iowa, that Brownie inadvertently invented pink lemonade, an achievement which would stand him in good stead for the rest of his long life, and Tiny Tim, the only real friend he had in this godforsaken world, caught a blow intended for someone else, the repercussions of which also had a lifelong effect on Brownie.

The invention happened this way:

Brownie, who always had a changing list of duties, was assigned that day to make lemonade. Even in early morning it was clear it was going to be a scorcher and they'd go through gallons and gallons of the stuff, at three cents a glass, providing what Mr. Snipes always referred to as "a small but dependable profit." Brownie had done this chore many times before so he knew exactly what to do. In a corner of the farmer's field where the circus had set up, he gathered together what he'd need: a twenty-gallon galvanized zinc laundry tub, a hose connected to a cold water tap, a hundred or so fresh lemons bought the evening before at the town's Piggly Wiggly store, a knife to cut them with, and a big sack of sugar. He set to work slicing and squeezing and within half an hour was almost done. He was mixing in the sugar with a big wooden ladle when fate took a hand. A skiff of breeze blew through what had been an unnaturally still morning, even for Iowa, which was often becalmed. Near where Brownie was working was the tent of Armand DeSoto, the lion tamer. Outside the tent, between two makeshift poles, Armand's wife and assistant, Mitzi, had hung a clothesline. On the line, along with some of her lacy undies, which Brownie had noticed with appreciation, imagining Mitzie in them, hung a pair of Armand's red flannel long underwear, the trap fluttering open the better to dry. Even in the height of summer, when many men chose to sleep in the nude, Armand, who suffered from chilblains, preferred the comfort of flannel. The morning had been so calm, Mitzi hadn't bothered to pin her husband's underwear, but had loosely arranged them over the clothesline. Now, the skiff of wind lifted the long johns gently from the line, blew them silently, like a huge, sprung-winged red bird, the twenty or so feet across the trampled-down field and, as if suddenly exhausted, dropped them into the galvanized tub of lemonade Brownie was stirring.

Later, in retelling this story—a story Brownie would tell hundreds of times during the many years of his life, to hangers-on at the bar plying him with beers; to lazy boys drinking cokes on the porch of the general store he would open in Three Bridges, Ohio; to schoolchildren he'd be invited to inspire with his tale of American ingenuity; and to newspaper reporters who never tired of rehashing the amazing sequence of events for a front page story around Independence Day, the day he claimed the remarkable event occurred—Brownie would always wonder aloud why it was that, during such a hot spell, Armand was still wearing flannel long johns. He didn't mention the lion-tamer's chilblains. "It was like it was sorta parta a plan," he would say, shrugging his bony shoulders. "Sumpin bigger'n you an me."

Immediately, the pigment in the flannel began to infuse the lemonade with a soft pink hue. Startled, Brownie took a step backwards, tripped over the bucket of squeezed-out lemons and went sprawling forward into the tub. Fortunately, he was working bare-chested and the only addition to the mixture from this mishap was some sweat, which, as he dried himself off with his shirt and assessed the damage, he decided was hardly worth mentioning. His attention was fixed on the deepening shade of pink the lemonade had become, even as he fished out the long johns, which were, he observed, clean. They'd been washed, so what harm could they have caused? And whatever harm there might be in the dye surely was trumped by the opportunity he saw flashing before his eyes.

That afternoon, lemonade—"pink lemonade, exclusive to Snipes and Snipes Big Top and World of Wonders!"— went for a nickel a glass, a sixty-six-percent increase from the usual three cents—and every drop was sold. An American institution was born, that simply and swiftly. It became a staple of the S&SBT&WoW midway, though ever after Aug. 14, the pink was produced by the direct addition of red food colour. Brownie didn't think it ever tasted quite as good as his first batch—whether that was due to the flannel underwear or his own sweat, he didn't know—but he really had no say in the matter.

What happened with Tim was no less accidental. With the circus folk all abuzz over Brownie's invention that afternoon, and the midway more crowded than usual as word spread, the freak show went on, but without Brownie's usual presence, as Mr. Snipes had assigned him to make more lemonade. Instead, the task of introducing Tim fell to the regular barker, Tim-Buck-Two Smith. Buck, as the other carnies called him, was a lean, gangly pro who had introduced any number of freaks over the years, but he'd never introduced Tim before and bungled it, proclaiming Tim "the Wild Boy of Boston," rather than Borneo.

This set off a chorus of laughter in the crowd, which unnerved Tim, who was already unsettled by Brownie's absence. Tim was working with snakes at this show, an aquarium full of good-sized, slithering, entwined garters and milks. After charging onstage and growling at the crowd, he reached into the aquarium, pulled out a snake, waved it at the suckers in the front row and, without further ado, dispatched it. Ordinarily, after biting the head off an unfortunate snake or chicken, he would spit it out on the stage, but today, still rattled by the laughter, he directed it at one of the front-row rubes, a big man with poorly fitting dentures and manure-stained gumboots over his overalls.

Pandemonium broke out. The rube, his dignity ruffled, charged onto the stage, where he was promptly leveled by Buck, who delivered a surprisingly powerful haymaker. The big man went down like a half ton of bricks, his false teeth rattling out of his gaping mouth. Two of his friends, dressed in similar overalls and gumboots, stormed the stage and one of them put Buck in a hammerlock while the other rained blows on him. The big man struggled up and, from somewhere, produced a length of two-by-four—later, no one could say with certainty where it had come from—and began to wave it around spastically, making him look like he was fending off a swarm of wasps. By this time, the freaks, led by Sweet Lorraine, the fat lady, and the blaringly high-pitched Siamese twins, Marvin and Melvin, were shrieking bloody murder and several carnies from adjacent tents poured in, yodeling their famous rallying cry, "Hey, Rube," and adding to the melee. Fists flew and there was pandemonium on the freak show stage. If Brownie had been there, he would have taken Tim by the hand and led him behind the curtain to safety. But, to his everlasting regret, Brownie was up to his elbows again in lemonade.

✎

It would be wrong to say Tiny Tim ran away to join the circus, that old romantic conceit. Rather, he was on the move and the circus found him.

Biting the heads off chickens and snakes would come natural to him, and he found his niche in the freak show with little effort. The circus became his family for the short time he had left on this earth, the other freaks in the side-show his siblings.

Tim never had much family, just a desiccated great-aunt who'd raised him on a sorry excuse for a farm after all the rest perished in an odd outbreak of smallpox that hit Rapid City, South Dakota, in 1929, a full decade after it had run its course in most of the rest of the country. Tim had been an infant lifted from his dying mother's breast so she could gasp out her final hours in some semblance of comfort. He was somehow immune to the pox. Great-Aunt Hilda was good enough to him, and he shed the usual tears when she died, but he hit the road without looking back or giving consideration to his inheritance: stingy, unproductive land, tumble-down buildings, and a manure-spreader full of debt.

He'd wandered into Minot, North Dakota, on an unusually hot day in early June, just as the Snipes & Snipes Big Top and World of Wonders was pulling up stakes after a five-day run at the exhibition grounds, and found a few hours' worth of work tearing down and lifting. He was only thirteen and still a growing boy, but he was already six foot five, two hundred and ten pounds. His body was all out of whack, arms longer than they should be for the rest of his body. That and his smallish head with sparse hair and a shuffle walk combined to make him look almost more ape than man. When he went to collect his two dollars of pay, the assistant manager, a shrewd-eyed, bowlegged man called Chilly, sized him up, thought he saw some possibilities, and told him to collect his gear and get on the train if he was of a mind to.

"Don't have no gear," Tim said.

"Jist get on, then," Chilly said, shaking his head.

Tim met Brownie that very first night out of Minot. The rumble and lurch of the train set the boy's stomach on edge right away. He rushed to the end of the car and the platform outside to heave. Brownie was already standing there, smoking a hand-rolled cigarette and plucking bits of tobacco from his tongue, a nervous gesture that would stay with him all his life, long after he developed a cough and quit smoking.

There was nothing freakish about Brownie. He was determinedly normal looking, the sort of man who is all but invisible in a crowd. He had an average build, though he was wiry and strong. He wore nondescript clothes, had bland features and weak eyes behind plain wire glasses—all of which made him pretty much perfect for his chosen line of work, which was pickpocket. By day, he was a general roustabout and carnie. He helped to throw up and break down the big tops and other tents wherever they landed, then tended the three-balls-for-a-nickel booth on the midway where knocking over weighted ten pins could earn a fellow a teddy bear for his girl. The light-fingering was on his own and would have earned him a one-way ticket to hell-and-gone if Chilly or Mr. Snipes had ever got wind of it. There was always plenty of boosting going on at any midway, but the Snipes circus officially frowned on it as bad for business. Aloysius Snipes, the father of the current owner, had been a practicing Methodist.

On his breaks, Brownie would stroll through the crowds and rake in a few extra bucks in the form of wallets, pocket watches, and even the occasional bracelet from the slender wrist of a young woman. He was almost nineteen, already a man of the world, having been on his own since he was fifteen, when he decided the last beating from his father was the last he was going to tolerate. He came from somewhere in Ohio, but he had been on the sunny side of the Mississippi since leaving home and wasn't inclined to go back. He had tried to enlist in the army but a dripping penis kept him out. He was sent away with a shot of penicillin and a prescription for more. The army doctor told him to try again in a few months, but Brownie was not the sort of man to knock a second time on doors.

Tim had also tried to enlist. Convincing the recruiters he was eighteen was no problem. His feet, however, were unusually small and delicate, and flat, which was no wonder, given the weight they had to support.

"You are a big sunuvabitch, that's fer sure," Brownie observed after Tim had emptied himself.

"Whassit to you?" Tim asked. He peered at Brownie with suspicion although he could see at a glance there was no harm to the fellow.

"Wha, you think yer the first shithead to spill his guts onna train?" Brownie asked mildly. Despite his inclinations, which were avaricious, he had an empathetic streak in him.

He posed the question meaning to imply that he himself had been sick, thereby establishing a bond, without actually saying so. Against inclination, Brownie didn't want to tell a lie.

"I ain't no shithead," Tim retorted.

"Well, who the fuck sez you is? Anyone does, you jist tell him back, 'takes one ta know one.'"

The young man and the hulking boy exchanged glances—a glare from Tim, a mild half smile from Brownie. Gradually, Tim's glare softened and transformed itself into a sheepish grin.

"Well, OK then," he said.

"How the hell old are you, anyways?" Brownie wanted to know.

"Eighteen. And a half."

"Is that right? And still all that moss growin' on you?"

"Well, seventeen."

"Seventeen, you say. Well, well."

"Did I say seventeen? Sixteen, I meant."

"All right, then."

"A feller can't be too careful."

"That's for damn rights. Smoke?"

Tim had never tried, but now seemed like the time. He nodded and watched with interest as Brownie expertly filled a paper with tobacco from a draw-string bag and rolled one, leering as he passed the tip of his tongue over the length of the perfectly formed cigarette. "Jist as sweet as schoolgirl pussy," he remarked.

Brownie lit the rollie for him and Tim took a puff that set off a fit of coughing. He got it under control, took another puff and swallowed. As Brownie watched, a bemused look on his face, the boy commenced to turn grey.

"Say, tha's an attractive shade a green," Brownie said. "Really sets off them black eyes a yers."

To Tim's surprise, there were still some dregs in his stomach, but not for long.

By the time the train pulled into White Grass, in the damp dark before dawn, the two had become good enough friends for Brownie to invite Tim to bunk in with him in his tent. Brownie took the boy under his wing, letting him help with the set-up and the routine of his day in the ball-throw game, but not with the hoisting, which was a solitary pursuit, and not something a boy as big as a barn and clumsy as a one-armed juggler could succeed at. Tim had been hired without any special duties assigned to him. Mr. Snipes, the owner, had him pegged for the freak show but he agreed to let Tim learn the ropes around the circus for a week or so with Brownie as his guide.

In those days, the circus lived on the rails; where the tracks didn't go, no circus ever went, but any place that had them was bound to get a circus sooner or later, big or small. Snipes & Snipes Big Top and World of Wonders, named after Mr. Snipes' father and uncle, who'd been high wire artists, was big enough that it stopped in Minot, a good-sized town even in the Forties, but small enough that it stopped in White Grass, which was little more than a shadow on the road, although Brownie told Tim they'd stopped in places even smaller, places no bigger than a wad of tobacco spit. Only a few hundred people lived in White Grass itself, but the surrounding villages and farms provided enough rubes to fill its three churches on Sundays, to cram the hockey rink to the rafters Saturday nights and make any events the ladies auxiliaries put on a success. From Brownie's point of view, a stop in a blur like White Grass wasn't worth the threadbare, mostly empty wallets he'd boost, but to Mr. Snipes it was a payday that drew in a few thousand suckers to his tents—that's what he called customers, in the Barnum and Bailey tradition—and paid expenses for the day with a bit of profit thrown in. "That's what bizness is," Mr. Snipes liked to say. "Work hard and go to bed with a little more in your pocket than when you woke up. Keep that up all your life and you die a rich man."

That's exactly how it went for Brownie that day, in fact. He lucked into a wallet stuffed with greenbacks—albeit Washingtons—and immediately took it as a sign that Tim was a lucky charm. "You stick wit' me," he told the boy as he introduced him to whiskey (more throwing up) and poon, in the form of Lulu, the palomino bareback rider (a more pleasurable reaction). By this time, he'd sussed out that Tim was still a long way from the advertised sixteen.

After a week of this routine, Mr. Snipes called the lumbering boy to his railway car, part living quarters, part circus office, and Brownie slouched along. Everyone had expected—everyone except Tim himself—that he'd be groomed to be a strongman in the sideshow, but to every-one's surprise—again, Tim excepted—he wasn't all that strong. Whether there was a congenital weakness within his blood and bones or merely that he had not yet grown properly into his frame wasn't clear.

"Damn if you ain't no stronger than my mama," observed Chilly, after Tim had huffed and puffed but failed to lift a medium-weight barbell very far off the floor, the biceps of his thick arms trembling with the effort. Even Brownie, who was a good one third narrower and lighter than Tim, could swing it to his shoulders,

"I think it's the snakes and mice fer you, my boy," Mr. Snipes said. The circus folk didn't like to use the term "geek" among themselves, although it had no especially bad connotations beyond what it was. In the parlance of the Snipes & Snipes Big Top and World of Wonders, Tim was to be an "animal handler."

It was mentioned in passing, if not exactly explained to him, that the last fellow to play that role had run off with the woman who'd been the knife-thrower's assistant, and both jobs had gone begging for weeks. The circus had been short a strong man even longer, the last muscular fellow to play that role having enlisted soon after Pearl Harbor. Strong men had been scarce as tits on a bull ever since. The exact duties of the animal handler weren't mentioned.

"Whatcha mean, snakes?" Tim mumbled. He cast his eyes down to his feet, which were shod in a cast-off pair of boy's boots Brownie had scrounged for him.

The owner and his assistant cleared their throats but Brownie put his hand on Tim's arm. "I'll fill'm in, if tha's OK, Mr. Snipes. Me'n Tim here, we got a way of knowin' each other."

"No hanky panky now," Chilly said, taking off his cap to scratch his pate, which was a bit like a sun-parched meadow covered in tumble weed.

"That okay with you, boy?" Mr. Snipes asked. Unlike his assistant, who, wearing dungarees and a torn T-shirt still looked like the roustabout he'd been, the owner was dressed in an ill-fitting black suit with a bright red tie, the latter, Brownie told Tim, all the better to disguise ketchup stains. Mr. Snipes doubled as the ringmaster, at which times he'd be decked out in a spiffy tuxedo with black satin stripes on the pants legs, but with the same red tie.

"You lissen to Brownie now," Mr. Snipes said. "He'll set you straight. Meals, a place to sleep, pocket money. We'll see about pay when we see what kinda draw you are. That okay?"

Tim went away from this meeting feeling a little confused. Of the animals he'd seen so far, there were the palominos, of course, Lulu's charges, plus a pair of flea-bitten

lions, the chimps who worked with the clowns, and one
sorry-looking elephant with open sores on the tough hide of
his backside. However, they all had handlers, and Tim didn't
really see himself up to looking after any of them anyway,
except maybe the horses, especially if that meant spending
more time with Lulu. So he was completely surprised
when Brownie took him into a railcar that reeked of chicken
manure. At one end of the car was a cage filled with scrawny
bantams. Brownie opened the cage door just wide enough
to reach in, grab a hen by the neck and pull it out. "Now
you jist watch," he instructed. Tim did, his mouth gaping
open as Brownie stuffed the protesting chicken's head into
his mouth, bit down and a moment later spit out head and
blood, followed by a spate of coughing and loose feathers.
Brownie threw the headless chicken onto the floor, where,
with blood spurting from its neck, it played out the sad herky
jerky ritual of its death dance, a dance Tim had seen any
number of times before, back home on Great-Aunt Hilda's
farm. On those occasions, though, the decapitations were
performed by Harold, the half-witted hired hand who had
attended to Hilda, with the aid of a short-handled hatchet.
The chicken would then be stripped of its feathers by Tim
and roasted with sage and rosemary stuffing by his aunt,
transformed in the space of a few hours from smelly raucous
bird to a plateful of tasty dinner. Tim had no problem
with any of that, but what he'd just seen was something else
entirely and the gorge rose dangerously in his throat.

"I'm suppose' to do that? I can't."

"Oh, sure you can," Brownie insisted, "just close yer
eyes and pretend yer muff-divin'."

Tim had no idea what Brownie was talking about, but,
with his mentor's prompting and to his satisfaction, the boy
took to his new duties quickly. "Yer a natural," Brownie told

him, to which Tim responded with a disarming grin, wiping feathers and blood from his mouth. He was fitted out with a fake leopard skin loin cloth and a frightwig which would have to do, Brownie told him, until his own hair grew longer. Mr Snipes added the "Tiny" to Tim's name and dubbed him the Wild Boy of Borneo. Taking on new duties himself, Brownie became his handler, personal valet, and announcer. At the beginning of the show, which took place not under the big top itself but in a smaller, adjacent tent, Brownie would bark his spiel to draw in the rubes, then introduce Tim: "Ladies and gents, now, direct from the untamed wilds of Borneo, wherever the hell that is, Snipes and Snipes Big Top and World of Wonders brings you its newest wonder...Tiny Tim, the Wild Boy of Borneo." Tim would then come roaring out onto a makeshift stage. He would be three quarters naked, his body daubed with brightly coloured grease paint. To all appearances, he was one hundred percent feral. Brownie would pull back a curtain revealing a pen crammed with half a dozen panicked chickens, one of which Tim quickly scooped up and dispatched, to gasps from the crowd.

Within a few days of Tim's debut, the circus train was stopped in Great Falls, a large enough town to provide a new supply of chickens, and some garter snakes and mice, which were purchased from small boys at a nickel each and free admission. In the absence of the last geek, there had been no need to keep such creatures on hand.

$$\mathscr{J}$$

Tim took to his job like the well-known duck to water. He was just a bit disappointed but later relieved to learn that he was not the headliner of the freak show but merely the bait. After he did his act—which, despite its high drama, took hardly more than a minute—the rubes would be enticed into paying their quarters for the real show, which featured Oswald, the Dolphin Boy, whose flipper-like appendages had come with him into this world; Sweet Lorraine, "the Biggest Little Momma West of the Mississippi," whose 400-plus pounds were distributed over a four-foot, six-inch frame that jiggled like Christmas pudding when she belted out a song like Sophie Tucker; Alphonse, the cross-eyed albino dwarf who spoke with a stutter and did amazing card tricks; and Marvin and Melvin, the morose Siamese twins joined at the tailbone. These stars of the S&SBT&WoW and the others were pros, with well-practiced routines that kept audiences howling. Marvin and Melvin, for example, had perfected several of Laurel and Hardy's skits and did a hysterical version of Abbott and Costello's "Who's on First?"

There was no way Tim, who could barely stitch three words together, could have kept up with them, though Brownie assured him he would learn over time. "Ain't nothin' to it," he said. "It's jist a matter a rememb'rin' which one's the rube, which is the con."

Tim pondered that, then asked, "How do those two guys shit?" referring to Melvin and Marvin. He had the good grace to do it out of their earshot.

"Beats all hell outta me," Brownie said. It wasn't something he'd ever thought about before or wanted to know now.

Weeks passed, the summer deepened, Tim became adept with the snakes and mice as well as the chickens, adding new thrills to his repertoire. Gradually, he and Brownie developed a routine to augment the theatrical violence of his act with war-whoops, high-footed dancing and general tom-foolery to fill Tim's time on stage to a full five minutes. The highlight of this was "the interview," in which Brownie would fire off questions like "Tim, wha's yer favor-it food?" or "whaddya like best, big fella, blondes, brunettes er redheads?" to which Tim would reply with grunts, leers and a range of other exaggerated facial expressions that drove the crowd wild.

The friendship between Tim and Brownie grew, as did the boy's comfort level around the other freaks. He became especially fond of Sweet Lorraine, upon whose massive bosom his head would often lay as the circus train rattled through the night, and the other riders of the freak car suppressed their giggles. Lorraine had been unlucky in love a number of times, but hope continues to swell in a woman's heart, even one so well upholstered. As for Tim's own desires, they lay more in the direction of the stock car that carried the horses and the enticing Lulu. But she had troubles of her own, mostly in the hot-headed, intensely jealous forms of Lorenzo and Leopold, two of the high wire flyers. The woman they worked with in the air, Lolanda, was their aunt, and their affections and urges lay with Lulu.

Sometimes, late at night, as the train rattled through the fragrant Midwestern countryside, the other freaks who shared their car snoring fitfully, Brownie would awaken to a noise, peer down to find the berth below empty, and he'd swing his legs over with a sigh and hop down. He'd find Tim on the platform, his huge, shapeless body wracked with the sobs of a lonely teenaged boy. Brownie was not that far removed from those feelings himself—though he'd never been one for tears—not to want to offer clumsy consolation. He'd watch the passing countryside, awash in moonlight and shadow, flash by and think of his older sister Velma, who had a harelip. He would remember how, after he'd taken a beating from his father and found refuge in the loft of the barn, she would follow and wrap him in her arms, rocking him. There had been an unspoken closeness between him and Velma. As he entered into his teens it had become a dangerous one. Since he'd left home, there'd been no communication between them, and he rarely even thought of her. Seeing Tim crying these nights on the circus train would send him instantly back to that hayloft, though, and a twinge of pain would course through him. Now here he was in the awkward role of comforter.

Brownie had no real sense of why Tim was crying—the boy had never spoken of his past or circumstances—but that didn't matter. Brownie felt a closeness with him that allowed the pain to be shared. There was no question of his taking Tim in his arms, but he stood beside the boy until the shuddering of those giant shoulders ceased. Then Brownie would lay a hand on the boy's bare arm and sometimes Tim would put his own hand on top of Brownie's. No word passed between them, but Brownie could feel the hole that had existed inside his gut since leaving home close a bit. After a while, Brownie would tilt his chin toward the east and the first glimmerings of light, and that would be the signal that would send them back into the car of sleeping freaks and their berths.

Through all the melee that erupted in the freak show tent that day in August in What Cheer, Tim stood transfixed at the edge of the stage, snake slime dripping from his mouth, the limp remains of the garter still gripped in his fist. Fists were flying around him, but for some reason—well, perhaps it was his imposing height and bulk—no one attacked him. The big man whose indignation had set things off directed his rage at one of the carnies whose foot was planted squarely on the rube's dentures. He was still armed with the length of two-by-four but, though he swung it with force, his aim was off. The piece of wood deflected off the carnie's shoulder and went flying, ricocheting against the floor, then bouncing up, catching Tim square on the jaw. He went down like a dynamited building, with a thud and a cloud of dust. No one noticed right away, as the fight raged on, until Sweet Lorraine's keening brought sudden order. Tim just lay there.

As the dust settled, it quickly became clear he wouldn't be getting up.

Lorraine was the first one to reach Tim's side, but she was quickly joined by some of the carnies, all to no avail. He was dead. It was almost an hour before news reached Brownie, though; he was still squeezing lemons. By that time, Tim's body had already been removed and there was nothing for him to do.

The doctors at the hospital in Cedar Rapids explained later that Tim's jaw was made of glass, a fairly common flaw in the make-up of very big men. The force of its shattering had sent shock waves through his system, all the way back to his heart, which exploded. He was three weeks, two days shy of his fourteenth birthday.

*

Brownie stayed with the circus for the rest of the season but he didn't go to Florida with the rest of them after Labour Day. During those final weeks, he was treated with kid gloves: a bit like a celebrity, for his amazing discovery, a bit like someone who's lost a brother and is locked in grief. Not that Brownie showed any sign of mourning. At the funeral, he was stoical, and afterwards seemed to shrug it off. You can't fool circus folk, though. They know all about the clowns who are crying on the inside.

Still, Brownie was loyal, and stuck it out. When the

circus train turned south, though, he stood on the cinders beside the tracks with his carpet bag, watching as it faded into the distance. At the funeral, he'd declined the invitation to say a few words, instead just listened as Mr. Snipes extolled Tim as someone who was "new to the circus but seemed born to it. He had a lot of promise."

"Amen," cried Sweet Lorraine, who hadn't eaten a bite for days. Some of the freaks wondered who was hurting worse, Lorraine or Brownie. But of course they were inclined to her side, and it was on her they lavished their sympathy. Brownie understood that and didn't resent it. He was circus through and through.

But he'd had had enough of carnie life. He drifted into Des Moines, then Kansas City and St. Louis, hoisting, small-time grifting and eventually getting involved in a couple medium-sized cons that earned him a grubstake, enough to buy something. He landed in Three Bridges, on the Licking River in west central Ohio, not far from Bluffton, where John Dillinger, a man he'd read about and admired, had robbed a bank of some $6,000 on Aug. 14, 1933, a memorable day for Brownie because it was his tenth birthday. He bought the general store from a man known in the area as Whitey, and changed its name to Brownie's. Three Bridges was only a couple hours' drive from the pimple on a hill where he'd grown up. From that safe distance, he would occasionally telephone his mother, who now, to her and everyone else's good fortune, was a widow. He paid her a visit once or twice, and even looked up the sister he'd been partial to, who, despite the harelip, was married, with children of her own. She lived not far away in Bowling Green.

Brownie was far from a braggart, but word somehow got out about the lemonade and his fame was set. His store sold a few groceries, tobacco, newspapers and magazines, odds and ends. The coffee pot was always on. Strangely, though: he had a cooler full of pop and, in the summer, tubs of ice cream, but never sold lemonade, of any colour.

He developed a friendship with a mulatto woman in Tecumseh, the next town over, but they never married. Occasionally, a circus would come through Tecumseh, or Flemington, which lay in the other direction, but Brownie was disinclined to go. Years passed. He grew old. In all weather but the worst, he liked to sit on the porch of his store, especially in the evening, when the soft light diffused the sound of voices drifting on the breeze. He would roll a cigarette or two, always smiling a little as he meditatively licked the seam. The road in front of his store led to the river, the bridges and, just a pebble's toss further, crossed the railroad tracks, the Ohio Central. From where he sat, Brownie could see the road, the tracks, the tree-fringed horizon. He seemed to be watching for something.

TALKING TO GOD

There is the heartbreaking pale blue of abandoned robin's egg, the toothachy blue of the enormous, unfettered sky, the imagination-deep blue of a mountain lake, the thrilling icy blue of Paul Newman's eyes, which Corie has seen in a number of films her mother brings home from the library on DVD, but there is no blue like that of a field of Saskatchewan flax in the waning days of July. Of that, she is certain. One day the field is lush green, the next it has erupted into a sea of blue, each flower unfolding itself into a small brave declaration of fidelity.

To Corie, these tiny small blue collisions are evidence not just of God's existence, which she understands has fallen into some doubt, but of His love. Certainly His love for her if not for all of the world, so much pleasure do they bring her. Rapturous, that's her word for the feeling they bring her.

She isn't thinking of any of that today, though, as she walks sure-footedly through the flax in a field on her friend Bernadette's parents' farm. She's traded in her summer flip-flops for her runners to spare her soles and ankles from the loose dirt and gopher holes. She has on a newish pair of jeans, slim but not too tight, and, rather than one of the t-shirts she lives in during the summer, this morning she chose a pretty cotton blouse, light blue with tiny yellow flowers.

"Where you off to, all dolled up?" her mother asked as Corie headed out of the house.

"Just a walk. It's such a beautiful day."

Her mother gave her a suspicious glance but said no more. She probably thinks I'm seeing a boy, Corie thought. What an idea.

Her eyes are on the horizon, and the hills to the southwest, which look to Corie as if an artist has swept a thin brush of azure across a canvas. Left to right or the other way around? She doesn't imagine the result would be any different. Corie is a student of detail; that is at least a conceit she enjoys. God is in the details, she read somewhere, but when she quoted that to her classmates, one of the boys, Charlie Lampman, laughed and corrected her: "no, no, the *devil* is in the details." Either way—and she has come to understand that both can be true simultaneously, though she is as certain that there is no devil as she is that there is a God—it means that detail is something to always be aware of, something worthy of pursuit.

She is not thinking now of either God or the devil, or even of the imaginary artist who may have painted the horizon, or the flax, or the dark-shrubbed coulee through which she passed on her way to the field, or of the fire-engine flash of the red-winged blackbirds in the cattails by the slough, or the dark comma of hawk circling above her against the azure sky. She's thinking, as she often does, of Rebecca, specifically of Rebecca's voice, the soft, singsong lilting of Hebrew prayer. Today, she's recalling yesterday's ceremony, with Rebecca's voice so clear and confident.

Al kiso lo yeisheiv zar, "and on His throne none other shall sit." She mouths the words, so unfamiliar and awkward in her mouth only a few months ago, now as easy on her tongue as soft plums. *Velo yinchalu od acheirim et kevodo,* "nor shall others inherit His glory." Rebecca, who was only a student herself until yesterday, has been helping her with the pronunciation. Now Rebecca is a woman, at least in God's eyes, and the eyes of her parents, her community. Corie, though, is still a girl, she's acutely conscious of that.

As she walks, her left hand goes to her neck, her slender fingers gingerly touching the small silver star hanging from a silver chain barely more substantial than a spider's thread, nesting in the hollow of her throat. Then her fingers slowly slide down the hard shelf of her breast bone. One by one, she opens the buttons of her blouse.

"Corie, what on earth is that gibberish coming out of your mouth?" her mother asked, the first time she heard the praying.

"It's not gibberish, it's Hebrew," she said, more sharply than she should have, and immediately regretted her words as much as the tone. Better, she realized, to have let her mother think it *was* gibberish.

She had been standing in front of the bathroom mirror, examining herself, and the words *modah ani lefanekha* had come without thought to her lips. She didn't remember the meaning—perhaps Rebecca hadn't translated the phrase— just that they were the opening few words of a prayer children recite when they wake up in the morning, happy to have a new day.

Corie had made the mistake of leaving the door open. With just her and her mother in the house, closing doors was not something usually necessary or approved of.

"Hebrew?" her mother asked. "The Jewish language?"

"It's not the *Jewish* language, Mom. It's the *Bible's* language."

"I thought that was Greek or Aram, Armic or something."

"Aramaic," Corie said, maybe just a bit smugly. "But that was later. Hebrew is what the people in the Bible were speaking. *Jesus* spoke Hebrew."

"Jesus was *Jewish*," her mother said. Now *she* sounded a trifle smug.

Corie's mother is a reasonable woman—as reasonable as a single mother in small-town Saskatchewan can be. She tries hard to understand her daughter, she always says, doesn't want to make the same mistakes her own parents made.

"But Biblical scholarship aside, Professor Smarty-Pants" she said, "why are you speaking Hebrew? And where did you learn it? From Beckie?"

"Rebecca," Corie corrected. "She's studying for her *bat mitzvah*. She goes into Regina twice a week and takes lessons."

"That's nice for her. I guess. What does all that have to do with you? And what's a *bat* whatchamcallit anyway? I thought it was *bar* whatchamacallit."

"*Mitzvah*. *Bar mitzvah*, Mom. A *mitzvah* is a command-ment—did you know there were six hundred and thirteen of them? Not just the Top Ten?"

"Top Ten! I'll give you top ten whacks, young lady. If Reverend Strickland could hear you."

"And it's a blessing, Mom, something good you do for someone, like, you know, helping an old lady like you across the street."

The mock glare between mother and daughter turned to grins.

"Anyway, *bar mitzvah*'s for boys, Mom, *bat mitzvah*'s for girls."

"Okay, glad we got that straight. And it is...?"

"It's like, you know, a ceremony. Very ancient. It's to mark when a girl becomes a woman. When she turns thirteen."

"Ah," her mother said. She looked at Corie closely, her eyes narrowing. "And all this has *what* to do with you exactly, honey?"

Corie frowned. When her mother smiled, she'd learned, it was best to be wary. "I was just thinking...."

"Yes?"

"That maybe..."

"Maybe what, Coralee?"

"That I could go into Regina with Rebecca..."

"And study Hebrew?

"And have a...."

"No, absolutely not. No confirmation, no baptism, no *bat* whatchamacallit. We're not Catholic, we're not Baptists, we're *definitely* not Jewish. We're United, and we don't do things like that."

✐

Corie pauses and looks over her shoulder to the road, far enough away now that, even should someone be driving by, they'd barely see her. Her bicycle is carefully hidden in a copse of cottonwood so her presence here is all but unmarked. She slips her arms out of the blouse's sleeves, shedding herself of it. Her bra is plain—the ugly training bra her mother bought for her—but Corie doesn't give that a thought. The sun beats down on her shoulders and back, creating a delicious, warm feeling. Simultaneously, a small breath of breeze wafts past, drying the sweat on her lightly freckled skin and ruffling the flax. She ties the blouse around her waist, sleeve to sleeve, and stretches her arms, luxuriating in the sensations just as she arrives at the point in the field where the flax gives way to a stretch of rough terrain, a narrow coulee clogged with chokecherry and wolf willow; its resin rises sharp in Corie's nostrils. On the other side, another serene field of flax awaits her.

Making her way through the coulee, she's on the alert for snakes, one of the few creatures of the earth she isn't crazy about. Milk snakes and garters live under the rocks. There've been reports of the occasional rattler spotted near Chopin, though usually they aren't found this far north. Bobby Northrup, who's a year ahead of her in school, told her about almost stepping on a rattlesnake when he was camping with his family in the Alberta Badlands last summer, an experience Corie devoutly wishes to avoid. She shivers at the thought, and wonders suddenly about the snake in the Bible story, the serpent tempting Eve. What kind was it? If it had rattled its tail, Eve would have been scared off and saved the world a lot of trouble. Corie smiles, remembering that in the Bible, the serpent was not yet a legless, hissing, slithery creature—that was its punishment later. The Bible doesn't say what the serpent that spoke to Eve looked like. There was so much the Bible left out.

She pauses for a moment, certain she's seen motion out of the corner of her eye, something fast and dark, perhaps there, behind that rock. But when she looks, there's nothing, just a flurry of birds swirling above the cattails fringing the slough below. Her friend Bernadette has told Corie about feeding peanuts to chickadees so tame they'd perched on her outstretched hand. Bernadette has an uncle who's a monk at a monastery near Humboldt. Her family went to visit him last winter and he took them for a walk along a line of tall fir trees filled with the bold birds.

Corie thinks now of an Irish prayer she's heard: "May God keep you in the palm of His hand." Having a bird perch in the palm of *your* hand would be a little like having God there, just for a moment, she thinks.

She looks around but there are no chickadees in the flax she's approaching, just a few sparrows quarrelling in the branches of a wolf willow at the edge of the coulee. They don't let her get too close.

Since that first conversation with her mother about the *bat mitzvah,* they've had variations of that discussion—it's not quite an argument—a number of times, but her mother, who sometimes relents on matters important to Corie, has been showing no signs of softening on this. She first said no to babysitting, to pierced ears, to occasional lipstick, but gave in on all three.

"Religion is not something people trade in for better models like some other ideas," her mother said, leaving Corie unsure what exactly she meant.

"What about the missionaries?" she asked. "In Africa, and, you know, Latin America? Isn't that all about getting people to trade up?"

"That's a little different, Coralee. We are not exactly savages. *Trade up!* Oh, my."

Corie doesn't think what Rebecca went through has anything to do with religion really, not exclusively, anyway. Rather, religion was the suit of clothes in which the experience was dressed, she thinks, but she didn't say that to her mother. She's thought about it a lot. It seems to her there is much more involved. The girl-to-woman thing. The ceremony is something like an initiation into life, regardless of sex, an initiation into the world, the universe. Like a door opening onto something unexpected but natural, not something to be feared. Like a test that changes something for you, maybe changes everything.

Or is that what religion is?

Corie and her mother go to the United Church, where there's a woman minister, Reverend Lois Strickland, who seems more like a teacher than someone who's a conduit between humans and God, which is what Bernadette, who's Catholic, says their priest is. Their minister is chubby and kindly, with a soft voice, who always seems so reasonable. In Sunday School, when she teaches the Bible stories, she always makes it clear they may be true, but may be not. Perhaps they're tales with a moral, like Aesop's fables, or metaphors—metaphor, that's a word Corie likes.

Corie knows there's also a dark side to religion. Rebecca and Rebecca's mother, who Corie likes a lot, have told her there are people who don't like Jews, who say and do hateful things, partly because they just don't like Jews, "just like some people are hateful to Indians and black people and other people who they think are different," and partly because they take exception to their religion. "For no good reason, really," Mrs. Miller explained. She's the librarian at the high school and knows lots of stuff.

"You know, the Bible calls Jews the Chosen people," Mrs. Miller told her. "Some people resent that." She smiled wryly. "They have no idea what *chosen* entails."

Corie has seen enough television and read enough novels to know about the hateful things people are capable of. She has heard about the Holocaust and other terrible crimes. She has even heard her own friends sometimes make cracks about the handful of Indian kids who are bused to their school in Chopin. One day last winter, standing in front of the drugstore with Rebecca and Janice Goodale and some of the other Grade Sevens, Janice had called out to Laurie Bear, who was walking by on her own, "Why don't you go home to your precious Rez," stretching the "z" out so the word rumbled in Corie's ears.

Laurie is a solitary girl, plain looking, with a heaviness in her face, and a shy way of speaking. She's also the only Indian kid in Corie's grade, and just started at the Chopin school that year. So she doesn't already know a ton of kids. All of this combines to make her permanently on the outside of any group of girls in the school hallways, the schoolyard, and even the streets of Chopin. Corie is conscious of this, conscious that there's something about this situation that bothers her, but she isn't sure what it is, nor has she done anything to change it.

The other girls laughed at Janice's remark, except for Rebecca, who turned on her heels and started walking fast in the opposite direction. Corie ran to catch up. "Where you two runnin' off to?" Janice called after them, her voice still buzzing. *Hateful,* that was the word that formed in Corie's head, though neither she nor Rebecca had come to Laurie Bear's defence, or said anything to her the next day at school. Or to each other about it, other than Rebecca's curt "Janice Goodale is such a bitch."

Corie thought about all this when her mother made her comment about religion. She's pretty sure her mother isn't like that, doesn't dislike Jews or Indians or anyone else for no good reason. She isn't the sort of person who says hateful things—Corie's never heard her do that—or has hateful thoughts. But Corie sensed that, for whatever reason, religion was not a good subject to pursue.

Instead, she resolved to make her own *bat mitzvah*, not

in a synagogue, as Rebecca would, or in her own church or with anyone's assistance. She's pretty sure that, even if her mother gave her permission, she wouldn't have been able to do it anyway. When she blurted out her intention to Rebecca, her friend giggled. "Duh. Earth to Corie. It's for Jews. You'd have to convert first." Corie hadn't thought about that.

But that's all right. Reverend Strickland says a church is just a building, a place for people to meet, that there isn't anything holy or even special about it. "You can worship God anywhere," she said once. "Inside, outside, anywhere. It's between you and God."

Rebecca said when she was standing at the Bible—she called it the Torah—reading in Hebrew, she felt as if she were talking directly to God, and, for that moment, He was listening only to her. "It felt just...rapturous," Rebecca said, with a tentative smile, as if she'd been caught doing something illicit. Corie craves that, that feeling of rapture. What she's going to do, she decided, would be just between her and God.

🎤

Corie knows she's in the process of becoming a woman. Her mother had the awkward talk with her over a year earlier, letting her know what to expect, and things have occurred much as she said they would. Corie has been intensely aware of the changes in her body—the gradual shift in her shape from that of a long, thin vertical rectangle, all sharp angles and edges, to that of an ellipse, just slightly rounded. Only a few months ago, blood came, expected but a surprise nonetheless, and frightening. Frightening and exhilarating all at once. Only her breasts are disappointing. Her nipples are sensitive as they rub against her pyjamas, and there's some swelling but it's barely noticeable compared to Rebecca's or Bernadette's. Her breasts make Corie think of the tulip bulbs she and her mother planted along the front walk. In the spring, green shoots erupted from the raked soil, then they hesitated for days before continuing their upward growth.

Having come to a spot that seems right, a small natural dip in the field the size of a backyard deck and almost perfectly round, Corie raises her right hand to her chest, as if swearing a pledge, and feels her breast through her bra, making her skin tingle. Feeling suddenly vulnerable, she looks around quickly, then turns herself in a full circle, but there's no one within sight. This field of flax is sheltered by the coulee she walked through and another at the far end, with stands of trees on its sides. The field, she thinks, is like a secret garden, and this small depression is even more protected. She's chosen well. She and Rebecca and Bernadette found this spot a couple of years ago. They call it their special spot, perfect for picnics or just getting away on their own. But Bernie is away in Calgary visiting relatives and there's no reason why Rebecca would be out this way today, nor any reason for Bernie's father to come here until harvest, still a few weeks away.

Corie drops to her knees, then sits back on her heels and gazes off again toward the horizon and the purple blur of hills beyond the stand of black fir. For several minutes she sits as still as she can, repeating the mantra she's prepared, *Beyado afkid rucho,* "into His hand I commend my soul, *be'eit ishan va'a'ira,* "when I sleep and when I wake."

Then she takes off her bra.

🎤

"So God doesn't ever say anything back?" Corie asked.

"No, silly, He has better things to do." Rebecca laughed.

She'd been telling Corie that the language lessons were funny because she didn't ever really learn anything. "I mean, I learned how to say the words, and I learned what the whole thing meant, but not what the *words* actually mean. Except for a few sentences. It's not like if God were to speak to me I'd know what He was saying or know what to say back. I mean, we couldn't exactly have a conversation."

Corie made a face. "You mean God talks to you?"

"No, silly, I just said He doesn't."

"But, like, you mean He could? He might?"

"Might? Sure, why not? You know, in the Bible, didn't He talk to Moses and Abraham and, I don't know, Isaac? And Noah and, Job? Did he talk to Job? I think so."

"That was all a long time ago," Corie said doubtfully, "I mean, a zillion years ago. And that's if it's even true."

"My Mom says some things in the Bible are true and some aren't, they're just stories to teach a lesson," Rebecca said. "Like, we're supposed to know which is which."

"Our minister says pretty much the same. She says they're metaphors."

"But even in your Christian stuff, God talks to people," Rebecca protested. "And that's not all that long ago, just two thousand years, right? I mean, isn't He supposed to have talked to Jesus and Mary and stuff? And St. Peter or somebody on the road to Damascus or some place?"

The girls were in Rebecca's room, sitting on her bed. Rebecca puffed up her cheeks and shook her head, made her voice go deep till it cracked: "You there, girl, wha's-your-name, God here. Whassup, babe?"

"Well, at least you get to talk to Him," Corie said when they'd stopped laughing.

"I talk, He listens," Rebecca agreed. "It's like being on the phone but the receiver isn't working."

It didn't seem fair. A one-way conversation was no conversation at all. Her mother had said that once when Corie was sulking.

Still, she likes the idea of talking to God in a language that might be God's own, and in a formal way. Corie has never been one to indulge in selfish prayers—"please God, let me pass this test," "please, God, let it be sunny on my birthday"—or, in truth, to think about God much at all, until recently, when Rebecca started her trips to Regina to get ready for her *bat mitzvah*. Something about it caught Corie's imagination.

Nor has she thought much about Jesus. The whole Jesus story—virgin birth, three wise men, parables and miracles, crucifixion and resurrection—has always seemed weird to her, creeped her out.

"You don't have to believe in Christ to be a Christian," her mother said once. "I mean, you believe in what he said, what he stood for, what his story means. But you don't have to believe there really was a Jesus or that if there was he was God's son, immortal and all that stuff."

"That's just a story?" Corie asked. "A metaphor?"

"Maybe. I don't know. Make up your own mind."

She hasn't yet. Hasn't made up her own mind about God either, or a zillion other things, boys and sex and love among them.

Nuns, Corie once read, are brides of Christ. What, she's wondered, was the wedding night like? Did Jesus whisper to them? Stroke their skin or their hair? Did God give them instructions? What might God say to *her*, should He ever get the notion to break His silence? And what would she say in reply? There are so many things she's wondered about, is confused by—so many questions God might be just the person to ask, except that God isn't a person, Corie knows that. It seems silly, trivial maybe, but what she most wants to ask, it occurs to her now, is about Laurie Bear. Not about Laurie herself, really—why she's different from the other girls, so self-conscious and shy—but why she, Corie, wasn't able to say the things she wanted to that day when Janice Goodale was so mean.

✎

She stands facing the sun and lets it warm her breasts, a surprisingly pleasant feeling. *Breasts*—the word seems too big for the reality. "Be patient," her mother has counselled. "I didn't get them till I was almost fourteen, and then, bingo. And now look!"

Yesterday, on the first Saturday after Rebecca's thirteenth birthday, Corie was in the second pew of the Unitarian Church in Regina, where the Reform congregation the Millers belong to holds its services. She sat between Rebecca's mother and father, as her friend became a woman. The rabbi, a tall, cheerful woman from Edmonton, led Rebecca through the service, proclaiming that God was smiling on her student today, but Rebecca, looking nervous and proud, was the star attraction. She stood at the enormous Torah scroll with a silver pointer underlining the script she read, stumbling over a word or two but mostly with an assurance Corie envied, giving a talk at the end. She was, she said, "proud to be a woman, a Jew, a member of this congregation and community."

Corie was pleased for Rebecca and proud of her, but she felt oddly let down or envious—she wasn't sure what it was, just that her own thirteenth birthday had come and gone the previous month with practically no notice. "Hey, sweetie, you is a teenager," her mother had said, with a grin. "I guess now you're going to be impossible, huh?" There had certainly been no welcome to a community, no smile from God.

Afterwards, there was a party, with food and wine, and the girls got to have a few sips. Rebecca was beautiful in a blue velvet dress that fit so well, accentuating her breasts, so much bigger than Corie's, her hair brushed to gleaming, a five-pointed silver star at her throat, a birthday gift from her parents. Corie wore the same star, with the same silver chain. The Millers had reduced her to tears when, at the small party for Rebecca at their house three days before, they'd presented one to her as well.

"This is from all of us," Rebecca's father said, and Mrs. Miller gave Corie's arm a squeeze.

"You're a woman too," Rebecca said.

This morning, Corie stood naked in front of the bathroom mirror—the door closed—admiring the way the star caught the light. When she put the tips of her fingers to her throat, as she does now, both the star and the soft skin of the hollow in which it nestled felt warm.

She kicks off her runners now and wiggles her toes in the warm earth.

Beyado afkid rucho, Corie whispers, *be'eit ishan va'a'ira.*

She unties the blouse and tosses it aside, unzips her jeans and pulls them off. Then, with a final self-conscious glance around, slips her blue and white checked panties down her legs and steps out of them. She folds her jeans into a thick square and, flattening a small patch of flax, positions it beneath her, a cushion.

She feels—in a kaleidoscope of emotions that washes over her—embarrassed, foolish, proud. What's there to be proud of? Whatever is happening to her body has nothing to do with her—that is, she's had no hand in it. And there's so little to be proud of, at any rate. Still, that's the way she feels.

She stands for a minute posing, lifting one leg, then another, as she imagines a ballerina might, dipping this way, then that, raising her arms, then spreading them, thrusting out her chest, grinning. Awkwardly, wincing at the small pebbles and clumps of dirt biting at her soles, she curtsies to the left, the right, pirouettes once, twice, a third time. Then, mustering as much grace as she can, Corie arranges her body into an approximation of a lotus position on her folded jeans.

She gazes again toward the horizon, whispering the morning prayer, *Modah ani lefanekha*, then throws back her head and addresses the prayer to the heavens.

Slowly, she untangles herself, straightens her legs and lies back into the embrace of the lustrous blue flowers, her head toward the east. She lies still for a moment, her eyes filling up with a perfect, implacable sky, blue as God's eye. She spreads out her arms and awaits the rapture.

BRIGHT LIGHTS ON BROADWAY

Had a massive heart attack last year.

Damn near died! I was taken to the hospital in a car at two a.m. by my friend, Mabel Austin, a crusty old gal who takes sass from no one and spares no one her own. She rushed inside and got the security and another man to get me on a cart. I was sitting for what seemed a long, long time on the edge of the car seat in a parking lot outside of the Emergency door, expecting to get jumped by a mugger. I was going to go with a piece of him in my teeth.

Also, I was weighing my chances of making it, or not making it.

Out of my mind with pain but at the same time thinking damn clear.

No fright, though. I was ready to go but regretted I hadn't made some arrangements to dodge the mortuary and morticians. I've made them now. I've collected my medical history (most of it, anyway), my body goes to a medical college. When the med student looks at it and wonders what the hell this guy did, what he went through, he will have the documents to tell him. And quite a story it is, too, what with a few scars I picked up walking up and down the

Korean Peninsula in a machine-gun rainstorm. Well, that was a long time ago.

They put me under with Demerol and it was a pleasure to let go of that pain, I can tell you that. I became a junky for a few days while in Intensive Care. That was okay.

While I was going under, I called for my Mabel. But the doctors were too busy doing a quadruple bypass or something of that sort on me to get her until later. Mabel told the surgeon that she'd actually meant to take me to the other hospital, about twice as far away, but got her signals crossed somehow. He told her that if she had she most likely would have arrived with a dead man beside her.

Pretty close, but I did not see St. Peter, nor the Golden Gates, didn't hear any harps or other types of heavenly music. I was just waiting for some guy to jump me in the parking lot, and even that didn't happen.

Afterwards, though, I couldn't shake the feeling that I'd been robbed after all, stripped of something valuable I'd never be able to reclaim.

Still, all in all, I came out okay. Nothing like a close call to sharpen the mind. Isn't that what they say? Focus it? I came home from the hospital with a certain resolve. Live a better life, be a better fellow. When you're as old as I am, it's easy to make resolutions—you only have the rest of your life to stick with them, after all.

I've never been much of a drinker, certainly no one who ever had to go to an AA meeting, but I've had a few friends who've had their sorry lives turned around. There's one of the steps of the big twelve where you go round asking people to forgive you. Asking for trouble, seems to me. Happened to me more than once. Fella comes along says he wants me to forgive him for such and such, something I never was even aware of or was but had forgotten about. Might still be stuck in this guy's craw, but to me it was never a big deal. But now, he calls it to my attention, maybe I get sore. Hell, no, I don't forgive you! See what I mean? In my case, as it happens, I'm an easy-going sort, and forgiving by nature. But what if you aren't?

What if a fella came along and says, "Look, I slept with your wife, oh, years back, I was a drunk then, didn't know what I was doing. I want to apologize, heartfelt as all get out. Please forgive me." Well, depending on your temperament, you might deck this fella or worse, and do the same to your wife later. Or, if you have a sense of humour, you might say, "Whatd'ya mean, you didn't know what you were doing?"

Rife with danger, that's the way I see the whole exercise.

It's not something that appeals to me, that's for damn sure. I do something wrong—and I sure as hell have done my share—I try to say sorry right there. Don't want boils under my skin.

But I did come out of that heart attack with one particular grievance on my mind. It wasn't even all that bad a thing, measured on the scale of grievances and sins, crimes and misdemeanours. It sure as hell wasn't something that had been eating away at me for years. I'd forgotten all about it, and so, I was pretty sure, had the other person involved. And the third party, the one who actually had the dirty done to, I'm pretty sure he never knew sweet tweet about it. What's the vocabulary for this sort of thing anyway? I'm the offending party, I guess, what the cops call the *perpetrator*—now there's a dandy word. The other party in on it, the co-conspirator? Accomplice? And the other fella, he's the receiving party? The offendee? Victim? Maybe just the poor sap, how's that?

Sitting in Mabel's car, hospital parking lot, two in the morning, waiting for someone to jump me. You don't need a

Ph.D. to know who the hell that someone is. And for some strange reason, I'm thinking about Arnold Whatshisname, Arnold Arnold Arnold…Peterson, that's it. Almost said Amundson, but that's someone else entirely. Arnie Peterson, good old boy, as they say, from up my neck of the woods, big strong ox of a Swede, a fair to middling second baseman on our high school team and a decent slugger, that Arnie Peterson. Haven't thought about him in probably fifty years. And the offence I'm coming clean about now happened years before that. I'm talking really ancient history. Arnie Peterson whose wife I slept with, yes, for real, that summer after high school, back in Tecumseh County, Iowa, where I grew up. A little spit-in-the-dust burg no wider than squashed roadkill called Torraville. Torridville, we used to call it, though it was any-thing but. Girl was Linda Rae Boyd. She used to write LRB on the cover of her scribblers, like that meant something. They married in June, day after graduation. Mid-July and already they're into their first fight. She's at the roadhouse, pissed out of her head. I give her a lift in my dad's pickup. But she doesn't want to go home. I'm still living with my folks so I can't take her there. We stop at a motel on Highway 7 near the crossing. I spend half a week's pay from the barbershop where I had my first job for a room, but man, was it worth it. One sweet fuck, best I'd had, not that I'd had too many, only eighteen then myself. I'd had a few but nothing like that, so, *memorable*, that would be the word for it. She was the cutest little thing, so you could hardly blame me. Still, she was married, and I knew it. Next morning, she was hung over as a mule and filled with self-loathing, you might say. "Don't you never tell Arnie," she hisses, makes me swear. "He's never to know. It would kill him." That's what she says, *it would kill him,* but it's her own ass she's worried about, I'm thinking. But maybe I was being uncharitable. Well, the future of the marriage, let's put it that way, she was thinking of that, not so much of him, of Arnie and his sensitive feelings.

Well, that was all over sixty years ago, yeah, sixty. She went home and I have no idea what she told him, what he believed. I know they were still together a few months later when my draft notice came and I went off to Korea. I didn't get back home for two years and when I did I ran into them down by the Piggly Wiggly one day, the two of them together, with two kids, a little boy on Arnie's hip, a little girl in Linda Rae's arms. Little boy looked to be a little shy of two, so the thought did cross my mind that he might be mine. "Cute little fella," I remarked, and I noticed that Linda Rae shot me a dirty look. I never saw any of them Petersons again—well, maybe I did see one of their kids. My folks sold the farm and moved to Des Moines and I had no reason to go back to Torraville. I haven't been in that part of the world since.

The only reason I had occasion to think about Arnie again, about seven or eight years later, is I was in Des Moines visiting my folks and I happened to see this kid on the street, boy about ten or so, and damn if he didn't look a lot like me! I was with my sister and she spotted him first, grabbed my arm. She was pale. "Look like you saw a ghost, Irene," I said. "Well, I think I did, or something like it," she says back. "Just look at that boy over there, Charley. He's the spitting image of you, same nose, same forelock, everything. Looks just like you did when you were that age." Irene—she's gone now, but she was six years older than me, so she'd have reason to remember. Irene wanted to collar the kid, ask him who his folks were, but I had a flash of who they might be and wasn't in a big hurry to find out. While we were talking this out, the kid slipped from view, so it became a dead issue, though Irene kept shaking her head about him all afternoon. Then I was off, and the whole thing slipped out of my mind again. Like I say, ancient history.

This is cockeyed, I know. Sixty years worth of water under the bridge for starters. Haven't thought about Arnie—the *aggrieved party*, that's the term—or Linda Rae—hardly the innocent bystander—or anything about the whole thing in forever. I don't know if Arnie ever knew, if he ever felt aggrieved. I don't even know if he's still alive. But here he is jumping around in my head as that fist is getting tighter and tighter around my chest. Who the hell invited *you* in? Then I was in a dark tunnel for some time—and no bright lights beckoning me to another world, nothing like that, just darkness—and when I wake up in the hospital bed there's Arnie again, poking around in my head. *Still here, are you?*

I am a man of eighty-one years, without heirs. I had three fine children, by two different wives. First son, Warren, died in Vietnam. He was nineteen years old, just about the same age I was when I had that moment of glory, you might call it, with Linda Rae. Next son, Billy, killed in an automobile crash that also took two other lives. My precious daughter Pearl—breast cancer got her. Not even thirty, and ain't that enough to make you stop believing in whatever it is you was believing in? They say losing a child is the hardest thing—try three, why don't you? It sure as hell knocked the stuffing out of both wives, both marriages. Anyway, all of them gone without issue, as they say. So no grandkids. No nephews or nieces, either, for that matter, at least not with the Weinheimer name—Irene's two kids are named Alberts, after her husband Pete, and neither me nor my dad had any brothers. The family line ends here.

So, apologize? No, that's the farthest thing from my

mind. No, the crazy idea that's come into my head in that hospital bed in Post-Op Recovery or whatever the hell they call it, still locked in the silken arms of the Goddess Demerol, is that maybe I *do* have an heir. Maybe that little boy on Arnie Peterson's hip was *my* boy, and that when I saw that ten-year-old on the street in Des Moines, I came this close to finding out.

I'm not the sort of person who likes to let things fester. So even before I'm out of the hospital I'm putting my mind to the problem. What I know about the Internet, you could put in a thimble, but Mabel knows some. I've heard her say it's a good way of keeping up with people, finding them, even. I wouldn't have the first idea how, but maybe she does, I'm thinking.

"Peterson," she says. "Arnie Peterson, Arnold Peterson. Whatchamacallit, Iowa."

"Torraville. Tecumseh County."

"Talk about your needle in the haystack. And next you're going to tell me he's a butcher or a baker or a candle-stick maker."

"No idea what he did for a living. His dad had the gas station, so maybe he took that over."

"That's something to go on at least, Charley."

I'm out of Post Op and in the ICU now. The very next day, there's Mabel, that shit-eating grin she's famous for plastered all over her mug. She is a woman built more for comfort than speed now that she's a sixty-something charmer, she likes to say, but she was a beauty in her time, I'm pretty sure of that. You can see it in the line of her jaw, her cheekbones, those big aquamarine eyes. She's still a hand-some woman, and when she smiles that way it could thaw the heart of an iceberg. She is a one-woman global warming machine. What she sees in me is one of Life's Great Mysteries.

"Give me something harder next time," she says. She is positively gloating. Me, I don't have any idea what she's talking about.

"Your friend Arnie. I found him. Think I did."

"He's no friend, Mabel. Just this guy I'd like to catch up on."

"Whatever. Peterson's Esso and Fine Automotive Repair, Torraville, Iowa. The place is still in business."

"Fine Automotive Repair! That would be Linda Rae's doing, not Arnie's, that's for sure."

"Couldn't say. Here's the phone number." She hands me a piece of note paper.

"Damn, Mabel, you amaze me."

"Like I say, Charley, give me something tougher next time. I like a challenge. This was easy."

"And Arnie? He owns this place?"

"That I can't tell you. I didn't check tax records, didn't do a title search. But there's the number. Call it yourself. Want me to dial it for you? Where's the phone, anyway?"

"No, Mabel, I'm not feeling quite up to that yet. Thank you, though."

"And what did you say this is all about?"

"I *didn't* say. As you know."

"Must have slipped my mind. You'll let me know in your own sweet time, I suppose."

"In my own sweet time," I agreed.

I didn't know what I wanted to do. Didn't know if I wanted to phone before I'd thought the whole thing through, just on the impulse. Didn't know if I wanted to do it while still high as a kite. Didn't know if I wanted to do it while still in the shadow of death's door. But I've always been an impulse sort of guy, so I asked the nurse the next time she came in about getting a phone. They'd be putting me in a private room the next day, she said, and I could have one there, ten bucks extra. "Why, want to phone for a pizza?" she asks with a wink.

"Nope," I sass her right back, "a hooker."

When I did dial the number, had to do it three times. Hand trembling, eyesight a little foggy. *What the hell am I doing?* I'm thinking as it's ringing but someone answered before my feet had the chance to get too cold.

"Peterson Esso." A man's voice.

"I'm looking for Arnold, Arnie. Arnie Peterson."

"Help you? I'm George."

"George Peterson, you mean?"

"Yup, that's me."

"Sorry, I didn't know. I'm calling long distance. Didn't know if the Petersons still owned the place or sold it and the name went with it."

"Nope, still ours. 7-7-5, haven't seen that area code before. Where is that?"

"Reno. Calling from Reno, Nevada."

"You lose the bet?"

"What's that?"

"Lose the bet. You know, Reno, calling a gas station you don't know anything about in the middle of Nowheresville, Iowa."

"Oh, I get it. No, nothing like that. I live in Reno, but don't ask me how I wound up here, that's way too long a yarn for long distance. I'm not a gambler, though, never have been. Was a barber more than forty years, retired now. Hardly ever go into the casinos except to have breakfast at a place called the Plugged Nickel. Best eggs in town, real hash browns. No, nothing like that. My name's Charley Weinheimer, I used to live in Torraville, Nowheresville, as you call it."

"Weinheimer, that's quite a handle. Haven't heard it."

"No, my family's all long gone from there, you wouldn't have. Go to the high school, though, you might see my name on a plaque in the hallway, if it's still there, along with a bunch of others, Nineteen Fifty-One regional baseball champs. I was a pretty good shortstop."

"I'll take a look for that. My boy's in that school, I get over here from time to time. Weeheimer?"

"Weinheimer, Charley Weinheimer. Kids used to call me Windjammer."

"Windjammer! That's good, I like that."

"Then, later, because I got a mug a little bit like Walter Matthau—you know that actor?—people started calling me Charley Varrick after a gangster movie he was in."

"Think I like Windjammer better. What can I do for you, Windjammer? Having car trouble?"

"No, nothing like that. I was looking for Arnie, Arnold."

"That was my dad."

"*Was*, you say."

"Died, oh, six years ago now, I guess. Had a stroke, then another one."

"Sorry to hear that. And your mother, Linda Rae?"

"Ha ha, haven't heard her called that since I was a kid. She stopped using the Rae, don't know why. Just Linda."

"So she's still alive."

"She is. In the nursing home, though. No point your calling there. Alzheimer's. I'll tell her you called but she won't recognize your name. Half the time she doesn't know me."

"That's a crying shame. Really sorry to hear that. Very nice woman, your mother, beautiful woman. Both your folks, real nice, salt of the earth."

"That's very good of you to say, Windjammer."

"Been a long time since I been called that. Not much wind in my sails these days, tell the truth."

"I hear you, Windjammer."

"You had a sister too, am I right? Little sister?"

"Gloria. A little brother too, Charles. You're pretty well informed about my family."

"Not really. We all went to school together, Arnie, Linda Rae, me. Your dad's on that baseball plaque too, you know—second base. Hell, I'm sure you've seen it."

"Guess I have, now that you mention it."

"But that was millennia ago, seems like. I started working at the barber's—Dugan's Barber Shop, that's where I fell in love with scissors and razor blades. I don't suppose that's still there."

"There's a barber shop, well, more of a beauty shop really, unisex they call it these days. But it's not Dugan's."

"Anyway, there was the war—Korea, I mean. You probably heard about it. I went off, never really did ever get back other than for a visit. I remember running into your folks at the store, you two kids just ankle biters. Haven't been back there since."

"Was there something special you were calling about, Windjammer?"

"No, not really. I'm in hospital here, had a heart attack, a real doozer. Tends to concentrate the mind, as they say. Just had a yen to catch up with Arnie and Linda Rae."

"Well, I guess you missed them."

"I guess I did. Good talking to you, though. George, did you say?"

"Yep, George, my dad's father's name. No nicknames. Doesn't seem to be a short version of George."

"No. You have some kids of your own, George? Oh, you said you had a boy at the high school."

"Yep, two boys, little girl too."

"So no chance of the family name dying out anytime soon."

"No, no chance a that, Windjammer."

"And Charles, you say your little brother's name is Charles?"

"Yup, Charley, he's called."

"Well, I don't know him, but give him my regards. One Charley to another. Your sister too. Good talking to you, George."

Lunch came soon, cream of broccoli soup, green Jell-O, orange juice. It would be another day or two before I'd be back on solids and it seemed like it might be forever before I'd be gnawing on a steak again, if ever. Mabel came by. "You're awful quiet, old man," she said.

"Lot on my mind."

"That it?" She gave me a look, *that* look, that Mabel Austin look that says, "You have no secrets from me, old man, I can read you like bright lights on Broadway."

You live a long life. Four score years, that's the span of a man's life the Bible lays down. Some don't make it quite to there, some get a few gravy years. Whatever way it falls for you, it's still just a hiccup in time as God sees it, just a blink of His eye. And sometimes time flies. You know, a year or two can just fly by. But when you're living it, eighty years seems like a long time. I'm past that already. I'm not the sort of old man who people say "Oh, you look ten years younger than your age." I don't, all my years are on my mug. And some days I feel more like *ninety*-one.

You live a long life and as you go along, you never really know for sure what's important and what isn't. What you'll remember and what you'll forget. What matters and what don't. When you approach the end, you look back and you see the long view, things a little skewed.

I had two wives, loved them both dearly. I've got my good friend Mabel now. She's a blessing in my old age. What I did to earn her, I'll never know. There've been other girls and women along the way. Of them all, Linda Rae Boyd—Peterson, I mean, Linda Rae Peterson—was just about the least important. That's what I would have thought. But there you go.

FLIRTATION

Toni wakes with a start a little after five. She imagines her
stomach twisted in the kind of knots sheets are fashioned
into by escaping prisoners in Saturday morning cartoons,
or elopers in old-fashioned movies. It was the wine,
she's certain. Too much stress, rich food or wine, or any
combination of the three, are almost guaranteed to bring on
the pain she's come, with irony, to call her "handicap" and
is resolved to endure. The food at the conference centre is
certainly not rich in the epicurean sense, though the meat
is often fatty and swimming in gravy. And Toni's been as
relaxed as she's been in weeks, though often tired. She gets
one to two fewer hours of sleep than she really needs most
nights this week as she prepared herself for the conference
and her presentation.

But this particular attack, she's sure, was brought on by
the wine, by the four water tumblers of pungent red plonk
she'd sipped the night before over a period of as many hours.
It was almost as if she was willing herself to waken with
pain, to punish herself for the sins she was committing. Or
would have, given the chance.

Still, it was the company she found the most intoxicating.

She gasps and shoots up in bed with the first wrenches of pain, clapping a hand to her mouth in consideration of others in the rooms stretching in both directions from hers in the long dormitory corridor. As the spasm began to subside, she lies back in the sweat-drenched sheets to catch her breath and lets the thoughts slice through her brain like the edges of riffled cards. Now, with the pain reduced to manageable dimensions, she forces her shoulders up, slides her feet to the ground and sits on the edge of the bed taking the deep breaths both her doctor and her naturopath have advised. The pain recedes further into a dull throbbing, then shoots forward again, flames of it tentatively licking at her intestines. She struggles to her feet and lurches to the bathroom and the unpleasant relief of the toilet bowl. Thank God she didn't have an attack last night.

She's paying for it for sure. Not just the wine, the whole thing. But Ben looked so forlorn standing on the edge of the dance floor, she wasn't able to stop herself from going over and asking him to dance, even though she had warned herself to stay away. He had *dangerous man* writ large all over him. He was too good looking, too *interesting* looking for his own good. Or hers, rather.

"I don't dance," he shouted over the roar of the music. "Bum leg."

"Me neither, really. I'm going to pay for this in the morning."

"Yeah? You look like you do okay." She'd already had several turns on the floor, with one of her colleagues from Calgary, and he'd obviously noticed.

"I used to be a good dancer. But not so much anymore. Getting too old."

He laughed at her, a laugh she couldn't be sure was denial or confirmation.

"Fishing for compliments."

"No, really." She shook her head to allow a slight shift in the conversation's direction. "Does your wife mind? That you don't dance?"

"No wife." He shrugged. She'd thought he had the look of a loner, and there was no wedding ring on his long, fine fingers, but she liked to be certain.

"I used to get mad at my ex because he wouldn't dance," she said, glad for the chance to let him know she too was unattached. "It was the one physical thing I was good at. He was very physical, did all sorts of sports, but he wouldn't dance."

Ben squinted at her through squarish, tortoiseshell glasses, looking quizzical. "Why not?"

"I don't know. To punish me, I guess."

In fact, that was it exactly, if not at the beginning then certainly later on, when things were falling part between her and Allan.

The marriage had gone bad almost as soon as it had begun, as if bearing the seeds of its destruction within itself, like a plant that attracts the very insect that consumes it. For the year or so they'd lived together and the six months prior to that when they'd been engaged in the intoxicating dance of flirtation, getting to know each other and falling—if not in love necessarily, into *something*—everything had been perfect. They seemed so well suited to each other. Allan had been thoughtful, considerate, always sweet. Toni, who'd never had much success with men, was already well into her early thirties. She had started thinking she might be genetically programmed to follow the half dozen maiden aunts she had on both sides of the family. Maiden aunts! The phrase was offensive—and frightening. Then there was Allan, not actually on his knees, but proposing, presenting her with a ring, everything that, as a little girl, she'd been taught to expect and cherish. And she'd even thought she loved him. Maybe even really had.

Soon after the wedding, Allan had a promotion and he became increasingly absorbed in work, less attentive to her, causing the cloud of happiness on which she'd been coasting to begin to deflate. He was a mid-level bureaucrat in the department of health, one of those people who, at least in the eyes of the public, were dedicated to keeping Medicare dysfunctional. At first, she attributed the problems they were having, if they could even have been called that, to his work, but she soon realized if it weren't that it would have been something else. Allan had started to lose interest in her as soon as he'd secured her, that was the sort of man he was. The fact that she continued to be there, sharing bed and home, was a constant affront. He had no choice but to retaliate, to drive her away. This explanation was pop psychology, she knew, but it seemed dead on. She likened her marriage to a fabulous dinner, meticulously planned, lovingly prepared. On the table, a treat to the eye and nose, delicious in the eating, but then immediately bringing on an attack of indigestion.

Why then had she stayed at the table as long as she had? The loss of those three years was something Toni would never be able to fathom, any more than she could fathom the infrequent men she'd been attracted to since. Again, three was the magic number.

There'd been others, too, casual dates, even a few blind dates arranged by well-meaning friends, but only three serious relationships in what Toni and her best friend Dee laughingly referred to as "AA"—after Allan.

They'd gone, those three, if not exactly from bad to worse, surely from bad to bad. The one saving grace was that, in all three cases, she'd realized her failure of judgment early on and got out quickly. Less than a year of her life had been wasted on the first, an affable alcoholic who was cheerfully killing himself. It took her five months to realize the next one, a married man, would never leave his wife for her. She'd learned one lesson from that disaster, swearing she'd never be *that* stupid again. The final relationship had lasted a mere six weeks; he was sweet, attractive and attentive— much as Allan had been in their early months together—but so indecisive he left every decision to her. Not just which movies to go to but even what meals to order in restaurants. His birthday present to her was a gift certificate.

After breaking off with him, she'd sworn she was through with men and the heartbreak they invariably bring. She'd told herself that any number of times. Her last romance was already two years ago, so maybe she was learning.

Yet here she was flirting with Ben. So maybe not. "Never say never," Dee liked to say.

By the time they'd negotiated their way through the no-dancing banter, they were at the open bar and Ben was pouring wine into two tumblers—the wine glasses had long since run out—filling them almost to the brim. Then she followed him through the noisy, undulating crowd to a safe haven, down the corridor and out onto the front steps of the conference hall. There were lawns on either side of the semi-circular driveway. One side led down to gardens, planted but not yet in bloom. The other side led to the river that pulsed through the city, just as the Bow did in Calgary.

"I don't know why we're having this thing inside anyway," Ben said. "It's much nicer out here."

"Much." She gathered her skirt under her legs, sat on a hard marble step and took the cigarette he offered. His cupped hand brushed hers as she leaned into his match.

Since she'd quit, several years ago, cigarettes were only an occasional indulgence and something else she knew would contribute to morning-after discomfort. The music, wafting down the corridor and out the open doors, sounded softer, more appealing here. Ben settled into place beside her.

"I'm Toni, by the way."

"Oh, I know who you are."

She laughed. "I like the way you say that. It makes me feel notorious."

"I just meant I was at your presentation this morning. Good stuff."

"You're too kind. I thought it was pretty boring, myself." Toni had been one of four people on a panel on special education needs. She was hardly an authority, but she was the author of a program that had caused a bit of a stir in the Calgary public school district and enough attention among colleagues in the field across the country to get her invited to the conference. The panel had gone on and on, especially the man from Winnipeg. Even the moderator couldn't shut him up. She'd noticed Ben in the sparse audience, looking at her intently.

"A couple of them were, yeah. Not you, though."

"Now you *are* being too kind. But aren't you going to say who *you* are?" She was grinning. Ben had been one of the conference's main speakers. His name and picture were on all the conference posters.

"Oh, I'm sorry, I'm Ben...."

"Stop, stop. I'm just teasing. I was at your talk this afternoon. Didn't you hear my clapping? I was one of the loudest."

"Touché. OK, now that we've established a mutual admiration society, where do we go from here?"

"Is it just me, or has the conversation taken a sudden and decided turn here?"

"I did notice a step-up in intensity, now that you mention it." He grinned. "But isn't that what my talk was about? I thought you said you were listening."

Toni had already decided she liked this man and she was starting to wonder what his faults were, and how long it might be before they became obvious. And just how serious they would be.

"Oh, I was listening, all right. Maybe this is an illustration of that gap between theory and practice you cited."

They smiled at each other, both of them a little at a loss for words. This, Toni thought, was where the flirting either fizzles out or goes up a step to something more serious.

Now, she thinks ruefully, as she washes down a headache pill with tepid water from the bathroom tap, she's paying for attempting to close the gap.

Brushing her hair after her shower, her stomach feeling a bit settled, Toni reflects that her nerves were seriously frazzled even before she got to the conference three days earlier, repeating a familiar pattern. Nothing serious—there hardly ever was—only a series of small disasters leading inexorably up to this morning's stomach cramps and diarrhea.

For so meticulously well prepared and punctual a person, she'd been uncharacteristically late calling a cab. Then the cab had taken an unusually long time coming, which meant she barely made the plane. The extensive security at the airport had further exacerbated things— she liked to crochet on the plane to relax but this time her wooden hook was confiscated.

Then she'd gotten into a major hassle over the peanuts.

This came as a complete, appalling surprise, because the

travel agent had assured her none of the airlines served peanuts any more.

"Oh, no, that would just be asking for trouble," the woman had replied to Toni's question.

So she was completely taken aback when the stewardess, who had already served sodas and coffees, came back with an offer of cookies or peanuts. Toni, in a window seat, was wearing a headset and listening to a Bach cantata or she'd have been alerted to what was heading her way earlier.

"But I'm completely allergic," she cried.

The stewardess reacted as if she'd been stung, jerking the proffered basket away just as the man seated to Toni's right was reaching for it. "Oh, I'm terribly sorry." She hesitated, unsure what to do.

Toni, already feeling her throat starting to tighten, looked beseechingly at her seatmates, a middle-aged man and woman in holiday clothes. The woman's expression was blank, as if she'd been startled out of a deep thought, but the man looked hostile. "I'm so sorry," she blurted, echoing the stewardess, "I could go into anaphylactic shock. Thanks for being understanding."

But the man in the middle didn't look like he understood anything.

"*I'll* have the nuts," he said loudly. He turned to his wife. "You want the nuts too, Doris?" Then, to the stewardess: "She'll have nuts too."

"But...." Toni began.

"I'm sorry, sir, the cookies are very good." The stewardess had several of the small packages in her hand and was already offering them, and a second stewardess, alerted by the commotion, had joined her in the cramped aisle and was starting to collect unopened packages of peanuts from the rows right in front of them.

"I could die," Toni said, miserably, but the man, through either innocent or willful ignorance, ignored her.

"Listen, lady, I've got a right to eat those damned peanuts. You hear about the Charter of Rights? This isn't the Soviet goddamned Union, not yet anyway."

If she hadn't been feeling so breathlessly panicky, Toni would have burst out laughing. Telling Ben about it last night, she was able to laugh, although a chill went through her at the same time.

"So you really could have died?" he asked.

"Oh, yes," she said, suppressing her amazement at his ignorance. It wasn't personal, she knew.

"And this yahoo going on about his constitutional rights."

There was a bitter edge to Ben's tone that surprised her, and makes her wonder now what grievances with the world *he* has. All she really knows about him is what was printed in the conference program brochure: professor of ethnography and literacy at Dalhousie, degrees from Alberta, York and Harvard, author of half a dozen books she was only vaguely aware of, frequent conference speaker. Even though she'd been to his talk, Toni isn't even really sure what ethnography is. She picks the much-handled brochure up from the dresser and re-examines his small photo.

"No wife," he said, but that can conceal as much as it reveals. Ben might have had one, or two or three. Or he's gay, a problem she's encountered with attractive men once or twice before. Doesn't dance. "Bum leg," he said, and she did think she detected a slight limp. In his mid to late forties, she guesses, maybe even past the Big 5-0 barrier, a good ten years older than her. That was not a liability. Lives far away—that can be as much a positive as a negative.

What else? Drank as much wine as she did last night—

a drinking problem? No, she doesn't think so, and who knows, he may be feeling some discomfort from the wine this morning too, maybe even as much as she is. Smokes, but only had a few, and thoughtful enough to always ask her if she minded. Obviously brainy, but not an interrupter, as brainy men often are. Not filled with that overbearing sense of self and entitlement so many interesting men seem to be weighted down with. Beyond that, what?

That's really all she knows, except for his sense of humour nicely in synch with hers. Awfully good looking. Why isn't a man that good looking married, or with someone at least?

What is she getting herself into?

But all they'd done was talk. And drink wine. Too much of the latter.

Ben is already at a small corner table when Toni gets to the dining room. The sight of him causes a pleasant little flutter beneath her breastbone. She goes through the line quickly, avoiding acidic juice and choosing weak tea rather than coffee, and just one slice of dry toast. She heads for his table, nodding at a few people she knows, trying hard to avoid direct eye contact. She also tries not to look at the remains of a plate of bacon, eggs, and fried potatoes in front of him. No upset stomach for him, obviously.

"Good morning." He makes that slight move forward that passes for a man's getting up for a woman these days, then settles back. "That's all you have for breakfast?"

"That seems like an awfully intimate question," Toni replies, immediately aghast at her own flirtatiousness. "For this hour of the day, that is." She smiles, pours herself a glass of water from the pitcher and washes down a handful of pills. She notices him watching with interest. "Don't ask."

"I already had my pills," he says with a crooked smile.

Toni pours just enough milk into her tea to turn its colour from bronze to muddy brown. She takes a tentative sip, then a small bite of her toast. He's still watching her, with the same look of open interest. It's not adoration, no, but definitely more than mere curiosity. He's laid his glasses beside his coffee cup and there are dark shadows under his eyes she didn't notice the night before. His sandy hair is neatly brushed, his cheeks freshly shaved, the smell of after-shave lotion spicy but muted. She imagines that, were she to ask him to stop using it, he'd happily comply.

"You look tired," she says.

"I am. Didn't sleep so well."

Toni smiles. "Too much wine?"

"That too, maybe. But I've been thinking."

"Oh, God."

He laughs. "No, seriously. This is not what it might seem."

"It never is, is it?"

"True. You going to listen to me or not?"

"I am." She takes another sip of tea, another bite of toast. Her stomach, thank God, is behaving itself.

"So." He takes a deep breath. "Two middle-aged people, unmarried if not necessarily unattached."

"Unattached here," Toni says, perhaps a beat too quickly. She thinks she can see the general direction this is heading and isn't displeased.

"Okay. Two middle-aged people, *unattached*. A little burnt around the edges." He gestures to the crusts of toast on his plate. "Between them, the better part of a pharmacy. Their best days behind them"—he holds up a stop-sign hand—"or so they both *thought*. But still plenty of good days ahead, maybe even their *real* best days. If"– a pregnant pause—"if they allow them to come."

"And your point is?" Toni is amazed at how closely Ben's little speech echoes the one she play-acted herself, first while sitting on the toilet, then in the shower.

"Oh, there has to be a point?" He laughs. "I'm just analyzing the situation."

"Spoken like a true academic."

"Hey, that's what I do. But, listen, seriously...Toni..." He pronounces her name with such gravity, she feels herself leaning toward him, as if he were the medicine she needs.

"Wait a second," Toni says.

She takes a deep breath and allows her mind to spool through the familiar film of her ailments, starting with the wine-induced pain in her gut this morning, through her frequently sore shoulder and knee, the fruits of a high school basketball injury and a skiing mishap, and the occasional bouts of panic attacks that plague her. She thinks too of the long periods of mourning her previous affairs have always thrown her into—they didn't kill her but when in the depths of them she sometimes felt like dying. "What doesn't kill you makes you stronger," her friend Dee is fond of repeating. Does love always have to end with banality? Toni's asked Dee that more than once in reply. The predictable answer was always the same, just a hollow laugh.

Then she makes up her mind. "Before you say any more," Toni says, laying her hand on Ben's arm, "I've been thinking too."

INTERFERENCE

My first job after university was at a newspaper in Michigan where I quickly fell into what felt like the welcome arms of an adopted family, a delicious situation I wasn't that familiar with from my own childhood as my parents and brothers had always been somewhat distant. The father figure in this new family was my boss, Si Cooperman; the mother figure was Vera Young, a feature writer who was as close to Si as any wife could be without actually being one. I didn't know just how close they were, not until much later.

Vera's dead now. She died last week, of cancer. And Si, I fear, is in the grip of some sort of dementia, so I guess that family is now officially over, although in truth it ended quite some time ago.

Si and Vera were the core of the paper's Sunday edition—Si its editor, Vera its main writer. After I'd been at the *Call-Bulletin* for several months and had proved my mettle, covering everything from cat shows to a particularly sensational murder, I was transferred from general news to work with them. When I reported to him on my first Tuesday morning, Si took a look at me, then another. "Lord love a duck, look what we have here." He clucked his tongue, laughed out loud—a full-bodied honest laugh that was famous in the newsroom—and, without actually lifting a hand, took me under his wing, as if I were a son he was glad to see finally come home.

"You look pretty green to me, boy," he said. That "boy," with all its dangerous implications, sounded amiable in his voice, almost affectionate, and I took no offence.

"Well, I *am* green."

"Good, just so's you know it. Vera," he called, "come meet Billy boy, the new greenie."

"Oh, he doesn't look any greener than the last one," Vera deadpanned, looking me over. Her role as foil to Si's rapier seemed practiced and comfortable.

"Yah, but how long did *he* last?" Si asked, winking.

We soon all became close.

Within an hour, Si had announced it was time for coffee break. Vera and I followed him downstairs to the staff cafeteria. Si treated. "This is the only time I'll buy your coffee, so enjoy it," he told me.

"I've been thinking about that murder of yours," he said as soon as we sat down. I looked up with interest. A doctor had shot his wife to death, apparently in a fit of jealous rage involving a plumber. I'd been on night shift the week it occurred and had done our first story, prying some juicy details out of neighbours and even a loose-lipped cop. I won praise from the managing editor, but then coverage of the murder had passed into the capable but not very imaginative hands of Mark Leone, the police reporter. The case was now beginning its slow journey through the court system, and Leone's routine stories were dry and jargon-filled, allowing the banality of the crime to overpower its drama.

"Leone's a hack," Si pronounced. "You keep an eye on it, dig into it, let's break some stuff on Sundays."

"Won't I be stepping on Mark's toes?"

"You let me worry about that," Si said.

Vera grinned at me. "Si's a regular fullback."

I didn't follow football close enough to know exactly what she meant but I intuited that he was good at interference.

The Sunday paper, which took all week to prepare, with its skeleton staff, always had a major feature story written by Vera, a lesser one done by me, and a variety of other pieces of varying length, most of them pretty fluffy, done by both of us. Over the course of the three years I worked there, I wrote stories on cancer survivors, autistic children, Vietnamese boat people, children in need of heart transplants, reunited twins, a shipwrecked sailor and a man who found his lost wedding ring, twenty years later, in the belly of a small-mouthed bass he caught in Lake Michigan. There was also plenty of fiftieth anniversary celebrations, hundredth birthdays and business expansions. The Sunday paper ran the usual syndicated stuff too: Dear Abby, a doctor column, something about science, puzzles, book reviews, several good national columnists and a few of our own, and the colour comics. Si handled most of that stuff, while Vera and I looked after the writing. The front of the paper, Pages One, Two and Three, and the back page of the classified section, which was always elastic, depending on how many ads were sold, right up to deadline, were filled Saturday afternoon and evening by Si and me—him functioning as news editor, me as general reporter—and another reporter, even more junior than I, who helped out with the obits and the routine cop checks.

That Saturday crew, which Vera was not a part of, was all male and operated with a somewhat different dynamic than that which prevailed Tuesday to Friday. There was a male bonding flavour to those afternoons, with a touch of locker room humour, and after we'd put the paper to bed the three of us, Si, me and the other young guy—that first year, it was Jim Wilson—would often go to a nearby tavern for a beer. Wilson was a toady, a pain in the ass, but we tolerated him. Like me, he was a recent journalism school grad, but from a considerably lesser school than the University of Michigan, where I'd gone. He had a habit of trying to sound more important than he was, replaying in the bar his takes on fairly routine stories as if the results were heroic. Still, there'd always be a lot of laughs at the bar, Si's booming laugh, Jim's and my smaller ones. But Jim, who only joined the Sunday crew on Saturday afternoons, wasn't really part of the family. In the newsroom on Saturday afternoons, and in the bar later, Si was careful to include Jim in everything, but the bond between him and me was much stronger. Jim clearly resented it. In less than a year, he moved on, to the sports department, and was replaced by another junior.

On weekdays, Si and Vera almost always had lunch together, just the two of them, in the lounge of the Barclay Hotel, two blocks away from the paper. Occasionally, I would be invited to join them. At these lunches, they would always order martinis, gin, very dry, one green olive, and there was never any off-colour talk. Si was always a complete gentleman around Vera, and he expected others to behave the same. At one of those lunches, I carelessly allowed the word "shit" to slip out. "Lord love a duck," Si snapped, and gave me a dirty look. That was all he needed to do. I continued to be an occasional guest, and a similar slip never happened again.

Although I had no evidence of it, I always assumed Si and Vera were lovers. Si had a wife at home, and two children, already in their late teens when I began at the paper, and Vera had a husband but was childless. I would meet both spouses when the paper held its annual Fourth of July picnic at Heritage Park and on other special occasions, and both couples were guests at my wedding. But I never heard Si or Vera make mention of their spouses other than in the most pragmatic of ways: "Bob painted the deck on Saturday," is the sort of thing Vera would report; "Oh, I'd better pick up some bread on my way home or Sheila will kill me," Si might say. But of Vera, Si would sometimes rhapsodize. Often, he would come over to my desk and thrust several sheets of copy in front of me as if it were a puppy he held by the scruff of the neck. "Look at this," he would say, the excitement in his voice just barely contained. "What an amazing piece. Vivid. That woman can really write." The implication, as I always heard it, was that I couldn't, or certainly not as well. "But what can't she do?"

It was a rhetorical question I couldn't answer. I did know some things she could do, including watching Si when he got up from his desk and walked across the newsroom, to the wire service teletype machines or the water cooler or the men's room. She watched him with admiring charlotte eyes that seemed to be seeing him for the first time, looking beyond his baggy chino trousers and crisp blue Oxford button-down shirt, seeing even beyond his skin. Was it a loving gaze? I thought so. But I never heard Vera praise Si, the way he did her. When we were at lunch together, for example, and Si excused himself, Vera never took the opportunity to let me know what a wonderful man our boss was. She never said anything about him at all. All she did was follow him with her eyes as far as she could, while asking me a question, usually work related, like "how are you getting on with that story we were talking about this morning?" This strategy, I quickly figured out, was to divert my attention from watching her watch him. It didn't really work, and gave me an opportunity to look directly at her.

I spent a lot of time looking at Vera, as did Si. She was a very handsome woman, in her late thirties, tall and slender but with pronounced hips that swayed as she walked across the newsroom in a tight straight skirt. She was always impeccably dressed in crisp pastel blouses, often with ruffles on the bodice that disguised the fullness of her bosom, and tailored jackets. Her chestnut hair hung down past her shoulders in sleek rolls of waves, a cut that made her seem younger than she was. When she walked, her hair was constantly in motion around her face, calling attention to it. During her strolls across the newsroom, to the water cooler, the women's room, the clipping morgue, Si would lift his eyes from whatever he was editing and affix them to those hips in a gaze that always struck me as more proprietary than lascivious. My eyes were also on her, as I said, and so were the eyes of half the other men in the newsroom at any given time. Si's gaze seemed to be saying, you can look, but don't touch.

Yet I never saw the two of them together outside of work, those weekday lunches and company social events. Nor was there any gossip about them, not that I was aware of, anyway. Still, the notion that they were lovers persisted in my imagination.

And if they weren't lovers in fact, I was sure, they were unrequited lovers, each in love with the other but prevented from acting on their desires by the realities of their marriages. When I was courting my own wife, I told her this theory about Si and Vera, and she thought it wonderfully romantic. "But don't *you* go falling in love with anyone else," she warned.

I mentioned that Si took me under his wing. When I was transferred to the Sunday department, I assumed that the assistant managing editor, Stu O'Hara, a red-faced man with a surprisingly mild disposition who had hired me, made that decision, but actually Si had asked for me. He'd read a few of my early stories, including the one on the murder, and thought I had some flair. Although I didn't find that out until some time later, I immediately sensed that Si had high expectations of me, and soon I was thinking of him as my mentor, even as a role model. I started wearing button-down Oxford shirts. I paid attention to everything he said—and did—and learned from him.

I like to think his faith in me was confirmed when I stumbled on a big lead in the murder story. The district attorney had argued against bail, as was routine in such cases, but to everyone's surprise it had been set at $1 million, and the doctor, a family physician with a sterling reputation, had been set free. Leone had routinely reported this. "Get over there," Si told me the next morning. "Talk to him."

I thought there was virtually no chance of my getting the doctor to talk, but it occurred to me that a colour piece on my attempt might make a good yarn; that was something that Leone would never take on. To my surprise, the good doctor, barred from returning to his practice until the case had run its course, was at home, alone and restless. He welcomed me in, eager to talk.

He seemed like a man high on caffeine, nicotine and lack of sleep, his eyes bloodshot and rimmed with red, his hands opening and closing in rapid-fire sequence as he talked, rambling on in what, despite its frequent incoherence, amounted to a confession. I knew there was little of what he said that was useable—a hunch the *Call-Bulletin*'s lawyer quickly confirmed that afternoon— but enough of it was to give me a pretty good story, which topped the front page that Sunday. The best part was the nugget, which ran as separate, boxed sidebar, that the judge who'd granted bail was a distant relative, something that was easy to confirm. That revelation led to the judge recusing himself. Another judge was appointed and a new bail hearing held but bail at $1 million continued. But, as Si liked to point out, the judge's relationship surely would have come out eventually and, if we hadn't reported it when we did, it might not have surfaced until midway through the trial, causing an uproar and forcing a mistrial. Leone didn't talk to me for weeks after my story appeared but there were no real repercussions. Vera had been right about Si's running interference.

Si is Jewish, I think—the fact that I don't know for sure puts the lie to my claim that we were once close—one of those New York intellectual types. He was born and raised in Brooklyn, went to NYU, and worked for several years at the *New York Post* as a reporter. Somewhere along the line he also spent time in the service, writing for *Stars and Stripes* in the peacetime years between Korea and Vietnam. He never talked about what had brought him out from New York to Michigan.

My name is William and most people call me Bill, but Si took to calling me Billy. "Time for coffee, Billy," he'd say in mid-morning. I'd drop whatever I was doing and follow him down to the cafeteria. Vera would only rarely join us. We'd find a table in the corner and, despite his vow to never buy me coffee again, he always paid. He would talk. I would listen, but occasionally sound off. These coffee sessions, which often began as a commentary on a piece I'd written and he'd just read, editing pencil in hand, often evolved into something resembling an Aesop fable, complete with a moral, punctuated frequently by Si's famous laugh—loud, uninhibited, honest.

One day I remember especially well. I was indignant over the way the paper had handled the suicide of a former city councilman who'd shot himself on the ninth hole of the country club. *Prominent resident dies suddenly while playing golf,* the headline read. There was no whiff of gunpowder in the story, written by Mark Leone.

Over coffee, I ranted, but Si just laughed. "This isn't j-school, Billy boy." He often would quote a line from Emily Dickinson: "Tell the truth, but tell it slant." He said it now and, for the first time, I understood. Si winked. "Just as true for us news hounds as it is for poets. Hell, truth hurts."

Si often told tales about Dads Kennedy, a newsroom legend of heroic proportions who'd been Si's best buddy for years. Dads had been a front-line correspondent in World War Two and was on first-name basis with many Michigan politicians. He could put down more alcohol than most men could carry, and had a prodigious sex life. Once, he was sent out to interview a *Playboy* Playmate of the Year who was on a promotional tour and didn't come back to work for three days. Working for one of the Detroit papers, he'd caused a commotion when he and a drinking buddy used their company credit cards to fly to Vegas for a long week-end. He'd won a slew of awards and come close to a Pulitzer for a story in which he intertwined the lives of the last man in Michigan to be executed and two young men: the son of the warden, who received his corneas, and the son of the lieutenant governor, who got his heart. Dads had worked for quite a few papers throughout the Midwest, big and small, invariably losing his job due to alcoholic misadventure, but he kept coming back to the *Call-Bulletin*, which was where he'd begun as a teenager, and which kept taking him back. He was that good.

"Lord love a duck, but could that man eat ice cream," Si said. "When he was drinking, it was the only thing he had an appetite for. I saw him put down a gallon of cherry vanilla once while he was working on a big murder story. He used to keep bottles stashed around the newsroom—in his desk drawer, of course, in a locker in the men's room, and in the false ceiling. But this night, he had a bottle openly on his desk and nobody said boo. Canadian Club and cherry vanilla from Marshall's ice cream parlour side by side. He kept sending the copy boy down to Marshall's for refills, half a pint at a time. He didn't like it soft."

Si sat back, finished off his coffee and brushed toast crumbs from his shirtfront.

"Of course, you can't keep that up forever, Billy. Eventually, the booze killed him."

I'd heard that any number of times from him, and there seemed to be a moral in there: go wild, but use caution.

🎤

After three years at the *Call-Bulletin*, I had turned into a pretty good newspaperman, I think. No Dads Kennedy, but solid, with some flair. I wrote a few stories I'm still proud of. Then, in a move I've always regretted, I left.

I was single when I began at the paper, just turned twenty-two. I soon met the woman who I'd marry. We bought a house, had a child—a wonderful little girl who's now a senior at Columbia. Then, though I'd heeded my wife's admonition not to fall in love with anyone else, the marriage began to go sour, for reasons I still don't fully understand. The arc of our marriage and that of my time at the paper more or less coincided. As my marriage began to falter, I found myself feeling restless and at loose ends. By coincidence, I had a job offer and I took it.

I had written quite a few medical stories, and several pieces about the local hospital. The PR man there, Bob Jamison, who'd once been a *Call-Bulletin* reporter himself, was retiring, and he recommended me as his replacement. Out of the blue, I got a phone call. It meant better hours, a Monday to Friday shift and considerably more pay— all of which I thought might help to save the marriage. It didn't.

Had I not been feeling that restlessness, had my marriage not been foundering, I probably wouldn't have taken the job. But I did. I've been at the hospital ever since.

Actually, the local hospital is now part of a multi-city conglomerate, that serves all of southeast Michigan, and I'm vice president of communication for the company. It doesn't have the adrenalin rush reporting does—I'm the guy reporters talk to now, slanting the story for them to best serve the hospital's purposes—but it has its satisfactions. Twenty years on, though, I still miss the newsroom.

I remarried, and that's worked out better. Had two more kids, both of them gems.

In the first few years after I left the paper, Si and I remained close, or at least as close as we had been. I continued to be invited occasionally to lunch with him and Vera, and every so often he and I would travel up to Detroit for a Tigers or Red Wings game. Once in a while, on a Saturday evening, I'd stop in at the tavern where Si and his new crew would go for a beer after getting the Sunday paper out, but I was an outsider there and never felt comfortable. Gradually my contact with Si lessened. He had never invited me and my first wife, or me alone after we separated, to dinner at his house, and I gradually came to realize we'd never really been that close. Our friendship had been limited to the office.

I was at his retirement party, of course, but that was a good three years ago. Nothing after that until just recently, a brief visit at the hospital, and then at Vera's funeral the other day.

I felt a little twinge of hurt that Si hadn't let me know about her cancer. We had once been family, after all. Instead, I heard through one of the doctors at the hospital who knew I'd once worked at the paper.

"That Vera Young, the columnist? She's over in cancer wing," he said. "She's in a bad way. You'd better hurry."

I have to admit, it was always Si and me who constituted my idea of the "Sunday family." I didn't really know Vera well. She was a private person and, when the three of us were together, she really only had eyes for Si. I felt enormous affection for her just the same. Whatever the exact nature of her role in the shaping of my life as a young man may have been, it was important.

I went right over to Oncology, and wasn't surprised to find Si in her room. There was no sign of her husband. It turned out that she had been in and out of hospital several times for a couple of years, and had already lost both breasts to surgery. For a time, she seemed to be doing all right after chemo and radiation, but then had gotten sick again, the cancer metastasizing. She'd been here in the cancer wing for over a week, and Si had been there every day, with her all through visiting hours.

Vera looked terrible. I could see the end wasn't far away. The last time I'd seen her—at Si's retirement party—she still looked pretty good for a woman almost sixty. Still had her figure, chestnut curls, her quick smile. "We miss you at the paper," she'd said, which I'm sure was completely untrue, but nice of her nonetheless. I'd been gone for almost twenty years and a lot of bright young guys must have passed through the Sunday department. With Si gone, she moved out of Sunday and was writing a three-times-a-week column, sort of Ellen Goodman style. Still the best writer on the paper. Now she was thin as a splinter, hair white and unkempt. Her face was gaunt and pained, the charlotte eyes, once so bright, clouded. She smiled when she saw me, but couldn't manage more than a few words. "Oh, Bill, so good of you to come." Si squeezed her hand as we talked. When Vera fell asleep, he reluctantly agreed to come down to the cafeteria for coffee. It was just like old times, except that this time I paid.

"I wish you'd let me know about Vera," I said. I kept my tone gentle, it wasn't an accusation.

Si didn't say anything. He looked at me, shrugged a little, then looked down and stirred his coffee. He didn't look so great either. He was thinner than he used to be. His hair, which had been going salt and pepper when I first knew him, was now completely white and sparse. Unhealthy looking dark pouches underlined his eyes.

Despite the weight of his years, he was in okay shape, Si told me. His own wife was sick, though, recovering from a stroke. Again, I expressed regret that I hadn't known. I recalled my old notion of his and Vera's unrequited love.

"Nothing you can do," Si said, a weary, resigned tone. "It's the end of everything." He spoke as if he were commenting on the collapse of civilization, rather than the approaching death of three old people.

Two weeks later, before I'd had a chance to visit her again, Vera died. Si was by her side at the end, I heard.

I mentioned I saw Si at the funeral, but it wasn't really

that. Vera's husband had her cremated without benefit of any sort of ceremony. I don't know what that says. Some of her friends at the paper organized a gathering at the Unitarian church on Maple Street, a celebration of her life they called it. We sat in pews and people who spoke did it from the pulpit. The church is pretty plain, unadorned, businesslike.

There was a pretty good turnout. Many people from the paper, some of whom I knew from the old days. Vera's husband wasn't there. There were several speakers, including Jim Wilson, who used to be the extra reporter on Saturdays; he's been a loyal employee all these years, and is now assistant managing editor, which grates me. Had I stayed, I'd be managing editor now probably, maybe editor. Of course Si spoke, though only briefly.

The eulogizers before him had kept things fairly light. They talked about what a great gal Vera was, a good friend, a fine reporter and writer. A few funny anecdotes, the sort of thing you'd expect. The famous tale of the time she button-holed Jackie Onassis in the ladies' room at the Barclay Hotel downtown for an exclusive.

When Si came up, he started off in the same vein. "Nobody at the paper knew Vera the way I did," he said. His statement floated over the crowd for a moment, its exact meaning elusive. Was Si leering, or was the light playing tricks? He looked exhausted. "Between us," he said, "we must have killed millions of words, and thousands of martinis." People laughed, but a little nervously.

Si was wearing a dark suit, the jacket crookedly buttoned. Everything about him looked rumpled. "She was a beautiful human being," he began again, his voice wavering, "a beautiful woman, a beautiful piece of ass…"

There was an audible gasp from the crowd.

"…and nobody knew *that* better than me."

Si stood with his hands on either side of the podium, gripping it to keep his balance. He glared out at the people in the pews defiantly. Then he turned and made his way slowly back to where he'd been sitting. Despite what he'd just said, he managed to retain a dignified aura.

There was one more speaker but I don't think anyone paid attention. Then that part was over and people moved noisily toward the stairs and down to the lower level, where food and drinks had been laid out.

Si went downstairs too, but he was alone, no surprise after what he'd said. I went to the bar and bought two glasses of Scotch and brought them over to where he was sitting. "Sorry, no gin, no olives," I said. He looked up with a blank expression but accepted the offered drink. "*L'chaim,*" he said gravely. And we both drank.

I'm not quite sure why, and I'm ashamed of myself now, but I was angry. What I told myself was that Si had somehow dishonoured his friendship with Vera—friendship, romance, affair, whatever it was. But now I think maybe I was feeling a twinge of jealousy. Perhaps I'd been half in love with her myself.

"That was a hell of a thing to say, Si," I said. "Are you getting senile?"

Si laughed, not the dry, brittle, bitter laugh as I might have expected, but a full-bodied hearty laugh—the old laugh Si Cooperman was famous for, the laugh I associated with his tales of Dads Kennedy's legendary exploits.

"What, telling the truth about somebody now is a sign of senility?" he asked. "I loved that woman. You know that."

"There's a proper time and place for everything, Si," I said.

"Billy, Billy," he said, a half smile playing on his lips.

"Still green. Lord love a duck." He finished off the scotch in his glass. "What better time and place than this?"

I went off, shaking my head, still feeling disgusted. But a few days have passed and now I'm not so sure. I think I'll call Si one of these days, to see if he'd like to go for lunch.

THE CONNOISSEUR OF LONGING

Many of Mandalstram's books were overlooked by his peers. A few were shortlisted for minor awards, an achievement and honor in itself, but didn't win. Fairly late in his life, he won a major award for a slim novella, *Disconsolate*—a delicate love story that was a revised version of a story he had written when he was in his twenties. The passion in the prize-winning book, so admired by the jurors, was from that early period of his life, when he had pursued an unrequited love affair with a woman from Madrid and had burned with the sort of ardour only a man in his twenties can experience. But the craft, those tricks of the writing trade which make a story compelling, was all from the later period of his life, the period of revision, a practice he had mastered. This blend of passion and craft worked well for Mandalstram. *Disconsolate*, the jurors wrote, ached with the agony of a spurned lover, exquisitely rendered, and Mandalstram himself, they wrote, was a "poet of the heartbroken, a connoisseur of longing."

He smiled at that latter phrase, "connoisseur of longing," which seemed to fit him like a well-tailored jacket. As he slept restlessly on award night in an unfamiliar hotel bed, in Toronto, the words chimed through his dreams like the cream-rich tones of a clavichord. He awoke amused by the possibilities. A publisher might create a Library of Longing, with paperback reprints of all his out-of-print books. The CBC might prepare a reality show, Canada Longs, with chipper Wendy Mesley as host and Mandelstram himself as featured guest. A restaurant might prepare a Menu of Longing, with dishes inspired by plots and character from Mandalstram's stories. He arose, turned on the electric coffee pot and showered. Then, feeling pampered in the hotel's fluffy white robe, with a cup of weak coffee by his elbow—oh, how he longed for something stronger!—he sat in sunlight at a small polished marble table and, on creamy hotel stationary, he began to make a list. This small pleasure was interrupted by another—the first of several telephone calls from the news media.

Back in Halifax, where he had lived for a decade since his third marriage failed, he found himself still propelled by the momentum of his unexpected victory. The money that accompanied the prize—more than he would ordinarily earn in two years!—was a godsend, but more important was the boost to his career. It would have been better, far better, to have had this triumph twenty years earlier, or fifteen, or even ten. But he still had another ten productive years in him, for another three, four, maybe five books if he approached them with more discipline than he ordinarily could harness.

He expected invitations to start rolling in: for lectures, interviews, workshops, residencies, festivals, readings of all sorts before all sorts of audiences. He'd had his share of that sort of thing, of course, but never enough to provide more than the most meager of livings. He'd always had to teach a class, take on an editing job for someone of lesser talent. On occasion, he even had to lower himself to the indignities of writing a review or article for the popular press. Now he looked forward to refusing those routine kinds of offers, to enjoying more of life's little comforts while, at the same time, being able to devote more time to his own work. He'd have to assess the new opportunities carefully. Perhaps he'd receive an unsolicited grant, maybe a call from one of the agents who hitherto had spurned him. He looked forward to the possible pleasure of telling one particularly nasty agent to fuck herself.

In the meantime, while he awaited these opportunities, he decided to allow euphoria to propel him into a regimen of inspiration and momentum. The backbreaking, spirit-snagging novel he'd been working on for several years, which had all but defeated him, now seemed manageable, its completion and publication inevitable. He would throw himself into work with a renewed vigour, informed by the sort of passion that had so impressed those jurors. Yes, passion was what had been missing from his latest work; passion, propped up by artful craft, could be his salvation.

But not just yet. His telephone was still ringing, interview requests from reporters and congratulations from friends and—this most delicious—acquaintances who now wished to be friends. Serious work was out of the question with such interruptions. And at any rate, a day or two of diversion, to savour the moment and let its meaning sink in, would do him good. A perverse, compulsive pleasure, perhaps, but pleasure nonetheless.

Mandalstram consulted the Internet and, fortified by a cup of espresso, telephoned his first wife, who lived now in Milan, where she had a thriving practice as a designer of high fashion, knowing full well what sort of response he was likely to induce. They hadn't spoken in over twenty years, and that only as the result of accident, but he had kept up with her comings and doings, another perverse pleasure.

"Louella," he announced, "it's Franklin."

"Calling to gloat?" Her voice sounded older, leathery, but with all of its old bite. To his disappointment, she didn't seem surprised to be hearing from him.

"Gloat?"

"I read about your triumph."

"Hardly that, my dear."

"Considering what came before it...."

"Well, yes. And thank you for the implied congratulations. But gloat, no, that isn't what I've called about."

"And that is?"

He hesitated, betraying himself. "To apologize. I am sorry. For..."

"Oh, fuck you, Franklin." She hung up.

Mandalstram was stunned by the sharpness of her response, though it did not extend far beyond the realm of what he had considered possible. He certainly had known she wouldn't be pleased to hear from him, regardless of the circumstances. They had both been young and inexperienced in their brief time together. She had come into his life during that bleak period when he was nursing the wounds inflicted on his heart by the Spanish woman. Their marriage had ended badly, on so sour a note that a stain on the abilities of both of them to form healthy relationships had remained for some time. Mandalstram had blamed Louella, she had blamed him. Over time, he had come to realize that probably neither of them was to blame. They had both merely been caught up in forces beyond their control. Louella, apparently, had not yet attained that stage of perspective and clarity.

Having worked his way through this brief analysis,

Mandalstram smiled and brewed himself another cup of strong coffee. This *was* a morning for indulgence. Although the call had not gone as he'd hoped, he still drew grim satisfaction from it.

Mandalstram's parents had been Holocaust survivors who were loathe to talk about their past. He was a bright, inquisitive child, with a fertile imagination, an only child often left to his own devices. And though his parents provided few clues, he grew up surmising that they were Jewish. Indeed, they attended a Reform synagogue and his father was a reliable contributor to the minion. It was only in his teenaged years that Mandalstram learned they weren't Jews. Berliners, intellectuals, journalists the both of them, they were Communists persecuted for their politics, not for their race or their faith. Mandalstram's father was an atheist, whose own parents had been Catholic farmers. His mother had been raised a Lutheran and came from a well respected middle-class family of lawyers and teachers. Good Aryan stock. True, the name Mandalstram did smack of Jewry, though it was in fact solidly Germanic, but had his father and mother not written inflammatory articles attacking National Socialism in a suspect periodical, they would likely have gone through that terrible period of history unscathed.

Instead, they rejected the chance to emigrate in an orderly fashion and later to flee in haste. They were rounded up and sent in cattle cars along with hundreds of fellow travelers to Bergen-Belsen, where, somehow, they managed to survive.

Prying even these minimal details out of his parents had been something of an achievement for the high-school-and-college-aged Mandalstram. He never learned anything of their lives in captivity, or the bargains they may have been forced to enter into.

After the war, the shattered couple was able to emigrate to the United States, where they attempted to rebuild their lives. They took up residence in a largely Jewish neighbourhood in the Bronx and devoted themselves—or so it seemed to their son—to a quiet pursuit of redemption. It was perhaps inevitable that these survivors of Hitler's death camps should seek the comforting company of other survivors, or so the teenaged Mandalstram conjectured. The elder Mandalstrams lived a quiet, humdrum existence, working as minor government functionaries—his mother as a clerk at the borough hall's property tax department, his father at the post office. As a child, teenager and young man, Mandalstram had chafed against the restraints of his parents' orderly lives. He had rebelled against it, but in time he'd come to understand it. As a refugee from the U.S. to Canada during the inflammatory years of the Vietnamese war, he found himself replicating their steps to a certain extent.

Mandalstram's parents were now dead. He had no living relatives on this side of the Atlantic that he was aware of, and no knowledge of any relatives on the other side. That was one area of his past that was immune, then, from his present preoccupation.

*

Mandalstram had no idea where his second wife, Margarita, was now. He mined his address book and, again, the Internet for clues, without success. He made a few calls, but the mutual friends he consulted either did not know her whereabouts or were disinclined to reveal them. His call to Arthur Behrens, an art school classmate of Margarita's, who had climbed through the ranks of the federal cultural bureaucracy and was now an assistant deputy minister, was typical.

"I don't think she would want to hear from you, Franklin—even if I knew where she was."

"Which you really don't, I presume?"

"Of course."

"Well, you said she wouldn't want to hear from me. I thought perhaps…"

"No, I'm not lying. If I did know, I'd say so, but wouldn't tell you where. I'd be willing to pass along a message, that's all. But as I said, I don't…"

"So what you're willing or not willing to do is irrelevant," Mandalstram interrupted.

"Yes, but your ill-temper does little to engender sympathy, quite frankly. Congratulations again on your prize. Now goodbye."

Mandalstram attempted to apologize for his impatience, but Behrens had already hung up. A few more calls were no more productive, only serving to abrade his nerves and cause him to reappraise his day's activities. What exactly was he after?

He put on his walking shoes and a warm jacket and set out from his small rented house for the waterfront, less than half a mile distant. It was along its serene shores, watching bobbing fishing boats and seagulls, that he often did his most creative thinking. There was a blustery wind but the temperature was unusually mild for November.

It was Mandalstram's affair with Margarita that had triggered the breakup with Louella, and his second marriage had ended just as badly as the first. Even worse, perhaps, because there was, to use a phrase he found delicious in its ironies, collateral damage. Again, they had been young, and ill prepared for the poverty-dogged relationship and the parenthood that had accompanied it. Margarita was a painter with a promising future and the detour that motherhood caused in her career embittered her, not toward the child, thankfully, but toward Mandalstram, as if everything that followed from that first passionate coming together had been his fault.

Of course, it had not helped that Mandalstram was a terrible father, incompetent and disinterested. After the breakup, he made half-hearted attempts to keep in touch with the child—a delightful little girl named Sunshine, whose blond ringlets and cherubic cheeks seemed almost contrived—but they had eventually become estranged. The last time he'd seen her, when she was nearing puberty, most of the shine had already rubbed off the girl, and she was cocooned in an impenetrable swirl of hurt and sulk. Mandalstram hadn't thought much about either his daughter or her mother in the years since, though Sunshine's birthday would always bring him pangs of guilt and regret. Now he found himself inexplicably filled with an intense longing to see the girl—who would, in fact, be a woman of close to thirty. According to one acquaintance he'd phoned, she lived in Southern California and was well-established as a publicist for Hollywood films. She often traveled abroad. Her name could be seen at the end of the occasional movie in the fast-moving welter of credits. Although she had disavowed her father, she inexplicably continued to use the Mandalstram name.

Mandalstram bought a chicken salad sandwich on a French baguette at an open-air stand near the dock. He leaned against a railing overlooking rocks and water and washed the sandwich down with a bottle of ice-cold locally produced root beer. This lunch was so simple and brought him such pleasure. Normally, it would have been beyond his means other than as a very occasional treat. He had hopes now of enjoying such a midday meal once or even twice a week.

He fed crusts of bread to gulls and ducks as he contemplated his next steps. Apology, he now realized, was the driving force behind this project, which was still taking shape in his head. At first, he'd thought of his attempts at reconnecting strictly as an exercise in clearing the decks, touching base with people who had been important to him at this significant moment in his life. It wasn't their congratulations or good wishes he was after. He'd thought he merely wanted to assure himself that things were unfolding as positively in their orbits as they were in his, so unusual was his good fortune. His clumsy attempt to apologize to his first wife for old crimes, real and imagined, had surprised him as much as it must have her. Now it was becoming clear to him that what he was after was, if not redemption or even forgiveness exactly, something along those lines. "Poet of the heartbroken," the jury had written, "a connoisseur of longing." He had focused on the latter, the longing part of that curious equation. Now, the former was resonating more. Was not giving voice to the heartbroken the special brief of the novelist?

At the same time, he realized, he wasn't exactly sure what those labels—so laudatory, on first reading—really meant. Had the jury intended some form of sly irony?

When Mandalstram had first begun to write, over thirty years earlier—first poetry, then moody, introspective stories, then complex, layered novels—his art was very much informed by the experience of his parents, though he knew so little of it. A large supporting cast of Jews, Communists, Germans and refugees from one disaster or another crept into his stories, usually as minor characters, though occasionally one would shoulder his way to the forefront. Many pieces involved children of Holocaust survivors; a story and several poems were actually set in concentration camps. One academic critic, writing about Mandalstram's third novel, identified exodus—flight, persecution, the refugee experience—as a major theme in his work. Still, when an article in *Books in Canada* mentioned his name in connection with a growing number of Canadian artists of various disciplines influenced by the Holocaust, he was surprised.

He began to be invited to do occasional readings at temples or participate in Jewish book fairs, and to be mentioned, along with better known writers, like Richler and the Cohens, Leonard and Matt, as representing a new Canadian Jewish literary renaissance, a misapprehension he did nothing to correct, and from that point on—the *Books in Canada* piece—the Holocaust specifically and genocide in general became central preoccupations in his work. The recent novel that had won the award was the first in almost two decades in which those themes had been entirely absent. It had been produced during a pause he had taken in a big novel, his most ambitious undertaking yet, overwhelming, really, that revolved around a large cast of Holocaust survivors, perpetrators and collaborators, and their children.

It was to this novel he now intended to return, with renewed vigour. But first he needed to play out the the process of reconnection he'd begun that morning.

~✐

Here was the score, as he recorded it on the back of that sheet of hotel stationary on which this plot had first been hatched, only a few days earlier. Wife one, a strike out; wife two and daughter, both missing in action. That left wife three, but Mandalstram wasn't ready to tackle that particular challenge, which might, he knew, prove to be the thorniest.

There had been a number of other women in his life, of course. He wasn't sure which of them he might want to now pursue. Nor had he given up on the search for his daughter. Should he find her, she might direct him to Margarita. He was thinking all this as he sat tossing pebbles into the placid water under his favourite tree, an expansive oak that leaned seaward from a spit of land jutting in the same direction. All the signs seemed to be directing him eastward, toward Europe, the familial homeland. With each pebble, he counted the concentric rings produced on the face of the water. There were other dusty corners of his life worth investigating, he thought. On the list he'd drawn up, after "wives," "lovers" and "family," he'd written "friends."

Mandalstram had been an indifferent and undistinguished student. Of his grade school and high school years in the Bronx, he had few pleasant recollections, and there were no teachers who stood out in his memory. Unlike some of his friends who spoke warmly of the influence one particular teacher or another had had on their lives, Mandalstram had encountered no such mentor, not even in college in the States, where he'd attended City College in Manhattan for two years before the furor over the war had overtaken his studies, or university in Canada, where he had obtained a degree, in comparative literature, from Concordia. A few professors had been friendly, certainly, but none to the extent that a friendship off campus had evolved. None had even been particularly encouraging, as far as he could recall.

As far as friends went, though, there was one old childhood

chum, whom he'd become reacquainted with out of the blue a few years earlier, and quite a few from later years, including a handful of close friends from student politics days, on both sides of the border. As he walked back toward his house, he sorted through various names and faces, drawing up a tentative list of people to call. At the top of the list was Hal Wolfowitz.

There was an email, several actually, he was looking for. They weren't in his in-basket or in the folder marked Friends, nor were they in Trash, where thousands of old email messages of all sorts gathered dust. Finally, though, in the Sent directory, he found an email he'd written in reply to one from Wolfowitz that contained a record of their previous exchanges.

Their correspondence had begun with a note from someone—the name had rung no immediate bell—asking if he was the Franklin Mandalstram who had once lived on West 183rd Street near the Grand Concourse in the Bronx? If he was, then perhaps he would recall the author of the email, Hal Wolfowitz, who had been a classmate and friend all through grade school. He was now a professor of history at the University of New Mexico, having traveled even further from the Bronx than Mandalstram had, at least in terms of miles.

Once having adjusted the context, he remembered Hal very well. As he recalled, they were not just friends but best friends through the lower grades and high school. They'd spent countless hours swapping comic books and records, talking baseball statistics and girls.

They'd exchanged several nostalgic emails since that first approach by Wolfowitz, mostly catching up and pondering

how it was that they had drifted apart and lost touch—
though none in the last year or two. Upon reading these
emails, Mandalstram decided the fault was chiefly his.
Now, having secured a phone number on the Internet,
he was listening to a phone ring in a university office
somewhere in Albuquerque. The voice that answered,
though, was female.

"Professor Wolfowitz, please," Mandalstram said.

There was a pause. "May I ask who's calling?"

"Franklin Mandalstram. I'm calling from Halifax, in
Canada. For Hal Wolfowitz? We're old friends."

Another pause. "I'm sorry to have to tell you then that
Professor Wolfowitz is dead."

"God," Mandalstram said.

"It just happened last week, a heart attack, at his desk.
The funeral was Monday."

Mandalstram poured himself a stiff shot of Bushmill's
Black Bush Irish whiskey, his drink of choice when he could
afford it, and bolted it back. Then he poured another glass
to sip from. This wasn't going well, and he was beginning
to wonder what exactly he was hoping to achieve. It was
only mid-afternoon, though, and having come this far, he
determined to persevere.

Mandalstram and Martin Semple had come to Canada
together as draft resisters in the early Seventies and had lived
together briefly in their first months in Montreal. Martin
had gone back to the States after the amnesty of 1977, but
they had kept in touch sporadically, though Mandalstram
couldn't remember the last time. Semple had finished
university, gone on for a doctorate in French literature and
was now a professor at NYU—presuming he too hadn't
prematurely died. The first entry in Mandalstram's address
book, a New York City number, was not in service; but a

second number, with an unfamiliar area code, produced a ring that was eventually answered by someone with a very young voice, sex undeterminable. After the usual semi-comic interplay—"is Mr. Semple there?" "Mr. Who?" "Well, let me speak to your father...?" and so on—Martin came on the line.

"Franklin?" he said after he finally understood who was calling. "What the hell do you want, you son of a bitch?" A question like that, pronounced in a jocular tone, could be the start of a pleasant, jokey conversation, but Martin's tone was not particularly jocular, making Mandalstram wary.

"I'm just calling to say hello, Marty."

"For Christ's sake, what is it?"

Mandalstram was confused. Unlike his first wife, whose enmity he fully understood, he had no recollection of any bad blood between him and Martin.

"Just that, Marty. No ulterior motives, honest. Not wanting to borrow money, asking no favours, nothing like that. Not even calling to spread gossip." Mandalstram chuckled, then paused to allow Martin to respond, but there was no response, so he went on. "Actually, there was something I've been wondering about, something I wanted to talk to you about."

"If it's about the money you owe me, forget it," Semple said. "I wrote that bad debt off long ago."

"Money? I didn't realize I owed you money, Marty. That I owe you, yes, of course, but money? I don't recall."

"Listen, like I said, forget it. Water over the bridge."

Mandalstram couldn't resist. "*Under*, isn't it?"

"What?"

"Water *under* the bridge. Isn't that the expression?"

"For fuck's sake, Franklin, what do you want?"

"Honestly, Marty, I just wanted to say hello. But if I owe

you money, I'd like to pay that back. It happens that I've recently come into some unexpected money. How much was it?"

"Didn't you hear what I said? Forget about it. I have."

"Well, then, I'd like to ask you about…well, you remember that year we lived together."

"How could I forget?

"And you remember Ingrid? That waitress you went around with for a while?"

There was no response.

"This will seem crazy, but do you remember, once we had a very brief argument over her?"

Again, silence from the other end of the line.

"I don't remember what I said exactly, but something about her that you took exception to. You probably don't even remember this, it was so trivial. I don't think we ever discussed it again."

More silence.

"Marty, you still there?"

Silence, then, finally, a frigid "I'm here."

"So, do you remember…."

"I remember you fucked my girlfriend, you asshole, I do remember that. I remember you didn't say anything about that."

"Martin, I…."

"I remember you fucked the woman who became my wife, shithead. And there was something you wanted to *ask* me? Forgiveness?"

"Well…."

"Listen, Franklin, don't call here again." With that, the line went dead.

Mandalstram was stunned. He only barely remembered having had sex with Ingrid, and had no idea she and Marty had gotten married. That must have happened after he went back to New York—she had followed? Mandalstram's memory of that period was murky at best. He hadn't even known they were serious, although that must have been why whatever he had said back then caused the argument. A brief trivial argument, at least that's what he had thought at the time.

Mandalstram went to the window in his bedroom, which had a better view of the street than the living room. He stood for a long time watching foot and vehicle traffic. A Buick from the Eighties pulled up across the street and expelled a man in an ill-fitting dark suit. The man consulted a piece of paper from his pocket, then re-entered the car, which sped away. A truck rumbled past, driven by a dark-skinned man whose arm swung like a symphony conductor's from his open window. Two boys on bicycles pedaled by, their laughter trailing after them in the balmy air. An attractive young woman in a polka dot dress walked down the street swinging her handbag, followed by an old woman in black who lived two houses down. A dog, a nondescript mutt, zigzagged across the street, then back, sniffing the air.

A dark stream of sadness coursed through Mandalstram as he watched the tableau of life, limited as it was on this particular street in this particular city, unfold before his eyes. In his mind, he drew a line through the name of his third wife, having determined to let that particular sleeping dog lie. He still had a longing to connect with his daughter— and he would, he determined—she was out there some-where, and he would find her. How many Mandalstrams could there be in Hollywood? And might not she actually be pleased to hear from her father, estranged though they were? But in other respects, he would leave the past alone. He had enough trouble coping with the heartbreak of the present, with his longing for a future.

GOD TELLING A JOKE

Hey, you t'ink *you* got *tsuris*? You don't know da meaning of trouble. Lissen ta dis, mistuh und missus.

My *landsman* Meyer, a lonely widower, is valking home along Delancy Street vun evening, lonely and blue and vishing somet'ing vunderful should come into his life, ven he passes a pet store and hears a sqvawking voice shouting out in Yiddish: "*Qvawwwwk...vus macht du...yeah, du...outside, standing like a putzel...eh?*"

Hey, you, with the steak sauce on your tie—you're laughing—what, you don't believe there are pet stores on Delancy Street? Cut me some slack, fer Yahway's sake. Do I tell you your business?

So vere vuz I? Oh, Meyer. He rubs his eyes and ears. Couldn't believe it. The proprietor, he's standing by the door and he's not one to let grass grow under his feet. He jumps out and grabs Meyer by the sleeve. "Come in here, fella, and let me show you this parrot. You won't believe your ears."

Meyer is not the kind of man, you should know, who frequents pet stores, or who knows from parrots. His idea of a bird to admire is a chicken, stewed in the pot with dumplings, the way his dear Ida made it every Friday night until her death two years ago. But he thinks maybe this is the something he's been yearning for, and he's intrigued, so he follows the proprietor inside and finds himself standing in front of an African Grey that cocks his little head and says: *"Vus? Kenst reddin Yiddish?"*

Meyer turns excitedly to the store owner. "You're right, I don't believe it. He speaks Yiddish, this parrot?"

"Vuh den?" the parrot says. "Chinese maybe?"

So you're wondering how this could be? Don't *hock my chinech*. He belonged to a Jewish pirate, maybe. How should I know? I'm just telling this story. What, you don't think there are Jewish pirates? Wait till the waiter brings you the bill.

And speaking of pirates…"This bird is for sale?" Meyer asks.

"Five hundred dollars," the pet store man says.

And without another moment's thought, Meyer pulls out his wallet and counts out five hundred dollars on the counter and carries the parrot in his cage away with him. All night, he talks with the parrot. In Yiddish—and I mean the real stuff, not my fractured Yidlish. He tells the parrot about his adventures coming to America. About how beautiful Ida was when she was a young bride. About his family, his ingrate son, the surgeon, and his high-and-mighty daughter-in-law, too good for a simple tailor to grace her Long Island home. About his years of working in the *shmatte* trade before he was able to open his own business. About Florida. The parrot listens with interest and makes a comment now and then. Of his own past, though, the parrot speaks little. To Meyer's direct questions, he replies, "Better you shouldn't know."

They share some walnuts, a little whiskey. The parrot loosens up and tells Meyer about life in the pet store, how he hates the weekends, when children poked at him with grubby fingers. Still, he shrugs, it was a living. He's a bit of a wise guy, this parrot, "Call me Ishmael," he says, but not a bad fellow. It's the first real conversation Meyer's had since Ida died and he feels happy. They both go to sleep, Meyer in his lonely bed, Ishmael on the perch in his cage, though Meyer leaves the door to the cage open.

Next morning, Meyer begins to put on his *tfillin* and saying his prayers. The parrot wants to know what he's doing, and when Meyer explains, Ishmael wants *tfillin* too. Meyer still knows his way around a scissors and sewing machine, so he sits right down and hand-makes a miniature set for the parrot. Next, Ishmael wants to learn to *daven*. Meyer is amazed but the parrot is a quick study and he learns every prayer. He wants to learn to read Hebrew so Meyer spends weeks and months, sitting and patiently teaching the parrot, instructing him in Torah, like he's a *bar mitzvah* boy. In time, Meyer comes to love and count on the parrot, as a friend and a Jew. He's been saved from his loneliness. He had thought his life was over but now... God has answered his prayer.

Now, listen. On the first morning of Rosh Hashana, the parrot demands to go to *shul* with Meyer. The old man explains that *shul* is not a place for a bird, but Ishmael argues that in God's eye he is as good a Jew as any other. Meyer relents and the parrot rides to *shul* on his shoulder. They make quite a spectacle, and Meyer is questioned by everyone, including the rabbi and the cantor. At first, they refuse to allow a bird into the building on the High Holy Days, but Meyer convinces them to let him in this one time, swearing that the parrot can *daven*.

"God's eye is on the sparrow," Meyer argues, "so why not a parrot?"

The rabbi relents, but Meyer's friends laugh at the thought of a parrot that can *daven*. Wagers are made, thousands of dollars, at even odds, that the parrot will not *daven*, can not speak Yiddish, let alone Hebrew. Even the rabbi, who disapproves of gambling on Rosh Hashana, puts up a hundred dollars.

All eyes are on the African Grey during services. Ishmael perches on Meyer's shoulder, wearing his silky white *tfillin*, as one prayer and song after another pass—but Meyer hears not a peep from the bird. He begins to become annoyed, slapping at his shoulder and mumbling under his breath, "*Daven*! So *daven* already."

Nothing.

"*Daven*... Ishmael, you can *daven*, so *daven*... come on, everybody's looking at us!" Still nothing.

After Rosh Hashana services are concluded, Meyer finds he owes his *shul* buddies and the rabbi over four thousand dollars. He sets off for home in a great grey huff. The parrot is silent, but finally, several blocks from the temple, it breaks out into song, an old Yiddish melody Meyer remembers from his own childhood, seemingly happy as a lark. Meyer stops and looks at him. "You miserable bird, you cost me over four thousand dollars. Why? After I made your *tfillin* and taught you the morning prayers, and taught you to read Hebrew and the Torah. And after you begged me to bring you to *shul* on Rosh Hashana, why? Why did you do this to me?"

"Don't be a *shmuck*, Meyer," the parrot replies. "Think of the great odds we'll get on Yom Kippur!"

That's the way I like to start my act. Believe me, even the hardest stone laughs at that one—whether it's Meyer they sympathize with or the parrot, I don't know. Sigmund Freud I'm not. I just tell the jokes.

Today, opening with that one, this old *shmuck* at a front table laughs so hard he almost swallows his dentures. "Please, Mister, don't laugh so hard," I tell him, "you should maybe get a heart attack before you pay the bill. Think of the poor waiter, his children at home without shoes, and you stiffing him!"

Old *shmuck*, gravy on his shirt, he just laughs even harder. I have not, I am here to tell you, lost my touch. Old *shmuck*—I should talk. This red-faced grandpa laughing till he pisses his pants is a teenager compared to me, but what's age anyway? Just a one-way ticket to the bone yard, that's all, so forget about it. Believe me, it won't forget about you.

Except it does seem to have forgotten me.

Here I sit, lonely hearted. Tried to shit but only farted.

God, I'm ready. I'm ready, already. This is not news, but He ain't listening.

#

You t'ink it's easy being God?

No. Make the world, in seven days no less, keep an eye on it, listen to prayers, smite big sinners, forgive the repentant, bring down plagues, keep an eye on those *fershlugganer* sparrows! One thing after another, if not one thing, the other. And always those venial sinners with their hands out, gimme gimme gimme.

Every once in a while, God likes to slip away and have some time for himself.

"Where should I go this time, I wonder?" He asks Gabriel.

God's favourite angel gazes out at the vast heavens. "Why not go to Mercury?"

"Mercury? You kidding me?" says God, "I went there twenty-five thousand years ago and got a terrible sunburn."

Gabriel says, "So how about Pluto?"

"Oh no!" says God, "I went there ten thousand years ago, remember? Sprained my ankle skiing."

"How about Earth then?" Gabe asks. He knows God is partial to that little blue planet.

"Earth! *Shlemiel!* What are you thinking?" God asks, incredulous, "I went there two thousand years ago, knocked up some Jewish chick and I've been hearing about it ever since."

I have not, as I say, lost my touch. Rusty maybe, but rust falls away. Timing a little off maybe, at the start, but one night, not even the whole night, and I'm back in tune. "Just like riding a bicycle," I tell Claudia. She rides a unicycle herself, so I figure she'll get the analogy. "That and sex both, you never forget. Timing too."

This is before I discover that she knows as much about sex as she does about bicycles.

"Ninety-nine-year-old men who ride bicycles break their fucking necks," Claudia says back, the mouth on that girl, I'm ashamed to say she's my great-granddaughter. I love that girl but I'm glad I'm not married to her. She can *kvetch* like her mother, who was a world champion. A lifetime with that mouth, with the chip on that shoulder? No thank you. And what kind of a name is Claudia for a nice Jewish girl anyway, not that she's so nice. Nice enough, my little *Claudela*, heh heh. As nice as she needs to be.

"Don't call me that, Salty," she tells me when I pretend to forget. She's always called me Salty—well, by *always* I mean years ago when she was little and now *now*. In between, we weren't in touch. My own son Herman, may he rest in peace, she called Grampa, the little she got to see of him, so what was left for me? "Great grampa," is too much of a mouthful for a three-year-old, "so call me Salty," I told her, and she did. Call me this, don't call me that, there's a lot of identity issues in this family, that's what Herman used to say. Him, Sigmund Freud he was, a framed diploma on the wall, a hundred-dollars-an-hour to prove it. What he would think of me coming out of retirement! "You don't have anything to prove, Pop," Doctor Herman would say.

That's true enough, I already proved what a flop I could be. On TV, I was a dog, I admit it. The wrong kind of face, a face made for radio. Movies, forget it—the wrong kind of physique. Radio, a few times, a guest on Benny, but never a sniff of a show of my own. Too Jewish, they said. You can be too Jewish? Take it up with God, why don't you? I do it all the time.

Still, at the Catskills I was always a hit, thank God for the Catskills. Long after Vaudeville faded, those mountains were still there. Grossinger's and those other hotels are all closed now—the last place New York Jews want to go now is where other Jews go. And Florida, no offence if you're the governor, gives me the willies. All those people waiting to die, all those crocodiles looking for revenge on the pocketbook-makers. No thank you. Bad enough being in retirement, going out of my mind, in the Bronx. Climbing the walls. Waiting to die. And waiting. Waiting.

And then Claudia comes along. Miracle Number One.

And then Sammy's. Miracle Number Two.

"Sammy's?" I ask.

"Sammy's Romanian," Claudia says. "You don't know it, Salty? It's a Jewish restaurant, not far from here. I'd've thought you'd hang out there all the time."

We're at her place—my place now too—and Angel's over. The two girls grin at each other, giggle. This is before I find out they're more than just friends.

"I should *shlep* all the way over here for a Jewish restaurant?" I say. "Believe me, a corned beef sandwich I can get in the Bronx."

"They have comics, Mr. Sellar," Angel says.

"Comics?"

The Chief Rabbi of Israel and the Pope are in a meeting in Rome.

What, you don't think it would happen? Why not, business is business. Macy maybe doesn't tell Gimbel, but that don't mean they don't do lunch.

So the Rabbi, he notices an unusually fancy phone on a side table in the Pope's private chambers. It's big, it's red, it's got lights on it, and there's no cord connecting it to the wall. A cell phone, the Rabbi thinks, but this isn't like any cell phone he's ever seen.

"So what's with the phone?" he asks the pontiff.

"Oh, that, that's my direct line to God," the Pope says, looking a little embarrassed maybe.

The Rabbi is skeptical. "Sure, sure," he says. "Maybe you should give him a call and order more coffee."

But the Holy Father protests he's not kidding, this is on the level, and he insists the Rabbi try it out. He picks up the receiver with a laugh but, to his great surprise, he finds himself immediately connected to God. The Rabbi holds a brief discussion with Him. They talk over the Palestinian situation, the *Intifada,* the Jerusalem question, but it turns out God's as stumped as Sharon. The Rabbi thanks God politely for His time and asks if maybe he too can have a direct line. "Sure," God says. "Why not?" They promise to keep in touch.

After hanging up, the Rabbi thanks the Pope profusely.

"This is great! But listen, I want to pay for my phone charges."

The Pope, of course, refuses, but the Rabbi insists and finally the Pope gives in. He checks a counter on the phone and says, "All right, the charges were 100,000 lira."

Seems a bit high, but the Chief Rabbi pulls out his chequebook and writes a cheque. As soon as he gets home, he asks God for a direct line too and gets it.

A few months later, the Pope is in Jerusalem on an official visit. In the Chief Rabbi's chambers, he sees a phone identical to his own. "Ah ha," he says.

"What can I say?" The Rabbi says, a bit sheepishly. "A good idea is a good idea."

The Pope remembers he has an urgent matter that requires divine consultation, something about priests thinking with their dicks, and asks if he can use the Rabbi's phone. The Rabbi gladly agrees, hands it over, and the Pope chats away with God for a good hour or more. God tells the Pope to tell those priests not to do it anymore.

After hanging up, remembering what happened the last time, the Pope offers to pay for the phone charges.

The Rabbi refuses, they quibble predictably but the rabbi insists there's no charge.

The Pope is incredulous. "How can that be?"

The Rabbi shrugs. "Local call."

Tonight, I'm on a roll. I got them eating out of my hand, which doesn't please the waiters all that much, but tough. This old *shmuck*, the one who laughed so hard before, this time he's purple in the face and I figure if the cops raid the joint now I'll get slapped with an assault charge. Assault with a deadly weapon. My tongue, it's a registered weapon.

"Salty, if you're going to live with me, you're going to

have to learn to shut up," Claudia told me. That was after we rediscovered each other and she came up with the idea of me moving in. She didn't have to ask twice, believe me, but still, shutting up's not so easy for me. All my life, my mouth's been my fortune. But ten years alone in that hell-hole in the Bronx—as if the Bronx wasn't bad enough—was enough to shut even me up. My own darling wife, Hannah, dead, all my sons dead, my last daughter in a nursing home, even the guy I was rooming with for a while, dead and gone, Billy Boxer, nee Boxbaum, another old Vaudeville trouper like me. Two old widowers keeping each other company, swapping jokes we heard so many times I could do his act, he could do mine. In our sleep.

He was just a senior citizen—me, I'm a postgraduate.

"I'll be quiet as a mouse, meek as a lamb," I promised *Claudela*, "and I won't even call you *Claudela*, if you insist."

She's got this place in the Lower East Side, that's what I call it, East Village she says, Alphabet City some people say. We could be in San Juan for all you'd know if you listened to people talking on the street. But it only looks tough, everybody I've met is sweet as candy, and the apartment's rent controlled. It still says Sadie Martinez on the mailbox, she's the tenant of record, and Claudia's the third or fourth sublet since the old lady died. She sends $500 a month to Sadie's daughter, who lives on Long Island somewhere, and *she* sends $400 to the landlord, who should only be getting $300, so everybody's happy. Even at $500, Claudie's making out like a bandit, but even $500 is a lot for a unicycle juggler on her own in the world, so having me share is a godsend for the girl, and she says she likes having me around. What, you think that's so hard to believe? I have my good moments.

A direct line to God! I should have one of those. "God," I'd say, "don't you think it's time you called me home, or sent me to hell, whatever's your pleasure? At ninety-nine, haven't I paid my dues?"

"Sidney," God would say—God doesn't like nicknames—"are you questioning the Divine Plan?"

"God forbid, God," I'd say.

"So shut up and go about your business," God would say. "I still have something in mind for you."

"Well, okay, okay, don't get sore," I'd say. "You da Man."

"And don't you forget it," God says.

"No, no, I don't forget," I say. "You fixed the game so I don't. Everybody I know is dead or so senile they're as good as. Me, my memory's as sharp as it ever was. I don't have the luxury of forgetting."

"So, you're so smart," God says. "Mr. Catskills. Maybe you can figure out what I got in mind."

Alas and alack, that smart I ain't.

*

In the old days, when this neighbourhood was ours, a madam at one of the brothels on Orchard Street opened the door to see an elderly Jewish man. His clothes are all disheveled and torn and he looked gaunt, needy.

"So can I help you?" the madam asks.

"I want Natalie," the old man replies in a hoarse croak.

"Sir, Natalie is one of our most expensive ladies. Perhaps someone else..."

"No," he insists. "It's got to be Natalie."

Just then, Natalie appears—and what a beauty she is, what a piece of, well, you know what I mean, excuse me, Lady—Natalie appears and announces to the old man that she charges a hundred dollars per visit. This is back when a hundred dollars was like a thousand dollars now, maybe two thousand dollars. A hundred dollars! It was a month's wages for a strong man. But this old man doesn't bat an eye, reaches into his pocket, and hands her ten ten-dollar bills. The two go up to a room for an hour, and then the man leaves, a big smile on his mug, a new spring in his step.

The next night, he appears again. And again, he asks to see Natalie. She's surprised to see him and explains that just because they had a good time together yesterday, that doesn't mean there's any discounts, this ain't Macy's bargain basement... the price is still a hundred dollars. Again the old man takes out the money, and the two go up to the room. Again, he leaves an hour later, an even bigger smile this time. He comes banging down the stairs like a man half his age!

When he shows up the third consecutive night, no one can believe it, all the ladies are in a tizzy. Again he hands Natalie the money and up to the room they go. At the end of the hour, Natalie questions the old man: "No one has ever used my services three nights in a row. Where are you from?"

The old man replies: "I am from Minsk."

"Really?" says Natalie. "*I'm* from Minsk. My sister still lives there."

"Yes, I know," the old man says. "She's a neighbour. She knew I was coming to America and gave me three hundred dollars to give to you."

I told you I'm hot tonight. Berle, he used to say "I got a million of 'em." That was inflation. I only got a thousand. But they're all good ones. And this isn't TV, I don't gotta worry about the censors and the sponsors.

By coincidence, the fellow who owns this place is named Milton. I come down here, look the place over, ask for an audition and I'm barely a minute into my act before I'm hired.

"Nice place you got here," I tell the fellow. "So why did you call it Sammy's?"

"What, I should call it Milton's?"

Everyone's a comedian. Still, he's got a point. Sammy's is the right name—that or Shlomo's, maybe.

Some young ladies are about to take their final vows to become nuns at the Cathedral when the bishop notices two Orthodox rabbis enter just before the mass begins, black hats, beards, long *payess* flapping over their ears. They slip quietly into seats at the back of the sanctuary.

The bishop wonders about them but doesn't have time to inquire before the mass begins. Later, when it's time for some announcements, he tells the assembled faithful he's delighted to see two rabbis in their midst, but is curious why they've come to witness the young ladies become the "brides of Christ."

The eldest of the rabbis slowly rises to his feet and explains, "Family of the groom."

You t'ink mebbe dat's hard ta believe? Trut' is stranger den fiction, brudder.

I mentioned Claudia? Now lissen ta dis. A genealogy lesson, no less. The Salter family tree.

Sidney—that's me—begat Herman. I mentioned I'm ninety-nine but maybe you don't believe me—a fine figure of a man like me, six foot three in a five-ten body, I don't look a day over ninety-eight. But Herman, if he'd lived, would be sixty-six now, and he was the baby of the family. Ruthie's the oldest, seventy-eight. I was a child bridegroom, barely out of my teens myself when she was born, and between Ruthie and Herman there were six others. Big families in those days—in those days, it wasn't just special phones to God that Jews and Catholics had in common. And my Hannah, from a good Litvak family she was, but I be damned if there wasn't some Catholic blood in her veins. Her father was a traveling man and the butcher who lived down the street was a big strapping Polack, blond hair and blue eyes—just like Hannah herself. A coincidence, sure. But that's another story.

Ruthie, Benjamin, Nathan, Sarah, the one stillborn we didn't name, Marvin, Lottie, Herman. One, two, three, four, five, six, seven, eight. Every one of them dead now except Ruthie, the oldest, the apple of her daddy's eye. Benjy killed in the war, in France. D-Day. Just a kid. Marvin in Korea. Sarah and Lottie both cancer, Sarah young, Lottie not so young. Nathan in that subway crash a few years ago, maybe you read about it. Herman AIDS—and no, don't get the wrong idea. You think any son of mine is a *faygeleh*? From a transfusion he got it, during dental surgery. "Dying is bad enough, Pop," was the last thing he said to me, "but the indignity...."

"Dying's not so bad," I told him back, "and don't you worry about indignity, Herman, you're my hero." I cried that day.

All gone but Ruthie, the oldest, her daddy's pride and joy. She's in an old-age home in Rockaway, her head as blank as a blackboard after the teacher's erased the lesson. Thank God she doesn't have my affliction. I was there to visit her last year but she didn't know me any more than you do. Less. You, at least, are laughing.

So all gone, more or less.

Now Herman, a fine man, he begat Carla. And what a piece of work that girl was. Thank God for laws against incest or my Hannah woulda had a problem on her hands, so appealing she was. I won't go into that. Some beauty she was, and some flirt, but all her life Carla was pissed off she was born too late to be a hippie. Ran away from home at fifteen, filled her head and her bloodstream with every drug you can name, LSD, DMD, DDT, CIA, and had a fine time but missed the Summer of Love, missed Haight-Ashbury when it meant something. Never forgave poor Herman and his good wife Cynthia for having her too late, way too late, Herman frittering away all that time in med school. Me she was willing to forgive, I don't know why. "Grandpa, you're the only Sellar worth any salt," she'd say, and she'd cackle.

If there are comic genes, she didn't get any of mine. But she did have her own twisted sense of humour. She didn't want to make the same mistake her parents did, so she had Claudia when she was seventeen, with no husband around to share the blame. Husband? Not even a boyfriend. "Who needs them, men?" she said, defiant. And when I had the temerity to point out the obvious once, "Bullshit," she said back. "A turkey baster works just as well. Better. It stays straight."

This explains Claudia's own mouth.

And her own attitude toward men, present company excepted.

So are you following this? Sidney begets Herman. Herman begets Carla. Carla begets Claudia—and not a minute too soon. Claudia takes Sidney under her wing.

"What goes around comes around," as Angel says.

Here's one.

This rabbi is apoplectic, beside himself. He stands up at the front of the *shul*, his face red with anger.

"Someone in this congregation has spread a rumor that

I belong to the KKK," he says, his voice shaking. "This is a horrible lie and one which a Jewish community cannot tolerate. I am embarrassed and do not intend to accept this. Now, I want the party who did this to stand and ask forgiveness from God and our Jewish community."

No one moves and the *shul* is silent. A pin dropping you can hear.

"Lying is a sin," the rabbi goes on. "Gossip is a sin. So is cowardice. Do you not have the nerve to face me and admit this is a falsehood? If you do, remember, you will be forgiven and you will feel relief in your heart. Now stand and confess your transgression!"

Again, the *shul* is quiet. But slowly, a gorgeous blonde with a body designed by Hugh Hefner rises in the third pew. She is a woman the rabbi knows well. Her head is bowed, and her voice quivers as she speaks.

"Rabbi, there has been a terrible misunderstanding," she says. "I never said you were a member of the Ku Klux Klan. I just told a couple of close friends that you were a wizard under the sheets."

"Salty, this is Angel," Claudia says, "Angel this is Salty."

"This is your grandfather?" Angel smirks. Everything that girl says comes out a smirk. "Cool."

"*Great*-grandfather," I correct her.

"Whatever."

Did I mention Claudia has tattoos? All over, but for every one she has, Angel has two—that's a lot of tattoos. Did I mention Claudia has a nose ring? Angel has a nose ring, a ring on her eyebrow, a stud on her tongue. It gives me shivers just looking at this girl. The thought of kissing her puts my teeth on edge. She gave the metal detector at the airport a heart attack. Did I mention Claudia wears a lot of black? Angel wears nothing but black. Even her tampons are black.

"Girls," I ask them, "did you ever hear about looking good to the opposite sex?"

"We're dykes, Salty," Claudia says. "I explained that to you."

"Yeah, yeah, I know. Just wait till the right man comes along. You'll change your mind. But whether it's boys or girls you like, there's still always the other one. So haven't you heard about looking good for the other one?"

"I think Claudia's pretty hot," Angel says.

"Angel's *beautiful*," Claudia says.

Go figure. Who can argue?

But then Angel shakes her head and says, "And so you're the one who was a comic?"

"Borscht Belt stuff," Claudia cuts in.

"Borscht Belt, even Borscht Suspenders," I say. "But whaddya mean *was*?"

"So, that's like standup?"

"These days it's more like sit-down," I admit.

"Like the stuff you see on Letterman?" Angel smirks.

"What's that?" I ask but Claudia is already interrupting again: "No, more like those corny old guys we saw at Sammy's that time."

"Sammy's?" I say.

The next thing I know, I'm down here having a *shnaps* with Milton. "Ten years already you been in business?" I'm aghast. "Why hasn't somebody told me?"

"I don't know," Milton says. "Where've you been? The Bronx?"

I let that one pass. "So you could use a good comic?"

"A good comic I could always use," Milton says. "Why, you know one?"

God is taking a break, having a beer, when one of the angels flies by and stops to talk.

"Good afternoon, God," the angel says.

"Gabe," God says, nodding his head.

"You look tired," the angel says. "What have you been up to?"

"I just finished my latest adjustment to that *cockamamy* new world I've created," God replies, wiping his brow. "I set up a 24-hour alternating pattern of light and darkness."

"Impressive," the angel says. "What's next?"

God shrugs. "I think I'll call it a day."

The older you get, the less sleep you need—you've probably heard that. At my age, I sleep practically not at all. I spend a lot of hours lying awake at night wondering why I'm still alive.

"You *shmuck*, God," I mumble under my breath, "*genug! Genug shayn.* Enough already! What, was it something I said? You *shmendrick*, God, you *shmegegge.* Strike me down, I dare you. Go on, I double dare you, you Holy *Dybbuk!*"

Nothing. Just the rumble of traffic passing on Avenue E. God doesn't take my dare, I don't take His.

"You think I'll let you off the hook, God? You think I've forgotten your promise? No, you sheep-fornicator, you won't let me forget."

Nothing, just the hissing of the radiators.

"All right, so maybe you didn't promise. But *I* did, damn it."

More hissing. More traffic. Somewhere in the apartment, a cockroach cocks its head.

"Damn you, God, damn *you.* Damn you *and* the angel you rode in on. This I say on behalf of Adam, Eve, Cain,

Abel, Job, Lot, Abraham, Noah, the combined populace of Sodom and Gomorrah, the Egyptian first-born, *all* the people you turned your back on. Not to mention the six million, may their memories be blessed. Too goddamned busy with the *shlimazel* sparrows to worry about the Chosen People! Damn you, you heartless *shmuck*."

Nothing. Just the gurgling of my stomach, a belch and a fart. Don't look for theological signs in plumbing, mechanical or human.

No, nothing. God may be home, but he ain't taking any calls. The Chief Rabbi and the Pope may have direct lines, but mine is disconnected.

And speaking of the Chief Rabbi, a rabbi dies, an old man with a good life, and after some time the congregation decides that the *rebetzin* should marry again. She was quite a bit younger than the rabbi, so it's not right that such a young woman should be unmarried. But, since it is a small village, the only available candidate is the local butcher, a bit beneath her standing. Still, he is a good man, with a decent income and a fine house, and the widow reluctantly accepts. She's used to living with a scholar, so things will be different, but life must go on.

After the marriage, on Friday night just after taking a bath in the *mikva*, the butcher tells his new bride, "Look, my mother always said that before the beginning of the *shabbes* it was a *mitzvah* to make love before going to the synagogue."

This was not something the rabbi, her esteemed husband, now deceased, would have ever suggested, but the good woman knows her place and willingly obliges.

When they return from *shul*, he tells her, "You know, according to my father, it is a *mitzvah* to make love before lighting the candles."

Again the new wife obliges her new husband. She's sure he'll be satisfied with this, twice in one day, but when it is time for bed that night he tells her, "My grandfather used to say that one should always make love on *shabbes* night, as an acknowledgement of God's power."

Finally they go to sleep. When they wake up the next morning, the new husband tells her, "My aunt says that a religious Jew always starts the *shabbes* by having sex. So let's do it."

On Sunday, after hearing about several more *mishpocheh* and their religious views, the new bride goes out to the market, where she meets a friend.

"*Nuuuu*, so how is the new husband?" the friend inquires.

"Well, an intellectual he isn't," the bride says, "but he comes from a wonderful family."

I'm not exactly a jinx, but practically everybody who's ever been around me is dead. My own folks, of course, long ago. *Mishpocheh* in the old country, dead in the camps. My sweet Hannah, may she rest in peace, ten years ago already, kidney failure. All the girls I cheated on her with—not that I'm admitting anything—they're gone too, except for one young tootsie, an old chicken now, has a part on a sitcom, which is the same as being dead. All my brothers and sisters. My children...them I told you about already. All my nieces and nephews—I think. Some I lost track of. All the people I worked with, all my friends, *everybody*. Even that grand-daughter of mine Carla, who should have been too tough to die. Everyone except Ruthie and Claudia—I told you about them, remember?

Nothing sinister about it, no plot: just wars, accidents, sickness, old age...all the same things people have been dying of for centuries. So how come not me?

And not just alive, but healthy. The ticker is strong, the plumbing works, aches and pains I got, sure, but most things work. And the memory...ah, I told you, I don't forget. Little things, sure, but most things I remember.

Like our first born, Ruthie. Three weeks home from the hospital and she's got a fever you could boil eggs with. I'm in a duo then, Salter and Boxer, sometimes on the road, but just then, as it happens, doing a regular bit at Minsky's midtown. Burlesque, yes, but you got something against pretty women? So I'm home. Hannah and I, we take the baby back to the hospital, the doctor goes white when he sees her. He doesn't know from what, just it doesn't look good.

I do my show but then I'm back at the hospital. In the middle of the night, Hannah is asleep in the waiting-room chair. I'm walking up and down the hall, up and down, and I stop finally at a window and look out, look up. There's the moon, full as your belly after a *seder*, and it makes me think of somebody's line, I forget whose, "the moon is a gold filling in God's mouth."

I look right up at it, and it's like I'm staring right into God's open mouth, right up to the Heavenly Tonsils, not so polite, I know, but I'm wondering why the hell He doesn't close his mouth when He's chewing. *That's* impolite.

"Listen, God," I say, "OK, let's trade. You spare Ruthie, take me instead."

I'm thinking, OK, this is it, if there's really a God He'll strike me down this minute. I'm not afraid, but I start to worry, Ruthie an orphan, Hannah a widow, who'll look after them? That rat Billy Boxer?

"OK, God," I say, "I'm not backing out, don't get me wrong, but let's think this through. If you think it's right to take me now, my darling wife a widow, my darling daughter an orphan, who am I to tell you your business. *You're* God. But if you think maybe that's not such a good idea, well then, OK, you take me whenever you want. I won't complain, whenever it is. Whenever you think the time is right."

I gaze at the moon a little longer, waiting for a sign of some sort—either I drop dead or a cloud passes over the moon, something.

But no, nothing.

Then I walk back down the hall and sit down next to Hannah and a few minutes later a nurse comes out, she's smiling, and do I have to tell you any more?

A bargain's a bargain. And here I am waiting to keep my end of it.

You'd think, though, that after all these years, God would have gotten back to me.

Well, maybe He's got other things on his mind, all those sparrows, rhinos making love, electric *eels* making love! What a *shmozzle* that must be.

So here I still am, still kicking.

Not that there's anything supernatural about it, it's just God telling a joke. "You're a healthy man for your age," my doctor tells me, "very healthy. But people are living longer these days. Nineties is not unheard of by any means, even a hundred. You've obviously taken care of yourself."

"But I haven't," I shrug. "Liquor, cigarettes, loose women, greasy food, late hours, everything you shouldn't do you can think of, I did it, and plenty."

"Well, you did *something* right," this doctor says.

This is Birnbaum, has his practice on Grand Concourse in the Bronx. For years, I went to Sam Cohen the father, and then Harvey Cohen the son. Both dead. For a while, I went to Bernie Cohen the cousin who took over the practice, but he sent me to Birnbaum, a gerontologist. I see him twice a year, just for a check-up—I don't know, is he checking me or am I checking him? I was there just a few weeks ago and believe me it's some *shlep* up there now that I'm in Manhattan.

He listens to my heart, takes my blood pressure, peers here and there, pokes and squeezes, makes satisfied noises. I tell him I'm working again. "The comeback kid, that's me," I grin.

"Good, Mr. Sellar, it's good to keep active."

Active, sure, but still, I tell him, this isn't golf, it's work, on my feet an hour a time, two shows a night, three nights a week, not full time on the assembly line, but *work*. "You ain't afraid it might not be too hard on the heart, maybe?" I ask.

Birnbaum knows not to bullshit a bullshitter. "Frankly, Mr. Sellar, at your age, I think you can do just about any-thing you want to. I mean, what have you got to lose?"

And that's it, the hammer right on the nail. What *do* I have to lose?

Croneberg, a retired cloakmaker, is on his way to Canarsie to visit his daughter and her family. He sits down next to a younger man on the subway. So many years in the *shmatte* business, he has an eye for clothes and he notices that the young man has a strange kind of shirt collar. What does an old Jew know from a priest!

After a few minutes, he smiles at his seatmate and asks, "Excuse me sir, but vy do you hev your shoit collah on beckvurts?"

The priest politely answers, "I wear this collar because I am a Father."

The old man thinks fondly of his children and many grandchildren and after a moment he responds, "Sir, excuse me, I em also a fodder, but I vear mine collar front-vays. So, *nu?* Vhy do you vear your collah so different?"

The priest thinks for a minute and says, "Sir, I am the father for many."

Croneberg quickly answers, "I, too, am the fodder from many. *Kineahora*, I have four sons, four daughters and too many grandchildren to count. But still I vear mine collah like everyone else. Vhy do you vear it dot vay?"

The priest is beginning to get exasperated. He blurts out, "Sir, I am the father for hundreds and hundreds of people!"

The old man is taken aback and falls silent for a long time. The train pulls into a station, stops, pulls out again. The next stop is the old man's. As he gets up, he leans over to the priest and says, "Misteh, maybe you should vear your pents on backvards, too!"

Oooh, I'm hot. Touch me, you get your finger burnt. I'm *on* tonight, *on*.

Here's the truth of the restaurant business. You can't make much of a living off food. It's drinks where you make your money. All my life, I've been a money-maker. That's why they kept having me back at Grossinger's, why Milton loves me. Anybody can make people laugh—I make them laugh so hard they get thirsty. When I'm on, the booze flows. And tonight I'm really *on,* so the bartender is working double-time, the waiters are losing weight, they're sweating so much. Tonight I can worry about a heart attack, a stroke maybe, but not job security.

"Salty, you don't have to work," Claudia tells me. "Your Social Security, what I make, it's enough." It's hard to believe she came out of her mother's womb, that one, she's so considerate.

Her math is lousy, though. What she makes busking, a

cockroach couldn't live on. Me and my Social Security were a godsend for her.

"I do," I tell her. "It's *not* working that's killing me, not working." She doesn't do drugs, this girl of mine, but her friend Angel does, so she understands. "It's my drug," I tell her. "I need that hit." That she can understand.

Still, Claudia worries about me, bless her heart. So does Angel.

"Don't worry, I'm not going to keel over," I tell her. "And if I do....?"

"Hey, you're the only great-grandfather I've got," Claudia says.

"And you're the only kid on the block to have one, too. Believe me, losing me won't kill *you*."

"*Salty!*"

"So, anybody ever tell you you're cute when you get mad?"

The last thing I ever thought was I'd wind up living with a nineteen-year-old girl—especially with a nose ring and tattoos. A girl who makes her living, such as it is, keeping balls and batons in the air. Every day, rain or shine, down at Tompkins Square Park, busking. You ever see a girl with a clown nose on a unicycle? In the snow? Juggling candles? Burning ones?

🎤

Four rabbis used to get together to discuss Torah. As it happened, three of them always agreed. The fourth, Rabbi Shmendrick, was always odd man out. One day, after losing an argument three to one as usual, he decides to appeal to a Higher Authority, you know Who I mean.

"Oh, God!" he cries. "I know in my heart that I am right and they are wrong! Please give me a sign to prove it to them!"

It's a beautiful, sunny day. As soon as the rabbi finishes his prayer, a storm cloud moves across the sky above the four men. It rumbles once and dissolves. "A sign from God!" cries Rabbi Shmendrick. "See, I'm right, I knew it!"

But the other three disagree, pointing out that storm clouds often form on hot days.

So the rabbi prays again: "Oh, God, I need a bigger sign. They're not convinced."

This time four storm clouds appear, rush toward each other to form one big cloud, and a bolt of lightning slams into a tree on a nearby hill.

"I told you!" cries the rabbi, but his friends insist nothing happened that could not be explained by natural causes. It's still three to one. Rabbi Shmendrick twists his hands in despair. "Oh God...," he cries out," but before he can say another word, the sky turns pitch black, the earth shakes, and a deep, booming voice intones, "HEEEEEEEE'S RIIIIIIGHT!"

The rabbi puts his hands on his hips, turns to the other three and says, "Well?"

"Big deal," replies one of the others, Rabbi Cohen. "So now it's three to two."

The phone rings one day and there's this squeaky voice at the other end, like a little girl. "This Salt Sellar?"

"It is, but no one's called me that in ten years. Who the hell is this?"

"Claudia. You probably don't remember me."

"Carla's Claudia? The hell I don't."

"Well, it's me, great-grandpa. Is it okay if I call you Salt?"

"No, that's too familiar. Salty's what I told you to call me years ago. So what are you up to, Claudia? I thought you were in San Francisco." That's where Carla and the little girl *shlepped* fifteen years ago, that's where Carla OD'd. Hannah was too sick but I went out there for the funeral. I would have brought the girl back with me but what do old people know about bringing up a child? It broke my heart, but I left her with the social workers.

She landed with foster parents, but that didn't work out.

"I've been with the circus but now I'm out on my own," Claudia tells me. She didn't tell me, not then, what exactly she was doing. Or why she left the circus. Or how she wound up here. It made my blood boil when she did.

"Show business runs in the family. You come by it honestly."

We talked some more and it came out she was living by herself, so was I. "Well that's silly," she said and I don't know what came over me but suddenly it seemed silly to me too. "You're all I have, Salty," she said.

"Is that right? *You're* all *I* have."

"Maybe you should call me Pepper," Claudia said.

Believe me, ninety-nine or no, I'm not the kind who wastes any time feeling sorry for himself, but I cried then, not so she could hear me, not because I *did* feel sorry for myself but because I suddenly realized how much reason I had to. Like I said, Miracle Number One. That day, I didn't curse God, didn't dare Him, didn't tell Him "enough already, enough! Take me, already!"

Damn, but this living is tricky work.

Years ago, *centuries* ago, long after they'd been kicked out of Spain, but long before Hitler, the Pope decreed that all the Jews had to leave Italy. Jews were well established in Italy so there was, of course, a huge outcry from the Jewish community, even many of the Gentiles were sympathetic. So the Pope offered a deal. He would have a religious debate with a leader of the Jewish community. If their leader won, the Jews would be permitted to stay in Italy. If the Pope won, the Jews would have to leave.

Well, the Jewish community met and picked an aged rabbi, Finkel Shmegegge, to represent them in the debate. Rabbi Shmegegge, however, could not speak Latin and the Pope could speak neither Hebrew nor Yiddish. Both men could speak Italian, of course, but it was considered too vulgar a language for serious religious discussion, so it was decided that this would be a "silent" debate.

On the day of the great debate, the Pope and Rabbi Shmegegge met in a great hall of the Vatican and sat opposite each other, the Pope surrounded by his cardinals, Rabbi Shmegegge flanked by a committee of rabbis. After a full motionless minute, the Pope raised his hand and showed three fingers. Rabbi Shmegegge looked back and raised one finger.

The Pope frowned.

Next, the Pope waved his finger around his head. Rabbi Shmegegge pointed to the floor.

The Pope shook his head. He then brought out a communion wafer and a chalice of wine. Rabbi Shmegegge responded by pulling out an apple and a jar of hot tea, wrapped in a rag.

With that, the Pope stood up and said with exasperation, "I concede the debate. This man has bested me. The Jews can stay."

Later, the Cardinals gathered around the Pope, asking him to explain what had happened. "You have eyes! Didn't you see for yourselves," the Pope said, annoyed.

"We're only cardinals," the chief cardinal said meekly. "We saw, but we didn't understand?"

The Pope was silent for a minute. Then, his temper cooled, he explained: "You saw, I held up three fingers, that was to represent the Trinity, of course. But that damned man responded by holding up one finger to remind me that there was still one God common to both our religions. You saw that. Then, you'll recall, I waved my finger in a circle, a halo, to show him that God was all around us. But the accursed man responded by pointing to the ground to show that God was also right here with us. Finally, as you saw, I pulled out the wine and the wafer to show that God absolves us of our sins. But he, wretched man, pulled out an apple to remind me of original sin. He had an answer for everything. What could I do?"

Meanwhile, the Jewish community crowded around Rabbi Shmegegge, asking what happened. "Well," said the good rabbi, with a laugh, "the Pope is not as formidable an opponent as I thought. First he said to me, 'You Jews have three days to get out of here.' I just told him, 'Up yours'. Then he tells me the whole city would be cleared of Jews. I said to him, 'No way, Your Excellency, the Jews...we stay right here!'"

"And then?" asked a woman.

"That was it, you saw," said Rabbi Shmegegge. "We broke for lunch."

And I take *my* break.

"I'm Salt Sellar and you're not. Thanks for being a great audience. Believe me, being here is a miracle for me. But I'm going to have a drink now—why don't you do the same. One or two or a dozen. Order another steak, maybe."

The place has been roaring—if I go any longer they'll be calling ambulances soon, and not for me. The old *shmuck* up front isn't the only red face in the crowd.

I don't drink like I used to, but I still like a highball when I'm working. Even Birnbaum says one or two a night can't hurt me. That used to be the way I felt about blondes—no, I'm kidding. Lots of vices, sure, but tomcatting on Hannah wasn't one of them. Well, once or twice, maybe. Now, I'm at the bar and Ernie the bartender is handing me the tall Canadian and Canada with lots of ice he knows I'm partial to. And standing next to me, looking good enough to eat, no whipped cream necessary, is this blonde, all teeth and tits, you should pardon the expression.

"That was *great*, Mr. Sellar."

Husky. Breathless. A better imitation of Marilyn Monroe Marilyn herself couldn't do.

"Salt," I tell her. "I'm Salt. Smile more, and I'll be Salty. Mr. Sellar's been dead a long time."

She laughs but even a bubblehead would know that line's not all that funny, and I'm not saying she *is* a bubblehead. She's no older than Claudia, though. And she looks like maybe she doesn't suffer from Claudia's peculiar persuasion.

"I'm Nancy," the blonde says. Nancy! What kind of a name is that? Curls, blue eyes, a smile so sweet you could lick it off her lips. The image of my Hannah, but seventy years ago. "You make me feel good. Can I buy you a drink?"

"I've got one, darling, as you can see." I salute her with the tall glass and take a big swallow. Man, I'm thirsty.

"The next one?"

"They're on the house for me. Maybe I can buy *you* one."

"I'd like that," the blonde says. "But I'd like to do something for you." Now, what the hell? This another miracle? What's God got up his sleeve for me this time? I mean, I can take a joke. But this is one punch line I don't know.

But I don't question God's mysterious ways. If this is the

way He has in mind for me to go, who am I to complain. God spoke to Abraham through an angel, so why not to me?

Lead on, Nancy. Lead on.

ACKNOWLEDGEMENTS

Some of these stories have been published, or are forthcoming, often in slightly different versions, in literary magazines:

"After the War," "Eclipse" and "God Telling a Joke" in *Grain*
"Bright Lights on Broadway" and "Romance" in *Found Press Quarterly* (online)
"Bucket of Blood" in *The Antigonish Review*
"The Connoiseur of Longing" in *Numero Cinq* (online)
"Desert Isle or The Compunction of Narrative" in *The Malahat Review*
"Interference" in *The New Quarterly*
"King of the Jews" in *Prairie Fire*
"Lightfoot and Goodbody, Improbable as it Sounds" in *Front Range* (Montana)
"Talking to God" in *Descant*

My thanks to Ron Smith for his sharp-eyed editing and to Dave Carpenter for the usual encouragement and support.

These stories were worked on, at various stages, at colonies organized by the Saskatchewan Writers Guild at Emma Lake, Christopher Lake and St. Peter's Abbey, all in Saskatchewan. Some were worked on as well during a month's residency at Toronto Artscape's Gibraltar Point studio on Toronto Island, and a similar residency at the Vermont Studio Center in Johnson, Vt. My thanks for the hospitality. Thanks also to the Saskatchewan Arts Board and the Canada Council for the Arts for financial support during the drafting and completion of some of these stories.

—Dave Margoshes

Dave Margoshes is a Saskatoon-area writer whose work has appeared widely in Canadian literary magazines and anthologies, including six times in the Best Canadian Stories volumes. He was a finalist for the Journey Prize in 2009. He's published fifteen books of poetry and fiction, including *Bix's Trumpet and Other Stories*, which won two prizes at the 2007 Saskatchewan Book Awards, including Book of the Year. He also won the Poetry Prize in 2010 for *Dimensions of an Orchard*, and has been nominated several other times for Saskatchewan Book Awards. His most recent title, a collection of linked short stories, *A Book of Great Worth*, was named one of Amazon.Ca's Top Hundred Books of the Year in 2012.